Searching for Love

by

Carolyn Rae

The New Horizons Series

Searching for Love

Cover Art by *Debbie Taylor*

The Wild Rose Press, Inc.
PO Box 708
Adams Basin, NY 14410-0708
Visit us at www.thewildrosepress.com

Publishing History
First Crimson Rose Edition, 2016
Print ISBN 978-1-5092-0865-4
Digital ISBN 978-1-5092-0866-1

The New Horizons Series
Published in the United States of America

Matt wouldn't believe…Christy was dead.

Wiping the sweat off his forehead with the hem of his T-shirt, Matt dragged himself into the last bar in this godforsaken, south-of-the-border town and ordered a drink.

Four days shot, and he was still rushing around and getting nowhere.

The stench of stale beer and cigarettes hung in the air. After swirling his whiskey and soda, he downed it in three gulps. The sharp burn stung his throat. The man in the mirror behind the bar was a stranger. The beginning of a beard shadowed his square jaw, and his red-rimmed brown eyes showed his exhaustion. Others in the tarnished looking glass didn't appear much better. One man wore a dirty shirt missing two buttons. Next to him a guy with nicotine-stained fingers hunched over the scarred wooden counter. La Cucaracha—this bar with its dirty plank floor and rickety wooden stools on the edge of El Jardin Bonito, Mexico, seemed full of losers.

Matt didn't want to be one of them, didn't want to give up. All that kept him going was that hotel clerk twenty miles south in Monterrey, who thought she recognized Christy from the photo Matt showed her. The clerk claimed she'd overheard someone who looked like her say something about going north to the next town. But so far the lead hadn't panned out.

If he didn't get results here, he had nowhere else to look. Staying away from the office much longer wouldn't sit well with the senior partners at his law firm. Could hire a private detective, but he needed to do this himself, and get his brother, accused of murdering Christy, out of jail.

Dedications

This book is dedicated to my critique partners,
Pepper, Jan, and Dorothy,
the DFW Writer's Workshop,
and my husband, Jack,
North Texas RWA and Dallas Area Romance Authors,
for their encouragement.
To Hebby, Karen, and Patricia.
And Dwight Swain,
who inspired me to write this story
with his talk about a bar in Mexico.
(My story's town is fictitious.)

Chapter One

Matt Larson wouldn't believe—didn't want to believe everyone was right—that Christy was dead.

Wiping the sweat off his forehead with the hem of his T-shirt, Matt dragged himself into the last bar in this godforsaken, south-of-the-border town and ordered a drink.

Four days shot, and he was still rushing around and getting nowhere.

The stench of stale beer and cigarettes hung in the air. After swirling his whiskey and soda, he downed it in three gulps. The sharp burn stung his throat. The man in the mirror behind the bar was a stranger. The beginning of a beard shadowed his square jaw, and his red-rimmed brown eyes showed his exhaustion. Others in the tarnished looking glass didn't appear much better. One man wore a dirty shirt missing two buttons. Next to him a guy with nicotine-stained fingers hunched over the scarred wooden counter. La Cucaracha—this bar with its dirty plank floor and rickety wooden stools on the edge of El Jardin Bonito, Mexico, seemed full of losers.

Matt didn't want to be one of them, didn't want to give up. All that kept him going was that hotel clerk twenty miles south in Monterrey who thought she recognized Christy from the photo Matt showed her. The clerk claimed she'd overheard someone who looked like her say something about going north to the next town.

But so far the lead hadn't panned out.

If he didn't get results here, he had nowhere else to look. Staying away from the office much longer wouldn't sit well with the senior partners at his law firm. Could hire a private detective, but he needed to do this himself, and get his brother, accused of murdering Christy, out of jail.

Damn Christy's sorry hide for disappearing. Damn her for running out on his brother. And damn her for leaving Gordon to face murder charges.

He motioned the bartender over, laid a ten-dollar bill on the wooden bar, and set a photo beside it. "Have you seen this woman?" Fingering his mustache, Matt waited.

The solemn bartender's fingers strayed to his cheek as he touched a thin scar running down the side of his face and glanced at the picture. "*Bonita*, pretty." The bartender shoved the photo back. "I not see her."

Matt sighed and snatched the bill. The drink soured in his stomach. What now? Maybe she really was dead. Could his brother have…what the hell was he thinking? Gordon might be ambitious, even ruthless when it came to politics, but murder? Matt wouldn't believe it; Christy had to be alive.

Her shrill voice had grated on Matt's ears as she shouted at Gordon, claiming he hadn't kept his promise to take her back to Monterrey for a weekend. Then she'd driven off in Gordon's truck with tires squealing and the radio blaring some country western song.

That was the last time Matt, or anyone else, saw her. Rising from the barstool, he pocketed Christy's picture and shoved away his empty glass. Alcohol hadn't dimmed his frustration. And it damn sure hadn't given him any ideas where to go next. He'd looked everywhere in this town. His faded T-shirt had perspiration stains. The image in the mirror showed the fatigue lines on his face echoing the desperation gnawing at his gut.

Someone tapped his shoulder. He turned to see a Mexican with skin the color of freshly brewed coffee and a bristly mustache as dark as the coffee grounds. "*Amigo*, maybe I see woman you talk of."

Matt handed the man his sister-in-law's picture. "Where did you see her?"

The man rubbed his thumb and forefinger together. Matt slapped a ten in his hand.

Grinning, the man nodded toward the center of town. "*El mercado*. She buy *un vestido*." At Matt's puzzled frown, he said, "Dress...*rojo*."

Matt didn't know much Spanish, but he knew *rojo* meant red. *Mercado* must be the marketplace. "*Gracias*." Excited to be getting closer, he quickened his steps.

In the open-air market, he strode past tables with mounds of red and yellow peppers, displays of colorful gourds, and a cart filled with baskets of pinto beans. Ripe melons wafted a tempting sweetness. The smell of sizzling tomato sauce made his stomach growl. He hadn't eaten all day, but he needed to find Christy. He handed over a few pesos for a cucumber he could take with him. Sweating in the hot sun, he dug out Christy's picture then headed toward a display of peasant dresses and stopped short.

Across the street, a fair-skinned blonde stood out amongst the brown-skinned natives. Her gently rounded hips undulated along with her hands as she haggled in

Spanish with a plump Mexican woman behind a table piled with colorful cloth goods. Picking his way past women with baskets, and others holding tight to children's hands, Matt hurried toward the blonde.

He'd found her.

Her determined chin stuck out, just as when he'd last seen her. She held up a brown dress covered with embroidered flowers in many colors. The dress contrasted well with her hair. He imagined how it would look hugging her nicely rounded hips. Hell, what was he thinking? He'd come here to find his brother's wife, not drool over her. She plunked coins in the woman's outstretched hand.

Christy was alive and safe. He could take her back and free his brother. His heart beating in anticipation, he strode toward her. "Christy, I'm so glad I found you. I'm returning you to San Antonio immediately." He touched her arm. "Police think Gordon killed you."

She spun around, shook off his hand, and glared at him. It wasn't Christy. Her sister's dangling strawberry-blonde hair gleamed in the sunlight. He could see the difference now. Christy's hair was a lighter blonde.

At Gordon and Christy's wedding, he'd watched Christy and her sister together. Valerie's ponytail, caught up in a beaded clasp, had swished over the shoulder of her bridesmaid's dress. She'd looked hot. Christy smiled and chatted with everyone, but he couldn't keep his eyes off Valerie. She seemed more steady, more down to earth. He liked that in a woman, except she'd avoided him as much as possible.

Her frown vanished. "Matt, I came to help you find my sister."

He swallowed. He'd never dreamed Valerie would

actually come to Mexico to hunt Christy, let alone offer to work with him. "Guess I could use some assistance. I've shown her picture all over town without any luck." He appreciated her lush figure, but her attitude said stay back. He paused. "Coming here alone is risky. It's not that I don't welcome your help, but—"

Her determined chin jutted out. "I can take care of myself."

He took a bite of the cucumber. "Someone might attack you."

In a flash, Valerie feigned a blow to his mid-section and tore the cucumber from his grasp. "If that had been a knife, I'd have you on the ground by now."

Seeing the belligerence etched in her face, he remembered she'd made it perfectly plain at his brother's wedding that she didn't like him any more than Gordon. Matt wanted Valerie to see he wasn't like his brother.

Valerie stepped back, probably wanting more distance between them.

"You're tough. Remind me not to tangle with you."

"I just passed the test for my second-degree black belt." Steadiness of purpose shone in her green eyes. "I don't care if anyone thinks coming here is risky. I'm not sitting at home waiting for news."

Nervously, she twisted a gold and silver ring around her finger. "I don't think she's dead. Maybe she's pregnant. That's why I want to find her soon. The blood the police found in Gordon's abandoned truck—maybe it wasn't from an injury—it could be from a threatened miscarriage."

Matt let out the breath he'd been holding. If he could prove that, he might get Gordon out of jail, but they needed to find Christy soon. He faced the plump, middle-aged woman wearing a white embroidered dress like the one she'd just sold Valerie. He held out the photo. "Have you seen or talked to this woman?"

"*No comprendo,*" the woman said.

"Let me," Valerie said. "I showed her Christy's picture, but yours is larger." She set his photo next to a pile of red and green serapes and pointed to it, then rattled off several sentences in Spanish.

The woman's face brightened. She chattered rapidly. Matt wished he'd studied Spanish. He didn't like depending on Valerie.

She faced him. "Maria here says she saw a woman looking like Christy with a man who had shaggy blond hair. He slammed down money, grabbed a red dress, threw it at the woman, and practically dragged her away."

"Did Maria see where they went? How long ago was it?" Matt asked.

Valerie asked the woman. Maria nodded, then spoke again, gesturing with her hands before returning the picture.

"About fifteen minutes ago," Valerie said. "She says they got in a red convertible with a license plate that said BAD BOY and talked about going to a restaurant. She pointed to that one on the next block. Anyhow, they drove down the street so fast people scrambled to get out of the way."

"Did she tell the police?"

Valerie rattled off more Spanish.

Maria shook her head. "*No policia,*" she said, then muttered something else.

"Maria thinks a husband has a right to make his

woman behave. I tried to tell her she wasn't with her husband." Valerie frowned, then whispered, "Stupid macho culture."

"Shhh. We may not agree with their customs, but we want people to help us, not dislike us." He pointed toward a small park and grasped her hand. "Come on. It will be faster if we cut through the park."

She frowned and yanked her hand loose, but hurried to keep up as they passed blankets spread with colorful scarves, baskets, and pottery for sale.

He couldn't blame her for pulling away after their less than stellar history. "Maybe we'll catch them there."

She stopped behind him. "Before we reach the restaurant, there's something else you should know." She was twirling that ring again.

"What?"

"Christy wouldn't disgrace him like this when he's running for mayor. I believe she's been kidnapped."

Chapter Two

Matt stood with his mouth hanging open in front of a sparkling fountain surrounded by red and yellow flowers. "Kidnapped? Why would you think that?"

She frowned, looking like she didn't want to have anything to do with him. Not surprising, since Gordon ditched her to marry her sister. Matt hoped she'd stick with him long enough to help find her sister.

Valerie took a deep breath and let it out slowly. "Before I left Dallas to come here, I got a collect call."

"A call? Who was it from?" He was worried about Gordon, but he did care about finding Christy. She probably thought he was only interested in saving his brother from the murder charge.

"The operator said it was from Christy Larson in Monterrey, but when I said hello, there was a click, and the line went dead. Maybe she was trying to call me, and someone stopped her. I don't think she left voluntarily. What if she's tied up and helpless?"

"If you think she's being held against her will, why hasn't anyone received a ransom demand? Maybe Maria saw some other woman instead of Christy. Maybe your sister's—"

"No. She can't be dead. We'll find her."

"They won't free Gordon unless we can show them she's alive." Matt rubbed the back of his neck. "The police don't even have a fricking body, but they threw him in jail anyway."

"How could they do that without proof she's dead?"

He shrugged. "The only evidence the D.A. has is a lot of blood in my brother's abandoned truck."

"How can they be sure it's Christy's blood?"

"Dad paid plenty to rush the DNA test. They confirmed it was Christy's blood, but I can't believe she's dead. I don't think she'd let Gordon rot in jail for a murder he didn't commit."

She gazed at Matt's brown eyes flecked with amber highlights. It took a few seconds to remember what she'd been about to say. "Just some blood in his truck—that doesn't seem like enough evidence to put him away."

Matt ran his fingers through his hair. "Neighbors claimed they heard them arguing an hour before she left her home in San Antonio. I'm sure the cops were under pressure to arrest someone."

"Why can't you get him out on bail?"

Matt frowned, discouraged. "I tried. I can still hear the rap of the judge's gavel and his booming voice saying, 'bail denied.' If you could only see Gordon, his face shadowed by prison bars—I've never seen him look so beaten—you'd understand how badly I want him out. We have to find Christy."

She kept on walking. "If we don't find her...are you...will you...defend him in court?"

He rubbed the back of his neck. "I've nailed a few abusive husbands and given their wives a fresh start, but I've never handled a murder case. A couple of my associates at the firm mentioned they'd help, but it's not looking good." He clamped his mouth shut. "I can just see the headlines. Mayoral Candidate Gordon Larson Slays Wife, Frank Carter a Shoo-in."

Valerie swallowed and touched his arm.

He tried to ignore the sudden tingle from her touch as she pulled her hand back. Was she thinking about seeing Christy's dead body on the front page?

"Oh, yeah, they'd print that, and more probably," Matt said. "If only the public could see the ruthless look in Frank Carter's eyes and the stubborn set of his chin when someone defies him. Believe me, I've seen it in court; they wouldn't vote for him. And if they listened to all the rumors about his connection to the criminal element, rumors most likely true, they'd vote him off the city council."

She walked beside him under a large tree, its shade barely moderating the sun's relentless heat. "Surely, with your associates helping, you can clear Gordon, even—" She brushed a tear from her cheek, then another. "Even if we can't find Christy."

Matt wiped beads of perspiration from his forehead. "We'll find her. Come on, we're wasting time."

A faint breeze stirred the leaves above them. Valerie pointed. "There's the restaurant Maria pointed to."

He stepped up his pace. "With Gordon in jail, his opposition will make the most of the pressure on the police to keep him locked up. He can't exactly campaign from there."

"Do you think pressure from Frank Carter is why the police arrested Gordon?"

"There's no telling what that SOB might do to win the election."

A few minutes later, Matt pulled open the door to the restaurant. As Valerie passed through, the worry in her soft green eyes pulled at his heart. Probably shouldn't have mentioned Frank Carter's underworld connections. It might make her worry even more.

He clamped his mouth shut and stepped inside. "Look at it from another angle. What if Christy hasn't been kidnapped? What if she left willingly? I don't think she'd come here by herself. Is there anyone your sister would be likely to run off with?"

Valerie glared at him. "She's married to Gordon. Why would she go away with someone?"

The restaurant with its white tablecloths, and framed oil paintings of bullfights was obviously the best one in town. No sign of Christy.

He turned to Valerie. "I hate to say this about your sister, but sometimes I wonder about her. Gordon took me to watch a fashion show she was in once. Some older man wearing a Rolex was there with another woman. I told Gordon Christy was flirting with the man, but my stubborn brother claimed she was just trying to get the guy to buy something."

"Flirting comes naturally to Christy. I'm sure she didn't mean anything by it."

Matt's gaze met hers. "Just like it didn't mean anything when she flirted with Gordon while he was dating you?"

The pained look on Valerie's face made him sorry he'd been so blunt. Gordon probably found it awkward to break up with Valerie to date her sister, but he'd fallen head over heels in love with Christy. According to Gordon, after he and Christy became engaged, family dinners at Christy's house were really strained. By the time the wedding rolled around, Matt figured Valerie had put that behind her. However, as maid of honor, she'd had been so frosty to him while he was best man, he'd needed a couple of drinks to feel warm again.

Obviously, she still hated his guts as well as Gordon's. He touched her arm. Seeing her flinch, he pulled back. "I'm sorry. I shouldn't have said that. At the fashion show, I was embarrassed to see how Christy behaved. Could she have gone off with someone else who'd treat her to a good time and buy her things?"

Sparks flashed in Valerie's eyes. A thoughtful look crossed her face. She twirled her ring with twisted bands of gold and silver. She faced him, her look defensive. "We had to do without a lot growing up. Christy's always liked nice things, but she wouldn't just take off with another man. She loves Gordon, really she does."

"But if she did, who might she go with?"

Valerie frowned. "The only one she might spend some time with is Buck Robbins. And on a vanity license plate BAD BOY is just the kind of statement he'd make."

"What's this Buck like?"

"Blond crew cut, good manners, dresses nice. Our parents thought he was perfect until they found out about his drinking binges and pot parties." She brushed a lock of hair from her forehead. "Mom forbade Christy to date him again. That was five years ago. I haven't seen him since, except at her wedding. Didn't you escort a drunken guest from the reception? That might've been Buck."

Matt nodded. "Hell, the guy slobbered all over your sister in the receiving line. What's he like when he's sober?"

"Christy claimed he only smoked pot occasionally. His daring escapades thrilled her. She snuck out to be with him the night he painted a caricature of Dolly Parton on a water tower."

"Matt shook his head. "Man, what a show off. I'll show Christy's picture to the hostess. You describe Buck. Your knowing Spanish will be a great help."

Matt held out the picture to the pixie-faced hostess. As Valerie described Buck, the hostess's brown eyes lit up. "*Si*, I mean yes. He was here." She pointed to the photo. "Her too. She laughed a lot—too much tequila. She was *borracha*."

"Drunk?" Valerie asked.

"*Si*."

Valerie shook her head. "Not real drunk I bet. She gets that way after only one drink. That's all she ever has. But I can't believe she'd be careless enough to drink even that much if she's pregnant."

"Pregnant? Neither she nor Gordon have said anything to me about that." He turned back to the hostess. "How long ago were they here?" Matt asked.

The hostess looked at her watch. "Twenty minutes maybe."

Valerie leaned forward. "Did they say where they were going?"

"La Cucaracha. The man, he wanted a *cerveza*. Tecate is a special kind of beer. We ran out of it here."

Matt grabbed Valerie's hand. "Come on, I know the place."

Outside, with her hand clasped in his, Matt liked the soft warmth of her fingers. He could almost feel as if she were a kindred spirit while they tried to save

13

Christy, but they'd never be close. No doubt she'd had more than enough dealings with Larson men. All she wanted from him was help finding Christy.

She pulled her hand away and hurried to keep up with his brisk pace. His determined chin jutted out as he strode down the street. There was no point trying to charm her. "Tell me more about this Buck."

"At my graduation, Buck marched into the high school auditorium wearing western boots and twirling a lariat. Everyone laughed, but Christy watched him in rapt attention. Later she told me he'd been the one who put hydrogen sulfide into the air-conditioning system a month earlier."

"Whew. Bet everyone poured out of the building to escape the rotten egg smell."

Valerie bit her lip. "It doesn't seem right to tell tales on my sister, but if we're going to find Christy, there's something else I'd better let you know. She dated Buck the night before she became engaged."

"What about after that?"

Valerie twisted her ring. "I don't think so."

He stopped in front of a weathered one-story building with slivers of red paint visible in places.

"You sure it's the right place? Christy wouldn't go in a place like this," Valerie said.

"I checked here earlier, but maybe they came by after I left. We'll ask again."

He held the door open, then followed her inside. Smells of dust, sweat, and cigarettes assaulted him. Fans whirred, but didn't cool the stuffy air. Knowing Christy, he couldn't imagine her sitting on one of those rickety barstools, but now he wasn't sure what Christy might do. Seeing only men at the bar, he scanned the scarred wooden tables.

No Christy. Matt's heart fell.

He spoke to the bartender. Fingering a jagged scar running down the side of his face, the wiry man said, "They left. The lady didn't like it here. Asked that blond gringo to take her someplace else."

"Did they say where they were going?"

The bartender nodded. "The hotel—to pack."

Matt turned to Valerie. "Let's go."

Outside, she said, "I don't get it. There's only one hotel in this town, the one where I've been staying. How come we didn't bump into each other?"

"Maybe this Buck character is keeping Christy out of sight."

"When we get to the hotel, I have a rental car we can use. I wasn't taking any chances of getting my new Miata rear-ended again after your Hummer accordion pleated it." She frowned.

Matt paused and stared at her, remembering the clashing of metal that barely dented his vehicle. He felt bad about messing up her car, but he'd already apologized once. That was enough. "You still steamed over that? My insurance company fixed your car as good as new. I checked. Turn in your rental car. We'll use mine."

She frowned. "I said I wanted to help—not obey your every command. It's my sister we're looking for. I insist on being part of any decision. Why take your rental car instead of mine? I have an Escort with air conditioning, and it gets good mileage."

He stared at her. "What if we have to chase them? Mine has air conditioning plus more power and more speed. Besides, it's closer. Turn here."

She followed him down a short street. "I hate to say it, but I guess you're right. I'll turn mine in, but it needs to go back to Monterrey."

"Pay someone at your hotel to return it."

She wrinkled her brows, but finally said, "Okay."

Matt led her to a red Mustang and held the door open.

She stared. "I'd expect you to rent something bigger."

"It's not a rental. I drove my car." He'd been in a hurry to get here after Gordon speculated about where Christy might have gone. Matt really needed to get his brother out of jail. He was still resentful his law firm hadn't agreed to lend him enough money to pay a bail bondsman a percentage of Gordon's million-dollar bail. Could his position at the firm be shaky?

Valerie slid inside. "What happened to your humongous Hummer?"

"Guzzled gas like a hippo, so I traded it." He drove to Hotel La Paloma.

Nearing the hotel, Matt's pulse raced. From what the bartender said, it sounded like Christy was with Buck. But if the blood in the truck was related to a possible miscarriage, why wouldn't Christy have gone to a hospital and called her family? And why would she run off with Buck?

Didn't she realize she was jeopardizing her life, and maybe the baby's by leaving then?" If she loved Gordon, why risk his run for mayor? And if she had come here with Buck, would the guy spend time with someone else's wife if she were pregnant? Maybe the baby was his. That was a chilling thought. Did Buck want to win her back or was he out to get revenge on

Gordon for marrying her?

Matt jerked the car to a stop in front of Hotel La Paloma. In a flash, Valerie climbed out and rushed inside. He followed. They'd find Christy and get some answers.

The lobby was deserted except for a clerk with long dark hair behind the desk. The clerk's face was hidden behind a novel titled *Wild at Heart* by Jane Graves. Matt sighed. That described Christy all right.

Matt grasped Valerie's wrist. "I checked here earlier, but the other desk clerk didn't understand much English."

"I'll see what I can find out." Valerie tapped on the counter. "Did a blonde American woman with a tall blond American man come here?"

The clerk brushed long, dark hair from her nametag, which said, Carmelita, and stared at her. Matt laid Christy's picture on the counter.

"*La mujer*," Valerie paused.

The woman looked down at the photograph. "*Si*, the *señora* and her husband, they paid the bill and left."

Valerie scowled. "Damn, my sister's not only wild at heart, but she's a liar."

Matt shrugged. "Hey, this is a small town in a Catholic country. She could hardly say he was her lover." He faced the clerk. "Did it look like he was forcing her to go with him?"

Carmelita shook her head. "She said she wanted to go home."

"Did they say where they were going?" Valerie asked.

Thank goodness, she was focused on asking the right questions.

17

The clerk pursed her lips. "They argued. She wanted to go to San Antonio in Texas. The man wanted to go to Houston."

Valerie snatched the photo and handed it to Matt. "That's just great. Which way do we go?"

Chapter Three

Valerie handed Christy's picture back to Matt and asked the hotel clerk. "How long ago did they leave?"

The woman looked at her watch. "About ten minutes."

Matt grabbed Valerie's hand. "Come on, we may catch them. With a license plate that says, BAD BOY they won't be hard to spot."

"I have to pack."

He ran his fingers through his brown waves. "We can't afford to lose any more time."

Valerie's chin jutted out. "Tell them to have my bill ready. I'll run upstairs and get my bag."

"Gordon's rotting in jail. I'm not taking a chance on missing your sister. If you're not here in ten minutes, I'm leaving."

Valerie scowled, but raced to the second floor. She slammed her things into her bag and ran downstairs. She tossed some money, a key, and a receipt on the counter and asked the clerk to have someone return her rental car. She followed Matt outside.

He looked at his watch. "Eight minutes. I'm impressed. Let's go."

As he maneuvered around an ancient, rusting car, Valerie closed the window, trying not to inhale the stirred up dust. The Mustang bounced along over the rutted road. Matt flipped a switch. The air conditioning fan ruffled her hair, and the cool air felt good on her neck.

Matt glanced her way. "That brown dress with all the flowers you bought...with your coloring, it should look good on you."

Imagine that, Matt complimenting her. The look in his brown eyes even seemed sincere. "Thanks." Maybe she could put up with him after all.

As he handed her the map, the touch of his fingers sent a tingle along her arm. She ignored that. She only wanted to find Christy.

He pointed to the map. "You be the navigator. This highway goes north to the border. After we get in the states, it leads to San Antonio and Houston. If we don't see them by the time the routes split, I'll have to choose which way to go. Tell me, besides high school pranks, what kind of man is this Buck?"

She didn't like the way Matt seemed to be making all the decisions without consulting her. She'd followed him across half of El Jardin Bonito, and now he was deciding which city they'd go to. It reminded her too much of Gordon. He had been bossy, demanding and domineering. From her few encounters with Matt, it looked as if the acorn didn't fall far from the tree. Gordon deserved whatever grief Christy gave him. And if Matt thought he was running this show, he had another think coming.

"Valerie, what else can you tell me about Buck?"

"He's likely to gamble on anything. He's a reckless driver, but he is a charmer. The one time he was at our house, he buttered me up while Christy finished dressing." She twisted her ring. "The boys buzzed around Christy. She'd concentrate on those from the wealthier parts of town. Buck was older and had enough money to show Christy a good time."

Matt waited for an old man to waddle across the road, then zoomed onto the highway. "So Buck's a wild card?"

"The excitement of the forbidden always appealed to my sister. Maybe it still does."

"You'd think having her husband run for mayor of a big city would be enough excitement."

Valerie sighed. "I guess not." She crossed her arms. "I can't understand why Christy would run off."

"I never saw her wild side until the night she left."

"I wish I'd been there. I might have talked her out of it. What happened?"

"Gordon, Christy, and I were going out to dinner together. I had just gone inside to meet them when she started screaming that she was tired of him always working late or giving a speech and never spending time with her."

"What did Gordon say to that?"

"Something about making money to support her and the baby they hoped to have, and that after the election he'd be home more. I don't know why she couldn't hold off until then."

"My sister never was very patient."

A red Corvette appeared ahead. Valerie squinted in the glare from the sun. "There it is. I can see the letters BAD BOY." Valerie grasped his arm, then let go. "We've caught up."

Matt stepped on the gas, and the car shot forward.

"Way to go, Earnhardt," she said.

"I'll keep a little distance from them and see where they go."

"Wish the cops would stop them for speeding or something."

"If he's as reckless as you say, he might run rather than stop. Then we'd lose them again."

The red convertible pulled farther ahead. "Matt, you'd better step on it." When Matt's car shot ahead, a siren sounded behind them.

Valerie clapped her hands. "Looks like I got my wish."

But the police car with flashing lights was tailing them, not the red car ahead.

"Hell, they'll delay us. Buck and Christy will get away." Matt eased the car to a stop and rolled down the window. "If he speaks to us in Spanish, you'd better talk."

A hulking policeman waddled up to them. The buttons on his uniform strained to contain his belly. His bushy eyebrows came close together in a frown. "You're American, no?"

Matt nodded. "Yes, sir."

"Show me your license and your passport." He glanced at Valerie. "The señorita too."

Valerie dug in her purse, then handed over the requested items.

Holding their documents, the policeman opened the door on Matt's side. "Get out."

"We better do as he says," Matt whispered and stepped from the car. "Is there a problem?"

"You were speeding. We got a report about the driver of a red sports car carrying cocaine. Open the trunk."

Valerie stepped out of the car. "Why didn't you stop the sports car ahead of us? It's red, too. Nothing's in our trunk except our bags."

Matt lifted the trunk lid. The officer opened their suitcases. His pudgy fingers pawed through her bras and panties, making her want to cringe.

He unzipped her cosmetic bag. "*Caramba.*" He held up a jar. "You will come with me."

"B-but," Valerie sputtered. "That's only bath salts…to use when I take a bath."

A stern frown made his round face appear sinister. "You gringos think you can fool us."

Valerie reached to grab the jar.

Matt snatched her arm back. "Don't argue."

"But we'll lose Buck and Christy."

"If we cooperate, he'll let us go sooner."

Valerie turned to the officer. "Sir, if you'll just sniff the contents—it smells like fresh ginger—you'll know I'm telling the truth. It was a gift I tucked it in my cosmetic bag and forgot about. That's probably why it's all clumped together."

"Smell does not matter. Cocaine could be mixed in." The cop stuffed Valerie's jar in his pocket, tossed their bags onto the backseat of the Mustang, then slammed the door. "Get in my car."

Valerie climbed into the back of the police car behind a wire grid. Matt's jaw clenched, but he locked his car and got in.

Valerie leaned against Matt and whispered, "How can he do this to us? We're American citizens. We can go to the American consulate and complain of harassment."

As the policeman started the engine, Matt glared at her. "What makes you think they will let us go there? For that matter, there probably isn't one within a

23

hundred miles of that godforsaken town." He drew a deep breath. "We're sunk now."

"We can't be far from the border. You should have tried to outrun him."

"Too risky. Maybe he's acting tough to show his superior he's checking all possible drug smugglers."

Imagining a tiny cinder block cell, she shuddered. "I've heard about Mexican jails. Heaven help us if they find a reason to hold us."

"We've done nothing wrong except speed. They'll probably fine us and let us go." The worried look on his face said he didn't believe that.

Valerie twisted the material of her skirt, then smoothed it out again. Not knowing what to expect made her heart pound. Her mouth grew dry. She clenched her hands into fists to keep them from shaking. She wanted to find her sister—she really did— but what had she gotten herself into? Was this her punishment for resenting her sister for taking Gordon from her?

As they pulled into town, knots mushroomed in Valerie's stomach. "They can't really throw us in jail, can they?"

"I don't know Mexican law, but I imagine they can hold us on suspicion for twenty-four hours, or maybe even forty-eight." He met her gaze. "That is, if they even follow regulations. Who knows what they'll do in El Jardin Bonito?"

Valerie gasped. "You're not making me feel any better."

"I just want you to know we may be in for a rough time. And there's not a damn thing I can do about it."

The officer parked in front of a frame building with

a sign that said *Policia.* He motioned for them to get out.

Valerie swallowed. "Do you suppose a bribe would get us loose?"

Matt shrugged. "Don't have much cash. Not sure it would do any good unless I had big bucks."

The officer motioned for them to hurry.

Inside they waited on hard wooden chairs. The officer stepped inside an office in front of them. The word Director was painted on top of the half-open door. Behind the desk sat a leaner man wearing a crisp uniform. Their Spanish was so rapid she only caught a few words here and there.

Matt's hand on her arm startled her. "What are they saying?"

"They plan to keep us twenty-four hours while they send my bath crystals to Monterrey to be tested. Do you suppose they'll allow us a phone call?"

He shrugged. "Who could I call? I doubt any of my colleagues know much about Mexican law."

Her stomach churned, and she twisted her ring. "Can't we demand to be taken to an embassy office in Monterrey?"

"That's twenty or thirty miles away and Monterey may not have one. We shouldn't make any demands. They might lock us up and forget about us for days, maybe without food."

Valerie met his gaze. "They can't do that, can they?"

"If we're under lock and key, they can do anything they want."

Visions of rape and torture scared her so much she couldn't speak. She wiped her clammy hands on her skirt, hoping she'd only have to fight one man at a time.

The officer came out of his supervisor's office and approached them. "We will hold you until the lab tests for illegal substances."

Valerie's spirits sank. She whispered to Matt, "I hope they're not going to throw us in jail."

Matt met her gaze. "Don't give him any ideas," he whispered.

The stern-faced deputy led them inside a small room with a desk, a small computer, and two chairs. At the door he paused. "You stay in this room. You have *dinero*? You can pay me five hundred dollars now and leave."

"How about fifty dollars?" Matt asked. "That's all I have."

The officer spat on the floor, splattering dust. "*No bueno*. You stay here." He left, slamming the door. Then a click sounded.

"Probably locked us in." Matt glanced at the tiny window. "And we can't get out that way."

Chapter Four

Feeling trapped, Valerie glanced around the small dingy room in the police station. "You're a lawyer. Aren't they trampling on our rights?"

"Can't be sure. I don't know Mexican law."

Valerie pointed to the computer. "Look, he left it on."

Matt moved the mouse. The screen lit up—with a game of solitaire. "I'll try to hook into the internet before he comes back."

He entered Monterrey + law. Tourist information flashed on the screen.

Valerie pointed to a picture of a canyon. "Canon de La Huasteca, that's where Christy said she wanted to go."

Matt squinted at the directions in small print. "Too far. It's on the Baja peninsula. Besides, after questioning that clerk in Monterrey, I'm sure she came here instead." He entered Nuevo Leon + law. "That's what state Monterrey is in."

He clicked a few more times and found Electronic Guide to Mexican Law. The screen went blank. It took five minutes to get the site again. He scanned through a Brief History of the Mexican Legal System, found the list of states, and then clicked on Nuevo Leon. "Bingo," he said, then peered closer. "Damn, it's in Spanish."

Valerie leaned over his shoulder. "See if there's an

English version. I can translate, but you'll understand that one better."

Matt returned to the earlier screen. "There is but you have to pay."

Noises at the door sent a chill through Valerie. "Uh-oh."

The door creaked open. "What are you doing?" the deputy barked.

Matt punched a few buttons, apparently trying to retrieve the computer game. The deputy's footsteps came closer. Valerie leaned over Matt, hoping to block the guard's view of the monitor.

The officer smoothed his uniform over a protruding belly and moved to stand beside Matt. "You lost my game."

Matt clicked the mouse again. "There's your game, sir." Matt stood, his chin jutting out. "Señor, tell us what we are charged with or let us go."

"Trafficking in unlawful drugs."

"B-but… Those are just bath crystals to make the water smell good."

Matt wiped perspiration from his forehead. "Nothing unlawful about taking a bath."

Valerie wished she were in a nice hotel doing that, her skin covered with soap bubbles. Instead, they were sinking in frontier justice.

The officer scowled. "*Callate*."

"He's telling you to shut up," Valerie whispered.

Matt frowned.

Valerie stepped closer to the man. "When can we leave?"

"When the laboratory finishes testing your crystals." He smirked and held out his hand. "Unless you give me five hundred dollars, you are our guests."

Matt ignored the bribery attempt.

Valerie frowned. "We don't feel like guests locked in here."

"You'd like private rooms? I can take you to our jail."

Matt stepped in front of her. "Never mind what she said. We will stay here."

"Señor." Valerie picked up paper and a pen. "What is your name?"

The deputy looked startled, but only for a moment. "Why you need to know?"

"We will want to tell your director how well you treated us—that you used proper procedure in interrogating prisoners."

"*Me llamo* Pedro Gonzales. How you know what is proper procedure? You are gringos."

"I presume you are supposed to ask questions, not do—"

Matt grabbed her arm. "Don't suggest anything."

The officer frowned. "We don't beat citizens who cooperate. Sit. I have questions."

Valerie bit her lip. They weren't even citizens. There could be a different standard for foreigners. She would try not to panic.

The policeman remained standing. "Tell me your names, where you are born, and why you come to Mexico."

After he and Valerie provided the information. Matt explained they were looking for his brother's wife and thought someone had kidnapped her.

"So talk to the police? The city pays us to take care of that."

Valerie leaned forward. "The people we talked to said they saw someone who looked like Christy, but she was with another man. We were trying to catch up with them when you stopped us."

"*Es una mujer mala*?"

"My sister is not bad." Valerie scowled and started to rise.

Matt stuck out his arm to block her. "I think she is being forced to travel with that man."

The deputy fingered his mustache. His stare threatened to intimidate her. "So why do you travel with a man not your husband?"

"What business is that of yours?" asked Valerie.

Matt frowned at her, but said nothing.

The officer said, "I ask questions to find out what you do in Mexico. We no want people who plan crimes in our country."

"We're not here for that," said Valerie. "We just want to find my sister."

"To shame her for traveling with man not her husband?"

Valerie looked at Matt. "Shall we tell him?"

"Tell me what?" The man's eyebrows moved closer together.

"My brother has been accused of murdering his wife," Matt said. "I want to find her to prove my brother is innocent."

"How do I know you do not try to save a criminal? Maybe he killed his wife. Your *familia* may be cursed with evil thoughts and bad deeds."

Matt clenched his fists. "My brother is not a murderer. If you hadn't stopped us, we could have caught up with the man we believe kidnapped Christy."

"Maybe your brother beat her, and she wanted to get away."

Matt scowled. "My brother does not beat his wife."

Valerie's chin jutted out. "We answered your questions. Now, please answer mine. When will you let us go?"

"When the laboratory has finished with your— what you call it—bath something?"

"Bath crystals."

Frowning, the officer turned off the computer. "You stay here. Do not touch anything." He left, locking the door behind him.

"Now what?" asked Valerie.

Matt turned on the computer. "I have to find that web page with Mexican law."

Valerie kept looking at the clock. "Hurry, we don't know when he might come back."

Two minutes later, he finally pulled up the page. Valerie stood beside him. "You have the same fragrance as those bath crystals. We're in so much trouble for a pleasant scent. Goodness knows how long we'll have to stay here."

Valerie sighed. "He might still throw us in jail."

"If so, I hope he lets us stay together instead of shoving us in with criminals."

Uneasiness shook her stomach. "I don't even want to think about that. Especially not now that it's getting dark."

"What difference does that make?"

"They seem to be shorthanded. Suppose they want to leave for the night and lock us in jail until morning?" Fear curdled in her stomach.

"Let's not worry about that until it happens."

An hour later, the officer brought them two burritos and two cups of coffee, then left.

While eating the meager fare, Valerie looked out the tiny window. Dusk came. Then darkness, unfettered with stars or moon. Thunder rumbled in the distance.

"I guess he means to leave us here for the night," Matt said. "We may have to sleep on the floor, but that beats being in a jail cell."

A click sounded from the door. He grasped Valerie's hand. "I won't let him separate us. I'll keep you safe if it's the last thing I do. I hope like hell it won't come to that."

The director, a tall, thin man with a stern-faced look, stepped inside. He looked Valerie over. His gaze dwelled on her chest for a long moment. She stood straight and proud, trying to ignore his lecherous look.

The director cleared his throat. "I regret to inform you that you must make use of our hospitality until tomorrow. The lab workers in Monterrey left for the day without testing the substance you were carrying."

Valerie twisted her fingers. "It's only bath crystals. If you smelled it, you could tell."

The director frowned. "The lab will find out. Come with me." He stood there tapping his foot.

Valerie rose and smoothed her skirt.

"Hurry up," he barked.

Spurred by his harsh tones, she moved quickly, careful not to step too close to him. Matt took her hand. Despite their situation, his firm grasp comforted her.

"It may not be as bad as you think. There should be beds," Matt whispered.

"Yeah. They probably have lice and bed bugs." She hunched her shoulders and made a face.

Jangling a ring of keys, the officer locked the door and led them to a doorway on the left. Inhaling smells of urine and cooking grease, she followed him down a narrow hall. Dusty air made breathing difficult.

The officer stopped before a door and opened it. Inside stood a metal double bed with coarse looking sheets. An open doorway revealed a toilet and washstand. "The lady can stay here, but I will lock her in."

Still smarting from the way he'd looked at her earlier, Valerie had visions of an unauthorized bed check in the middle of the night. She shook her head. "I want to stay with Matt."

The officer frowned. "You'll have to be in a cell then." He led them farther down the hall, which opened to a large area containing three barred cells.

Two held prisoners. From the smell of him, one was apparently sleeping off a drunken stupor. The second, dressed in a stained shirt and dirty trousers, stared at them.

The jailer stopped before the second cell and sorted his keys. Matt shook his head. "Put us in the empty cell."

The officer's eyes widened. He pointed to Valerie. "You and the lady?"

"Yes."

"*Es muy bonita.* How can I be sure you will behave?"

Matt glared at the officer. "I would not dishonor the lady in front of witnesses."

"If she has fire in her heart, she might scratch your eyes out."

He opened the door and gestured for Valerie to

enter. She stepped inside onto a dirty concrete floor and flinched. A rusted metal cot sagged in the corner. No telling what kind of vermin nested beneath. A dingy stain ringed the gray concrete wall about six inches from the floor. She pointed. "What's that from?"

"When hurricanes come, sometimes it rains hard, and the water comes in."

Thunder sounded again. She wouldn't cringe in front of the officer. She sat on the cot's thin mattress. A sheet with ragged edges and a blanket lay in a heap at the foot. A wooden bucket in the corner smelled of feces.

Their jailer shoved Matt inside and locked the door. The clank resounded against the concrete walls, followed by his footsteps on the dirty floor between the cells. At the doorway he turned. "You'll stay here until the lab completes the tests."

The drunk raised up and ran his hand through his grizzled unkempt hair. "Forget what he says. You're in this hell-hole to stay."

Chapter Five

Valerie gripped the bars as a drunk spit in the corner of his own cell. "How long have you been here?"

"Not sure. A year maybe. Better get used to it. You won't be leavin' any time soon." He flopped back down on his sagging cot.

"Things might get ugly," Matt said. "I can take it, but I worry about you."

She met his gaze. Would she be raped or tortured?

"I hope they don't do anything to break your fighting spirit. I could kick myself for not insisting you go back to Texas earlier."

The other prisoner, barely past his teens, moved to the front of his cell and fingered a straggly auburn goatee. "*Vas a comer la gata?*"

Matt turned and asked Valerie, "What's he saying?"

Valerie felt heat rising to her neck. "Never mind."

"Come on, tell me."

"Literally, it means are you going to eat the cat?"

Matt looked puzzled, and then nodded. "He means pussy, doesn't he?"

A mischievous smile lit up the young prisoner's face. His guffaws echoed against the cell walls. Even the officer laughed.

Valerie covered her heated cheeks with her hands.

There was no way they could sleep on that narrow cot without touching each other. Matt might be arrogant and conceited, but surely he wouldn't take advantage of her.

She couldn't even think about things like that now. More important, how long would they have to stay here, and could they stomach the food?

Matt grasped the bars again and spoke sharply to the departing officer. "Señor, we need another bed in here."

Valerie shot a surprised glance at Matt. Maybe, unlike Gordon, he had an ounce of compassion.

The officer shook his head. "No more beds."

Valerie rose. "What about the one in that room you showed me?"

"It will not fit."

Matt pointed to the cot. "That's not big enough for both of us."

Laughing, the younger prisoner rocked back and forth on his cot. "*Gata, gata.*"

Valerie felt her face flame, but she wouldn't let Matt stay up all night or sleep on the floor. Stepping next to Matt, she gripped the bars, and tried to ignore the welcome warmth of his arm touching hers. "I'll stay in the room you showed me earlier."

At least she could use the toilet in privacy. Maybe she could crawl out the window and escape to call the American embassy for help.

Their jailer's footsteps slapped against the floor. His key squeaked in the lock. She took one last look at Matt. Would she regret leaving his protection? She hoped not as she followed the director past the stone walls to that room.

Once she stepped inside, his key clicked in the lock. So much for trying to sneak out to use the computer in the other room. She shivered. Had she made a wise choice? She wouldn't let Deputy Gonzales take advantage of her. She wedged a chair under the knob of the hall door and then made use of the tiny bathroom. A pity the window was too small to squeeze through.

She didn't dare take off her dress and lie down in her slip. She wished for her suitcase with her toothbrush. Everything might be stolen from the car by the time they got back to it. She lay down.

She was almost asleep when a noise startled her. The chair she'd wedged under the doorknob rattled. Before she could jump out of bed, the chair crashed to the floor. The door flew open.

Silhouetted in the light from the hall, the wiry director's dark-eyes roved over her body. His lecherous grin made her heart pound. Cold shivers snaked down her back. She held her breath.

He stepped into the room. The whiskey smell on his breath unnerved her. He reeked of body odor. "You have red in your hair. You should be hot woman in bed."

Gritting her teeth at the thought of him touching her, she sat up, binding the sheet around her. She wanted to shout that she'd kick him in the nuts if he tried. Not smart. She clamped her mouth shut and waited, tense. Her pulse raced. If he tried anything, she'd beat the crap out of him—and probably be slammed into a cell for who knew how long.

Frowning, he stepped closer and stared. She tried to steady her heaving chest, but her breaths came in an uneven rhythm, which only made it seem worse. He met her gaze, his eyes dark, intimidating.

She swallowed. She'd try politeness. "If you'll excuse me, I'm very tired and wouldn't be good company. Please leave."

"But if you are nice to Enrique Ruiz…" He smiled. "You and your companion could leave in one hour."

She doubted him.

He played with a lock of her hair, and then ran his fingers down her arm.

She flinched at his touch. She moved her arm away. "There must be some kind of international law. Prisoners are not supposed to be molested."

"Who will dare call it that?" He held his head high, his expression arrogant. He grinned. "You will like it. I will make you scream. "

A shudder skittered down her spine. She straightened, trying not to let him know how scared she was.

His laugh echoed in the small room. "You are my prisoner. Gringas have no rights in Nuevo Leon." His dark eyes glittered in the dim light. He reached for her.

She squared her shoulders. "Don't touch me. If you try anything, I'll report you, and if necessary, I'll get a Mexican lawyer to file charges."

"Everyone knows who runs this town." A malicious grin creased his brown face. "Women say I am very persuasive. Call me hot lover."

"They must have spent too much time in the sun." She swung her feet to the floor and stood, bracing for action. "You're disgusting."

He snorted. "No one says that to Enrique Ruiz." He pulled out a knife, its sharp looking blade gleaming in the shaft of light from the hall.

She stepped closer and forced his arm up. The knife clattered to the floor.

Rage contorted his face. He snatched the knife. "You are bad woman. I teach you lesson."

Valerie planted her feet on the floor and flexed her knees for action. He came at her, his serrated blade raised to slash her face. She knocked the knife loose and crooked her leg around his. He fell. She grabbed the knife. Slashed his cheek before he could rise. Brandishing it toward him, she scowled. "Now get out and stay out. If you come back, I won't scream. I'll kill you." She took a step forward. Dared him to attack.

His mouth wide open, he wiped blood from his face. Frowning, he scrambled to his feet and backed toward the door. "I will call two officers to assist me. We'll make you wish you'd stayed in the cell with your gringo." Valerie stifled a gasp. Blood raced through her arteries. She gripped the knife until her knuckles turned white. She'd fought two in her last black belt test, but she couldn't fight off three. She'd be gang-raped, but she'd bloody a few faces before that happened.

She took a deep breath. Could she bluff him? Maybe he was bluffing. She met his gaze, matched him stare for stare. If the police chief had stayed on duty this late, she'd bet there weren't two more officers on duty. Holding the knife and threatening him, she could probably brazen her way out, but she wasn't leaving without Matt.

Legs tensed, body ready for action, she glared at him. "Someone would find out and leak information. You'd be charged with police brutality, lose your job."

His chin jutted out. "I do not think so. If you go

back quietly to the cell with Senor Matt, I won't call the other officers to subdue you. But if you try to attack me again, I will have you executed for resisting an officer of the law. Now give me that knife and walk ahead of me to the cell."

She shook her head. "I won't give up the knife unless you promise not to call any other officers. You'll get the knife back after I'm in the cell. And you must walk ahead of me all the way to the cell, unlock it, and stand back until after I have entered. Then I will slide it through the bars."

She waited. Would he agree to that?

He scowled. "No *puta* tells me what to do."

"I'm not a whore. Shall I take you down again?" She stared him down and waited.

His eyes flashed daggers at her. He met her stare for a few seconds. Then he took a few steps backward into the hall. "Go then."

She stepped outside the room and faced him. "You first." Again she waited.

He shook his head and pointed. She didn't budge. His tone quiet but forceful, he said, "Go, or I will call my deputies to drag you there."

Keeping her eyes on him, she backed down the hall toward the cells. She stopped in front of the one holding Matt.

Still scowling, the director unlocked the cell. "Get inside."

"Not until you back off."

Finally, he stepped away. She strode inside and turned to glare at him. Ruiz locked the cell door. The young prisoner across from them laughed. "Didn't get any, did you?"

Enrique Ruiz faced him. "*Callate.*"

Matt leaped from the cot. "What happened?"

Ruiz scowled at her. "Do not speak of it."

She glared back.

Ruiz held out his hand. "Give me the knife or I will call all the officers on duty to make you give it to me."

She thought about it for a minute. Maybe he would. She couldn't take the chance. "Stand back then. I will drop it on the floor."

Finally, he moved away a few steps. She tossed the knife through the bars. It hit the metal door at the far end of the hall and clanked to the floor, barely missing his foot. He flinched. She had to clamp her lips together to keep from grinning. Served him right, the bastard.

Mouth clenched in a tight line, he bent to pick it up, then turned and stalked back toward the offices. She let out the breath she'd been holding and released the tight hold on her muscles. Now she couldn't seem to stop shaking.

Matt took pulled her close to his side. His arm around her shoulders steadied her. "You look pale. Are you okay?"

Still breathing heavily, she nodded and tried to control her ragged breathing. She didn't like cutting someone's face, but she'd do it again if she had to.

"Was that blood on his face?" Matt asked. His hand slid down her arm in a caress, and his fingers grasped hers. His gaze roved over her. "I hope you didn't get hurt." The anxiety in his eyes warmed her heart. "What happened?"

"He thought he—" Her voice broke. She lifted her chin. Determined not to show any weakness, she glared at Ruiz. "The bastard thought he could get a little action. Well, I showed him a different kind of action."

Matt grinned. "I'm betting he got the worst of it."

Pausing at the door to the offices, Enrique Ruiz pivoted, and then marched back. A fierce scowl contorted his face. "Shut the hell up!" He turned and stomped back down the corridor. The other prisoners snickered, and Ruiz flipped off the light, leaving them in the darkness. Valerie inched toward the cot.

"I have to hand it to you," Matt said. "I don't know any women who'd best a man the way you did."

She smiled. Her ex-fiancé had never given her credit for anything.

"You've definitely made an enemy of the director." Matt's low tones reached her through the darkness. "It could be spring before we get out of this hell-hole."

Valerie's hands fisted on her hips. "Enemy or not, I wasn't letting el director, the police chief, or whatever he calls himself, rape me."

"Of course not." He let go of her hand. Springs creaked as he sat on the cot. "Come sit beside me."

Rustling sounds told her he was moving to make a place for her. Glad to realize she was no longer shaking, she edged toward his voice. The smell from the toilet bucket filled the fetid air. Not wanting to kick it accidentally, she inched toward him, her shoes scraping on the concrete.

He caught her hand, his strength imparting hope in the darkness. Somehow, they'd get out of here and find Christy. Standing beside the bed, she became conscious of the faint citrusy scent of his aftershave.

Amazed she could pick up that smell over the less pleasant ones, she felt for the mattress and came in contact with his hard thigh. She moved left, trying to put some distance between them before she sat.

She plopped down, but instead of sitting on the bed, she landed in his lap.

His arms went around her. She struggled to get up, but his arms held her more tightly. "I don't want you to fall. Not on this filthy floor. Who knows what germs you could pick up?"

His breath warmed her neck and shoulders. Somehow, in spite of everything, she felt safe in his arms. Together they'd make it through.

Warm gentle fingers caressed her arm, and he hardened beneath her. After Gordon's barbs, she didn't think any man would find her sexy, but obviously, Matt did. She wouldn't comment and embarrass Matt, but a warm glow spread through her. It was good to know he found her attractive, but all she wanted now was to know she was safe.

Matt's hands, firm, yet gentle, took hold of her chin. She hadn't thought she wanted more than comfort, but his lips came down on hers, warm, welcoming, tasting, and filling her heart with wonder. And his mouth, his glorious mouth, banished all thoughts of Ruiz. Grasping her shoulders, he deepened the kiss. He ravished her mouth as if he were starved for her and her alone. Lost in the feel of his lips moving over hers, she tangled her hands in his hair. His springy waves slid over her fingers. She let her mouth answer his unspoken question. She found him attractive, sexy, and his kiss more compelling than any other she'd ever had. She told him with her lips and her hands as she wrapped her arms around him. His hand caressing her breast sent shivers of delight all over her.

Her pulse raced. What a time to discover Matt was

attracted to her. How thrilling was that? Too bad they were in the worst of places to do more than kiss. Ruiz might come back to check on them at any time. Right now they needed to concentrate on escaping. Reluctantly, she shook off his hands and pushed to her feet. "We need to get out of here."

"I know, but we can't do anything about it tonight. Maybe tomorrow they'll have finished testing your bath salts. Might as well get some sleep."

"If we sit in the middle and lean away from each other, maybe we can at least rest."

"Good idea." He grasped her arm and guided her to sit beside him. She lay on the bed, leaving her feet dangling toward the floor. Sounds of the bed creaking told her he was doing the same.

"I'm not sleepy," she said. "Let's talk...about anything except this awful place. What kind of cases do you take?" Her lips still tingling from his kiss, she willed herself to concentrate on his words.

"Family law, personal injury, wrongful death, and a few criminal cases."

"How can you stand to defend criminals?"

"They need a fair trial, just like anyone else."

"Have you ever defended a murderer?"

"Not until now. Gordon told me he didn't kill Christy, and I believe him. He suggested I might find his wife in Monterrey. I'll do whatever it takes to get my brother exonerated."

"I don't think he's guilty either," Valerie said, "but what if that wasn't Christy we saw in that car? What if Gordon did commit murder?"

Matt swallowed. "I don't want to think about the possibility. Growing up, I was in a few fights with my brother. Gordon has a mean streak, and he can fight dirty, but I don't think he'd actually kill his wife. I want justice for him. Whatever that turns out to be."

"So, will your partners in the firm help with his defense?"

Matt frowned. "They'll give me advice, but I'm not a partner yet, so they won't bend over backwards to help. If I don't make a good showing at my brother's trial, it will look bad for me and even worse for Gordon." He sighed. "After I get Gordon acquitted, I need to bring in some big cases in order to stay there."

"How do you do that?"

"Network. Join several civic clubs and sit through their boring meetings."

"Wouldn't that be worth it if more business came your way?"

"Yeah, but that isn't all. I'd have to kiss up to our main partners, Brown and Smith, and tell them they're brilliant whether they are or not. That rubs me the wrong way."

"Can't you compliment them when they do something right?"

"It's not that simple. You don't understand."

"Don't understand what?"

"Politics at a big firm. Why the hell are you telling me what to do?"

"I wasn't. I was just suggesting—"

"Unless it's got something to do with escaping or finding your sister, I'd rather not hear about it."

"Why do men get so annoyed when a woman tries to help?

Matt was silent a moment. "Telling me what to do when you don't know the situation is insulting.

However, I wish I'd been there to help you fight off that bastard. I'd have done more than slash his face. I'd want to kill him."

"I don't think he'll try anything again," she said.

"He may be chief of police, but if el director tries to lay a hand on you again, he'll have to come through me."

Chapter Six

"He'll have to come through me." Matt's determined tones made her feel safer, but the bars of their cell wouldn't keep the director from dragging one of them for interrogation and torture.

He was still making all the decisions in the search for Christy. However, he didn't seem quite the arrogant jerk she'd thought him at the rehearsal dinner for Christy and Gordon.

She'd swallowed the lump in her throat and reminded herself Christy was family. Valerie had acted as a dutiful maid of honor, and hoped no one glimpsed the heartbreak behind her forced smile. However, she had to admit Matt stood up for her, claiming her late arrival was his fault because he'd rear-ended her. Walking beside him, as they followed the wedded couple, she'd tried to ignore his eyes on her. Standing beside her in the reception line, he'd smiled charmingly and whispered, "That dress, what color did you say it was...rust? It looks good on you." She couldn't help smiling back as she waved good-bye to the happy couple as they left for their honeymoon in Monterrey, Mexico.

Now, lying on that jail cot in the dark, she took comfort from the steel in Matt's voice when he vowed to protect her from that bastard police chief. She recalled his determination earlier while he accessed the internet. He'd been so frustrated when he couldn't glean enough information to make a claim that might get them out of jail. If she was imprisoned, she'd rather have Matt by her side any day. He might be domineering, but at least she could depend on him to protect her.

It must have been hours later when a ray of sun from a window at the end of the hall woke her. She felt deliciously warm. Blinking at the bright light, she figured Matt must have tucked the blanket around her. Then she realized he was lying beside her. His arm hugged her waist, and his muscular body heated her all the way down. Her legs were tangled with his, and his hardness pressed against her belly.

She shook his arm. "Wake up. We can't let el director find us like this."

He snuggled closer and kissed her cheek. "Why not?"

Reluctantly she eased away, her cheek still warm and tingling from his soft kiss. Why did his kiss make her feel so comforted, so safe, and even desirable? She wanted to taste his kiss again, see if she'd experience more of the same wonderful feeling, but this wasn't the time. They needed to be careful. They had to do everything they could to get out of here. "If that lecherous director finds us so cozy, who knows what he might do?"

Yawning, Matt snuggled closer, then pulled away and pushed up on his elbows. "Good point." He rose, supporting himself with one arm, then leaned back and looked at her with rapt attention. His lazy brown-eyed gaze bathed her face, awakening her senses better than the bright sun. "Got any ideas to get us out of here?"

Surprised, she stared. Was he actually asking for suggestions? That was a first. "We should demand to be released," she said, feeling cooler after he moved. Glancing at his lips, so help her, she wanted to feel then against hers once more. They'd be warm and insistent. She sighed.

He rested his chin in his hand. "It's worth a try," he said, but now his gaze seemed focused on her mouth. He touched her arm and leaned closer. She looked in his eyes. He was going to kiss her. Anticipation set her quivering.

The sound of rattling keys and footsteps snapped her to attention, setting her senses on alert. She sat up and put her feet on the floor.

Instead of Enrique, Pedro walked into the hallway. He unlocked the cell door and motioned for them to step out.

Where was he taking them? Shivers ran down her spine, itching and tingling in a way she couldn't ignore. Her stomach knotted. Valerie bit her lip, and then whispered," Do you think they'll shoot us because I fought the supervisor?"

Matt grasped her trembling hand and squeezed it. "I hope not. It might hurt."

How could he joke at a time like this?

Matt's stern face portrayed his control, but his fingers gripped hers. "Where are you taking us?"

Pedro beckoned them to follow. "Outside."

Matt whispered, "If you see men with rifles, run."

Her heart beat faster as Pedro led them through the lobby to the front door. Still holding Matt's hand, she tried not to think about not living to see another day. Or about the pain of being shot and dying. She wasn't ready to think about death. She wanted to live. It was time to concentrate on getting away. Outside stood the same old police vehicle that brought them here.

"Go, get in the car," Pedro barked.

Pulse racing, she halted. "Not until you tell us where you are taking us."

Pedro's jaw dropped. "You wish to stay here?"

Matt stepped in front of her. "The lady worries that we might be shot. Tell her she's wrong."

Pedro snorted. Arrows of apprehension prickled her arms. She glanced at the wall clock. Reminding her of schoolroom clocks when life was safe, it ticked slowly, maddeningly. She waited for Pedro to deny they faced execution.

Long seconds passed.

Matt gripped her hand harder. Now he looked anxious—no, make that scared. Meeting his gaze, she decided he must be as scared as she. "Maybe we should kiss goodbye now." He put his arm around her waist.

His arm comforted her, but it couldn't stop her from thinking about dying. About all the things she hadn't done—and might never do. She studied Pedro's face, trying to see the truth behind his solemn expression.

Pedro pointed a finger at Matt. "Do not kiss the woman. Not a good thing to do."

Matt scowled and clenched his hands into fists, then pulled her close. "Why the hell not?"

Pedro inclined his head toward the police station. "El director, Señor Ruiz—he fancies the lady. If you kiss her, he might not let you go."

Valerie stepped back and let out the breath she'd been holding. "You mean he's going to release us?"

Pedro nodded. "Go outside."

"Wait a minute," Matt said. "You haven't said where you're taking us."

Pedro held the door open. "You want to go back to your car, no?"

She nodded. "You walk out first. We'll follow."

Pedro frowned. "Do not tell me what to do." He motioned for them to step outside. "Get in the car."

"C'mon." Matt's warm hand on her back, urging her toward the car, helped calm her fear. But her heart still raced. She opened the back door of the car and slid in the backseat.

Matt walked to the car. He put one foot inside, then turned to look at Pedro, still standing near the police station door. Ruiz stepped out and turned to speak to Pedro. She heard *"Mátelos"* and *"coche,"* but couldn't make out the words in between.

Valerie guessed at the meaning and gasped.

"What did he say?" Matt asked.

"He said, *'Mátelos.'* He's going to kill us, then take our car." She struggled with the door handle on the side away from the police building. "We've got to get away."

The handle wouldn't give.

Her throat constricted. She didn't want to die. Not now. Not before they found her sister. Not here—far from family and friends. She grabbed the lock button and pulled. Unlike more modern police cars, it worked. She yanked the door open. "Come on. We can run behind those houses across the street."

She got out and glanced back. Matt scrambled across the seat behind her and out the door. Valerie ran across the road. Matt followed.

Shouts sounded behind them.

Heart pumping furiously, she dashed behind a house. She hoped the pounding footsteps she heard were Matt's.

He caught up. "Don't slow down, not until we're farther away."

She ran faster. Panting, she shoved her way through a tangled hedge of gray-green cenzia bushes into another yard. "Can you see anybody"—she gulped in several deep breaths—"coming after us?"

"I hear footsteps, but can't see anyone. Keep running."

She came out on a dirt street. Saw a row of small wood and tarpaper shacks. Looked up and down the street. No bushes to hide behind. "What now?"

He pointed between two houses. "That way."

She raced across hard-packed dirt with scraggly clumps of grass. Behind the homes, yards ran together. No fences to climb, thank goodness. A chicken pecked at something on the ground. Brown-skinned children were skipping rope and laughing. A dog chased a cat up a tree. As she ran past, the dog stood below, yapping at the cat. After ducking behind a large bush, she peeked back between two houses.

Ruiz stood in the middle of the street, his rifle slung over his shoulder. He looked both ways. Had he seen them? Could they outrun him?

She beckoned to Matt and pointed. "The director's got a gun."

Matt grabbed her hand and pointed to a steep hill topped by a large house. "Come on."

Valerie scrambled up the rugged hill of packed dirt and rocks. Her side hurt. Forced her to slow her pace.

Matt forged ahead. She tried to keep up. Picked her way around large rocks. Ignored the pebble and the sand in her shoe and the sand.

Finally, almost out of breath, she reached a four-foot cyclone fence surrounding a large yard. Begonias and roses bloomed in profusion. Beyond them stood a large brick house with a covered patio. Matt stood on the other side of the fence. "Hurry."

Still panting, she climbed over. About to jump down, she felt a tug on her skirt. It had caught on the curved wires protruding from the fence.

"C'mon, hurry."

"My skirt's caught." She struggled to free it, and then jumped down, ripping her skirt.

Matt cast an appreciative glance at the exposed curve of her thigh, then took her hand. "Let's ask these folks for help."

"What if they report us instead?"

"That's a chance we have to take." He gulped in air. "We can't keep running much longer." He looked back. "I don't see anyone chasing us now."

"That doesn't mean anything." Valerie hurried toward the house's back door. Beside it, yellow jasmine blossoms decorated a trellis, covering it and giving off a pleasant fragrance. "This place is huge. At least we're not in direct view from the houses below us."

"There's a smudge on your cheek. We don't want to look like tramps." With gentle fingers, he brushed it off, his brown eyes watching her intently. "There, that's better." A smile lit up his face. Things didn't seem quite so hopeless.

She smoothed her skirt, finger-combed her hair, then knocked on the door. No one answered.

From inside came sounds of a baby crying.

Matt nudged her. "Knock again."

She did. The door opened a crack.

A uniformed maid, or maybe a nanny, peeked out. "*Que quiere Usted?*"

"What did she say?" Matt asked.

"She's asking what we want." Valerie turned back to the nanny. "*Un telefono, por favor. Quiero* taxi."

The nanny beckoned her inside, but when he stepped forward, she shook her head. "*La señorita, si. Usted, no.*" She shut the door in his face.

****

Matt edged back toward the fence. Down the hill, Ruiz stood looking up. Matt ducked under the patio roof. His breath caught. Had Ruiz seen him? Matt peeked in the window. Valerie was using the telephone.

Ruiz started up the hill. He was huffing and puffing. Would a taxi get here in time? If the director got much closer he'd see Matt. Edging behind the trellis, Matt realized it wasn't much cover. He hoped Valerie could explain enough to relieve the nanny's fears so she'd let him in.

He knocked on the window. Valerie hung up and spoke to the woman holding the crying baby. Matt waited. Valerie rattled off more Spanish and pointed to him. The maid hesitated, and then finally let him in.

Pulse racing, he hurried in and shut the door behind him. "Ruiz is heading this way. Don't know if he saw me or not."

"The man on the phone said a taxi would be here in five minutes," Valerie said. "This woman's a nanny. She told me we could wait on the front porch."

"We'd better wait inside. Ask her to show us to the

front of the house."

Valerie talked to the nanny, who set down the now-quiet baby, and led them to the front door. Matt peeked outside. No taxi yet.

A knock sounded from the back.

Matt froze. Tugged at Valerie's hand. Edged toward the front door.

Valerie spoke in Spanish to the nanny. The woman shook her head. Valerie touched the nanny's arm. "Please don't let him in."

The baby's cries joined with insistent knocking. The woman hurried back. Sounds of a door being opened echoed through the house.

Valerie followed Matt out the front door. "He might search the house. Maybe we can hide behind the bushes."

Matt eased the door shut. A few low shrubs sat beside the concrete porch. His stomach tightened. How could he protect them with no weapon? And the taxi hadn't come.

Valerie ran down the three steps and crouched behind a cenzia bush dotted with lavender-pink flowers beside the porch. She motioned to him to join her.

He jumped off the porch and squeezed in beside her. He knelt in the soft dirt, and dampness seeped in around his knees. Must be a sprinkler system here.

Noises and loud voices came from inside. "What's he saying?" Matt asked.

"I can't make out anything but bad words. I must have really dented his macho ego."

The front door flew open. Ruiz stomped out. Let loose a string of curses.

Matt shrank behind the bush. He put his arm

around Valerie. Scooted her closer. Hoped Ruiz couldn't see them.

A taxi pulled up and honked, but Ruiz still stood on the porch. Inside the baby was crying, and sounds of the nanny trying to hush it came through the open door.

The taxi honked again. The chief paced the porch, glancing their way several times. How long would it be before he saw them through the bushes?

What could he do then to protect her?

Chapter Seven

Valerie crouched behind a bush. The taxi honked again. Director Ruiz stood on the three-step front porch. Soft branches poked her arm, and the fragrance of the lavender blooms teased her nose. She wanted to race to the taxi but didn't dare. She scrunched closer to Matt's warmth and protection.

The director reached into his shirt pocket. Would he pull out a gun? She held her breath. His pocket wasn't large enough for a gun, but might hold a cell phone. He could call for backup. For all she knew, he already had. He turned away from her, so she couldn't see what he pulled out. She bit her lip. Watched and waited.

She leaned closer to Matt. Whispered in his ear. "Should we run now? Before he calls for reinforcements?"

Matt shook his head and put a finger to his lips.

The chief looked in their direction. She froze. Sweat slid down between her breasts. Had he heard her?

Her heart pounded. Matt grasped her hand. His strong grip reassured her—for the moment at least. She strained to see through the dense gray-green foliage and saw a flicker of flame. Ruiz took a drag on his cigarette. The smoldering smell of the cigarette reached her nose immediately. Would he give up hunting them and return to the station?

The taxi honked again. The Mexican driver, tan and chubby, walked up to the director, who stood next to the porch steps. They spoke in rapid Spanish. Ruiz gestured up and down the road, and then asked the driver if he'd seen them. At least that sounded like what he was saying.

She held her breath. Had the driver spied them? Finally, the driver shook his head. She let out the breath she'd been holding. Now if the director would just leave, she'd feel safe.

The director touched the cut she'd slashed on his face in the jail. He cursed, calling her a whore. She clenched her hands into fists. She wanted to stomp out and strangle the bastard, but that wouldn't be smart. He was alone now, but sooner or later, he could have the full police force behind him.

More than likely she didn't have enough time to fight him and get away. Ruiz, a typical macho Mexican male, must hate that a woman had bested him. Probably he'd be too humiliated to let anyone know. Instead, he'd claim she was a streetwalker who resisted arrest.

What if she got away, but Matt didn't? If the police took it out on him, she'd never forgive herself. How would she explain to his brother, that Matt hadn't made it? She sighed.

Ruiz cursed. Shrugging, the taxi driver ambled back to his vehicle. The director bent to stub out his cigarette on the concrete porch step.

Through the bushes she could see his black eyes and frowning mouth. He rose and spoke into a cell phone.

Valerie tensed. Since he faced away from them,

she couldn't make out much of his conversation. Was he calling for reinforcements? She gripped Matt's hand tighter. They wouldn't have a chance of eluding a swarm of cops.

The director stepped inside the house and eased the door to, but not closed. The cab driver started the engine. It chugged noisily, and the cab inched forward. Matt tugged at her hand. "We need to catch that taxi."

"Can we make it before Ruiz sees us?"

"It's that or run some more."

"Okay, let's chance it."

They ran around the back of the taxi. "*Alto*," Valerie said.

The driver braked, and the taxi jerked to a stop.

"*Habla Inglés*?" she asked. After the driver nodded, they scrambled into the backseat.

The man turned toward them with a snaggle-toothed grin. "Where you want to go?"

"We left our car just north of town. Take us to the highway toward Texas," said Valerie. The driver stared at her, no doubt thinking they were crazy to leave their car on the road. Valerie wasn't wasting time explaining. The driver nodded and stepped on the accelerator. The taxi coughed and jerked. The driver stroked his full mustache and stepped on the gas again. Finally, the car crept forward.

Matt leaned toward her. "We could walk faster than this old rattletrap," he whispered.

Valerie put a finger to her lips. "Shhh."

"*Alto!*"

The director's shout jerked Valerie's head toward the window. Ruiz ran toward the taxi and pulled out his gun. The taxi lurched to a stop.

Knots twisted her stomach. Would they be shot after all? For all she knew her sister was still in the clutches of a madman and she was about to be killed. A lump formed in her throat. Her mother might not ever find out what happened to her two daughters.

Ruiz could handcuff them, then strip her naked and rape her before killing her. She clamped her eyes shut. Visions of Ruiz tearing her clothes and slamming into her made her stomach cramp.

He couldn't do it without a fight. Her throat tightened, and adrenaline coursed through her veins. She wasn't ready to die. She reached across Matt for the door handle.

"Don't," Matt said. "We can't outrun bullets. We'll have to talk our way out of this."

"Fat lot of good that will do."

"At least we can try."

Valerie swallowed and rolled the window down. "What do you want? You released us, didn't you?"

Ruiz scowled. "You did not pay the fine. You cannot go unless you pay the money. Give me the money now." He held out his hand.

Matt pulled out his wallet, handed over a fifty. "That's all I have." He turned to Valerie. "Hope you have enough for the taxi."

Ruiz grabbed the bill and frowned. "*Mas dinero.*"

"What's he saying?" Matt asked.

"He wants more money." She pulled a twenty from her wallet and held it out. Ruiz snatched it, almost tearing it."

The chief yanked open the front passenger door and planted his scrawny butt on the seat. He spoke to the driver, who gunned the engine. Now the car was moving too fast for them to jump out.

Valerie's breaths came in short spurts. She couldn't seem to get enough oxygen. "Where are you taking us?" Waiting for his answer, she held her breath. Hoped it wasn't jail again. She didn't want to fight him off yet another time. He might best her the next time while those two disgusting prisoners watched. Shivers shimmied down her spine.

Remembering the lust in his eyes and the rough way he'd grabbed her arm, she gagged. She cringed, and then straightened her back. What if he claimed submitting to him was the price of their release? She clamped her lips together. No way would she stand for that. She'd rather die first. What was she thinking? She didn't want to die. Her stomach knotted.

Ruiz spoke in rapid Spanish. She caught the words for bank and ATM as he pointed back the way they'd come. "*Si,*" said the driver and careened around a corner.

Would this postage-stamp-sized town even have an ATM?

Five minutes later, they pulled up in front of a bank built of rough-cut stone. Two spindly wooden pillars flanked the door. Pointing his gun at them, the director motioned for them to get out.

"We'd better do as he says," Matt said.

Pulse racing, Valerie was too scared to do anything else. Her legs seemed to be made of Jell-O. With effort, she forced them to support her as she climbed out.

A stern-faced Ruiz stood glaring at her as Matt scrambled out. "Go inside," demanded Ruiz. "Use your credit card. Get me three hundred dollars. That is your fine for speeding."

Matt exhaled slowly. "Whatever." His tone told her he was relieved that was all Ruiz wanted. Matt walked to the teller's window and laid his card on the chipped Formica counter. Ruiz stood beside him, gun in hand. Valerie stepped up beside them to interpret if necessary.

The teller looked at Ruiz and then at them. Ruiz spoke in Spanish to the clerk. "American?" the teller asked.

Matt nodded.

"You want three hundred dollars American money?"

Again Matt nodded and pushed his card forward. The clerk wrote something on a form and shoved it back. Matt signed it.

"ID, *por favor.*"

Matt held out his driver's license. The clerk took it and wrote on the form. Then he disappeared into the back with Matt's license and credit card. "I hope I get them back," he whispered to Valerie.

Ruiz spoke from behind him. "If he gives you money, he will return your ID and credit card."

"Then can we leave your lovely city?" Valerie asked, immediately regretting her sarcastic tone. They didn't need to antagonize him.

The clock on the wall behind the counter ticked off the seconds. They dragged on. Valerie shifted from one foot to the other. Drops of perspiration formed on her forehead. Why didn't this damn bank have air conditioning?

The director leaned against the wall, one hand on his holstered gun, the other fingering his badge. She studied his face. Would he let them go after Matt paid the fine?

She tried to slow her rapid breathing. Wouldn't do to let the director know she was afraid. She stared at the clock. The minute hand clicked, moving from one dot to the next.

Still the clerk didn't return.

What was taking so long? She was sure Matt didn't have a stolen card. And his driver's license must be authentic. He wouldn't last long at the law firm if it weren't. But what if he'd already maxed out the credit card like she had? Or, what if they kept his card and claimed it was stolen? Waiting, she held her breath. Walked around the small lobby.

And waited some more.

Finally, the clerk returned and handed Matt his card, license, and a handful of bills. Matt held out the money to Ruiz, who stuffed it in his shirt pocket. She heaved a sigh of relief. Was this the end of it? She hoped so. Her muscles were still tense, as if her body couldn't believe she was free at last.

Matt and Valerie followed the police chief outside. Waving the gun, he motioned for them to get in the taxi. After they did, the director spoke to the driver in Spanish, and slid into the front seat.

Valerie held her breath, then whispered to Matt, "Now what? Will he let us go?"

Matt shrugged and reached for her hand. That made her feel a bit safer. Her heart beat faster as the taxi rumbled on.

Five minutes later, the director stepped out in front of the police station. As he walked up the steps, Valerie finally let out the breath she'd been holding. The driver leaned over the backseat and stuck out his hand. "*Dinero*, give me money now."

Valerie fished out a five, and the driver nodded. As the car moved away from the police station and the chief, Valerie asked, "Do you think we're safe now?"

Matt nodded. "Unless we see a posse following us, or a sniper half hidden behind a building, we should be in the clear."

"Matt," she whispered. "The director didn't say anything about the bath crystals."

He put a hand on her shoulder. It felt reassuring. "They can't have found anything. Probably didn't want to lose face by admitting it. Three hundred for speeding is exorbitant. Ruiz will probably take a cut."

Up in front, the cab driver nodded. "*Si*. It is the way things happen." He gunned the engine. "Where you want to go?"

Matt pointed. "Take the highway out of town. We need to find our car."

"*Si*, Señor." He started the car again.

Valerie sighed. At least they were on their way out of town. She fingered her turquoise squash blossom necklace. The director had taken money, but at least he hadn't demanded she give him that. She remembered what he'd shouted to his deputy at the police station. Something kept niggling at her.

Then it dawned on her. She heaved a sigh of relief. "Matt, I finally realized what the chief said back at the police station. I thought he was saying *mátelos*, which means kill them, but what he must have said was *métalos*, which means put them. He must been telling Pedro to put us in the car and take us to the bank to get money to pay the fine. We weren't in danger of being shot after all."

Matt's eyebrows drew closer together. He scowled.

Uh-oh. She braced for the approaching storm.

Her muscles tensed. Should have told him she wasn't that fluent in Spanish. And she shouldn't have jumped to conclusions.

Matt's eyes widened, and his mouth dropped open. He glared at her. "That mad dash up the hill, and us crouching behind the bushes—it was all your fault." His voice rose a couple of notches. "Damn you. Should have got it right the first time, so we wouldn't have to run like the devil was after us. I got a stitch in my side doing that. It's a wonder I didn't get heartburn too."

Valerie nodded and waited for more criticism. She deserved it.

Then he leaned back and rubbed his chin. "Things must have looked treacherous back there. I don't know any Spanish, but they talked so fast I guess it would be easy to mistake what they said."

She felt better now. "Thanks for being so understanding."

Matt reached forward to touch the driver's arm. "Stop just around that bend, next to our car." However, after the driver made the curve, his car was gone. "Dammit."

Valerie's mouth dropped open. Should have known they weren't home free. "Where's your Mustang? If we don't have it, there's no way we can catch up with Buck and Christy. And we'll be stranded out here." She clenched her hands into fists. Could things get any worse?

Matt placed his hand on her shoulder, his touch strangely reassuring. "It's got to be somewhere near here." He turned to the driver. "Let's check farther down the road. Drive on, please."

Another mile and around another curve, she saw it. "There it is. Thank goodness. Matt, you must have been mistaken about where we left it."

Matt glared at her. "Never mind that. We found it. Get out."

Valerie fished in her purse for a five in an envelope in the bottom of her purse she'd been saving for an impulse buy. Handing it to the driver, she thanked him and followed Matt to the red Mustang.

Matt opened the door. A wave of hot air enveloped them. Matt got behind the wheel. He touched it, and then snatched his hand away. "Damn, that's hot."

Valerie scrambled into the front seat. "Ouch, the seat is burning my legs." She looked behind. "Oh no. My suitcase is gone. Damn, my clothes…" She glanced at her rumpled clothes, feeling grimy and sweaty.

Matt craned his neck, then glanced at the dashboard. "I'm surprised they didn't steal the radio too." He pushed the lever for the trunk and got out.

Seconds later he slid back in. "Nothing there but the spare tire. But we're alive and out of jail. We can buy more clothes."

"You're right. Let's go." She didn't relish doing without makeup and a toothbrush. Already her mouth felt gritty. Hot and sweaty, she really missed having a change of clothes.

Matt turned the key. The engine came to life, and the car jerked ahead. The bumpy ride jolted her.

He stopped the car. "Uh-oh, we've got a flat."

Valerie sighed. Would they ever get back to the U.S.? She stepped out and looked at the right front wheel. "It's on this side. I'll get rocks to brace the wheels." The hot sun beat down on her back and bare arms as she searched. After finding three big stones, she chocked them in front of the other three tires.

Matt pulled tools from the trunk. Deftly, he loosened the nuts and jacked the car up. With bulging muscles he lifted the wheel off.

He grinned. "Now this is something I can fix. We'll be on the road again in no time." His smile filled her heart with hope. If they hadn't been too far behind Christy and Buck—if indeed that was whom they'd seen—she and Matt might catch up with them yet. She crossed her fingers, hoping Buck and Christy had stopped somewhere for the night.

After dusting his hands, Matt climbed in and started the car again. "Don't know how far we can go on that doughnut spare tire. We really need to find a gas station to fix the flat. And the fuel needle is nearing empty."

They'd gone about ten miles when the engine coughed and sputtered. The car coasted to a stop.

Matt scowled. "Damn. We're out of gas, and there's no town in sight."

"I don't want to be stuck out in the middle of nowhere." Her heart sank. "Try again." She held her breath and listened.

He did. The engine coughed and then was silent.

She swallowed. They'd be sitting ducks for those highway bandits she'd heard about. "Now, what?" she asked.

"Get out. We walk. I'm not leaving you here alone. I don't remember seeing any gas stations on the way here, but that sign could be for one up ahead. Come on."

The hot sun beat down on Valerie as she got out.

She was already dirty and smelly, and perspiration formed on her forehead. "That's all we need, a long walk in the hot sun," she snapped. "Why didn't you fill up earlier when you saw the tank was getting empty?" She pointed a finger at his chest and frowned. "If you had, we wouldn't have run out of gas. Now we're easy pickings for any bandit who comes along."

Matt locked the door and pocketed the key. "Damn. You would have to bring that up." He scowled, and then kicked a rock. It skittered over the rough pavement before rolling onto the shoulder. "Give me a break, will you? I would have done it before leaving town, but we were rushing to catch Christy."

"You saw Christy drive off that day she left. When you heard Gordon and Christy arguing, did she act as if she were going to leave him?"

Matt shook his head. "I figured she was just blowing smoke. If I'd thought she was going to leave town, I'd have urged Gordon to go after her. I bet he's kicking himself for not doing that."

Valerie frowned. "He may be in jail, but at least he's safe and has a roof over his head." She glanced up at the hot sun beating down. "Which is more than we've got." She wiped perspiration from her forehead. 'Twould serve Gordon's conceited ass right for dumping her so quickly. "Hell, he was probably seeing Christy on the sly while he was still going with me." She gritted her teeth. How could she have been so blind? She kicked a pebble. "He can stew in jail for all I care."

Matt glared at her. "Think you know everything, don't you? We don't know why she left. As for my brother, who knows what scumbag might want to take a poke at him in jail? Might even be someone planted to beat up on him or worse."

She turned to face him. "Why would you think that?" She had to admit, if only to herself, as much as she despised Gordon, she didn't want him brutalized in jail.

He frowned. "Something political's going on. Your sister's disappearance may have been rigged to hurt Gordon's chances in the upcoming election."

Valerie rubbed the back of her neck. "I've been so worried about Christy I hadn't considered that. I can't believe my sister stayed away this long on her own. If she's with Buck, he must have forced her to go with him. Maybe he's not just reckless—maybe he's crazy. I don't really know him that well." She tried to ignore the knots growing inside. "I don't want to think about what he might do to her." Her voice broke.

"We can't know unless we find her—"

"Don't even say it. We have to find her…before something bad happens." Valerie swallowed, hoping nothing already had.

Matt reached out to touch her shoulder. "I've found it's always better to hope for the best, but plan for the worst."

"I'm trying not to think about the worst." She sighed. Tried not to imagine how awful she'd feel if Christy were dead. She just couldn't be.

Matt squeezed her shoulder. Despite their predicament, his touch reassured her and gave her hope they'd catch up with Christy and Buck before it was too late.

He met her gaze. "Maybe someone will give us a ride to the nearest gas station."

She glared at him. "On this lonely road? You've got to be kidding."

He kicked at a stone. "Well, then we'd better keep walking."

Valerie resisted the urge to grumble about him not buying gas sooner. After all, he hadn't shouted at her for the mistake in understanding the director's Spanish.

The sun beat down, and perspiration dribbled between her breasts. Through her sandal's paper-thin sole she felt the heat, every pebble, and every hard-baked ridge of dirt along the shoulder. She wished she'd taken time to change into her Nike's before leaving the hotel. And now they were gone.

Two cars zoomed by. They kept walking.

After what seemed like three miles, they finally reached a gas station—at least it looked like it had been at one time. Two dilapidated pumps with no roof overhead stood on a sparsely graveled driveway. Behind them a small stucco building crouched, as if ashamed to be associated with the rusty gas pumps. The place looked deserted.

Matt knocked on the wooden door. Its remnants of yellow paint matched the stucco walls. No one answered.

"Knock again," Valerie said. The hot breeze did nothing to cool her. How long would she have to go without a bath and deodorant? What she'd put on earlier wasn't stemming the perspiration. She held her arms away from her body, hoping she didn't stink to high heaven.

Matt tried again. Still nothing. Valerie tapped on the window. Finally shuffling sounds came from inside.

The door creaked open, and a brown-skinned,

weather-beaten face appeared. "*Que quiere?*"

"You talk to him," Matt said.

"*Habla Inglés?*" she asked.

"No."

Valerie explained in Spanish that they wanted to buy gasoline. His expression was blank until she mentioned petrol.

Then the man smiled and hobbled outside. He looked both ways. A puzzled look appeared on his face. "*Donde esta el coche?*"

"He wants to know where our car is," Valerie explained.

Matt pointed back the way they had come. The old man nodded as if to say he understood.

"Ask him," Matt said, "if he has a gas can we can borrow."

Valerie asked. The man shook his head, then went inside and shut the door.

Matt frowned. "You mean he won't let us borrow a gas can? I guess we could push the car here."

Valerie's jaw dropped. "We can't push it that far."

"Why not? It can't be much more than two miles."

"Seemed more like three to me." Hearing shuffling sounds, she stared at the door.

It creaked open. "Perhaps he found a can," Matt said.

The man stepped out carrying a bucket and a thin piece of stiff burlap.

Matt's sigh echoed against the yellow stucco walls. "I hope that holds enough to start the car."

Valerie fished out her last two dollar bills and gave them to the man. "*Gracias.*"

The man scowled and held the bucket behind his

back. "*Mas dinero*."

"No *tengo*."

"No petrol." He took a step back.

Matt tapped her on the shoulder. "Maybe he'll take my watch."

She shook her head. "That's a nice watch. I'd hate for you to give that up. I'll give him mine. I can buy another. Perhaps he has a wife or girlfriend."

The man pointed at her squash blossom turquoise necklace. "*Por mi espousa*."

"Don't give him that," Matt said. "It's too nice."

"He wants it for his wife. Let me try something else. She pointed to her watch. "*Quiere?*"

He shook his head.

Matt held out his watch.

"No." The man pointed to the necklace again.

She sighed, hating to give it up.

"Sorry, I guess that's all he wants. I'll buy you a new one after we get back."

It was nice of Matt to offer to replace it. Reaching back to unclasp it, she wondered if he knew how much they cost.

"Let me." He lifted her hair from the back of her neck. The touch of his gentle fingers was almost a caress. Welcoming the cooler air that lifted perspiration from her neck, she wondered how his hands would feel on her bare shoulders. Forget that. After her fiancé dumped her a year ago—it had taken a long time before she'd managed to stop feeling beat down. She wasn't ready to get that close to another man, especially not someone who ordered her around.

He brushed a lock from her forehead. "I hate to do this." He handed the necklace to the man. "That had better be enough."

The old man grinned, showing a gap between his yellowed teeth. Valerie said "Petrol *ahora*?" The man nodded and pointed to the gas pump. After Matt filled the pail and draped the burlap over the top, she walked beside him.

A shiny new Cadillac stopped, and a fashionably dressed woman, her hair beauty salon fresh, asked," Do you need a ride?"

Her male companion was obviously several years younger. Valerie wondered about their relationship. "We'd really appreciate it. We ran out of gas."

The woman stared at the bucket and then the rough, bumpy road. "That might spill. I don't want gasoline fumes all over my new car." She zoomed away, leaving a film of dust on Valerie's skin. How long before she could take a bath?

Matt set the pail down and brushed dust off his arms. While she'd been busy thinking only of herself, he probably felt hot and dusty too. She bent to clutch the handle of the bucket. "Let me carry that."

"It's not heavy."

"I'm sure your arms are tired."

He shook his head. "It can't be much farther."

By the time they reached the red Mustang, Valerie was still feeling guilty for misinterpreting the policemen's Spanish. If she hadn't done that, they might have gotten to the car sooner—before their things were stolen. Except the director would have still insisted on money for the fine. Their stuff probably disappeared right after they left. They could replace their belongings. At least they were safe and free.

Matt unlocked the door and pulled the gas tank

lever. He frowned. "How the hell are we going to pour the gas without spilling some? We need every bit to start the engine."

Chapter Eight

Matt wiped sweat from his brow and frowned at the rusty pail. "That bucketful won't get us out of Mexico unless we can pour it in the tank without spilling a drop."

He hated not being in control of the situation. "Valerie, you should have gone back to Dallas and let me find Christy." He ached for her and what she had dealt with at the prison. "You don't know how many times I've kicked myself for not insisting on that when I found you in El Jardin Bonito."

"Christy's my sister. You couldn't have stopped me."

"If you had driven back to Monterrey, you wouldn't have to fight off that strutting peacock."

Valerie clenched her hand into a fist. "Maybe now he'll think twice before he assaults another female prisoner."

Matt rubbed sweat from the back of his neck. He wished he'd talked her into staying with him in that jail cell in the first place. He could still feel the incredible warmth of her body against his on that jail cot. He could have made her sigh with delight—if they'd been anywhere else...

Valerie bent over and picked up a stick. He liked the way her breasts strained against her dress when she straightened. She might not look as sexy as her sister, but despite being outspoken, she was one hell of a woman. Except he had no room in his life for any kind of woman. He had to free his brother and secure his own place in the firm. Finding Christy and saving Gordon would take all his time and energy.

Valerie fished in her purse and pulled out her printed hotel receipt. After folding it around the stick like a funnel, she pushed it in the gas tank opening. "I'll hold this. You pour."

"That won't work."

"Wait and see."

To his amazement it did. Finally, he set the empty bucket down. "Valerie, you're a genius." Her smile spread over her face, awakening two cute dimples in her cheeks. He had a sudden urge to kiss her, but hugged her instead. He threw the bucket in the trunk and slid behind the wheel. "Let's go. We'll catch them yet."

She got in beside him. "How are we going to find them? They've a big head start."

He reached under the front seat and pulled out a small scuffed leather bag. "At least they left my ditty bag."

"Your what?"

He grinned. "My shaving kit with my cell phone inside."

"Why didn't you take the phone with us? We could have called someone."

He glared at Valerie. "Wasn't sure it would work there. And they might have thought it was some kind of bomb. Like an idiot, I thought they'd give us at least one phone call. Figured they'd take my cell phone if I kept it with me."

"Thank goodness they didn't bother anything else in my purse. They might have taken my wallet, but I had that and my passport in a hidden pouch strapped under my blouse. Except the cop who took my passport didn't give it back."

Matt grimaced. "Hope we don't have trouble crossing the border."

"Look at us. How could they think we're illegal aliens?"

"We'll worry about that later. We need to get a line on Christy and her ex-boyfriend."

"How can you do that?"

He grinned. This he could do something about. "I went to law school with a guy from San Antonio who practices criminal law. He might be able to check out the license plate." He handed the bag to her. "Find my phone. I stashed it there when we got arrested." Knowing what she'd find, he waited and tried not to smirk.

One by one she pulled out his shaving things, deodorant, toothbrush, and toothpaste. Gingerly she held up a giant fake cockroach and frowned. "Ugh, what's this?" She shuddered. "It looks gross. No wonder no one stole it."

He grinned. "Hand it over. It has legs like a real insect." He unfolded the brown pipe cleaners he'd glued to the bottom and held it near her arm. "Want to see how they feel?"

She jerked her arm back. "No way. You're sick."

"Ever since biology, insects have fascinated me. It's a great conversation piece."

"Not if you want to impress a woman."

"I just hope it works here." After pushing buttons

for directory assistance, he asked for his friend's number in San Antonio, and dialed it. The man was in a meeting so Matt left his name and number. "Hope he calls back soon." Matt started the engine. "We might as well head toward San Antonio."

In the next town they finally found a gas station to fix their flat and a bank with an ATM. Matt withdrew more cash with his credit card. He stopped at a restaurant that looked clean.

"I'm not very hungry, but I could eat a salad," she said.

"I wouldn't advise it," Matt said. "Better get hot food here." He ordered a bottle of beer. "We don't dare drink the water." She insisted on a salad, but drank a Coke instead of water.

His attorney friend called. "Joe," Matt said, "Can you check out a Texas license plate with the words BAD BOY?"

Joe cleared his throat. "My process server has access to car registrations. I'll call you back."

Matt and Valerie were almost to the border when the phone rang. The connection was poor, and Matt could hardly understand. "Car belongs to Alfred James Robbins. He has an address in San Antonio." Joe said. "Did time...rape...attempted murder." His voice trailed off.

"What's that again?" Matt asked, but the line went dead.

"Valerie, that Buck guy—is his name Alfred James Robbins?"

She nodded. "But he mostly went by Buck. I only hope Christy's with him."

"We can't be sure, but that's our only lead. They

could be anywhere by now." He didn't mention Buck's record—no use worrying Valerie.

"Christy can be very persuasive," Valerie said. "Buck was crazy about her. I bet she'll talk him into going to San Antonio instead of Houston."

"Hmmm. Wonder if Frank Carter put Buck up to it—"

"Put him up to what?"

"Frank Carter's running against Gordon for mayor. Anything he can do to stop my brother, he would."

"You think he'd dare arrange Christy's kidnapping?"

"Sure. He'd want to throw my brother off course so he'd lose the election, and now with a murder charge hanging over his head, he's sure to lose."

Valerie swallowed. "That's crazy—to kidnap her for political gain. Carter would be ruined if anyone found out."

"I'm not sure that's what happened. Just a wild guess."

"Somehow I can't see Buck getting thick with a big time politician."

"Carter's got a bunch of associates. All he'd have to do is put out the word." After having done time, Buck was a likely prospect. "He'd probably be glad to keep Christy out of circulation for a while for a few hundred." Matt hoped to hell that's all the guy would do.

Valerie looked thoughtful. "The last time Buck took her out, I know he was dying to get into her pants; she was still in high school but I'm sure she didn't let him."

"Must have thought he could score this time."

"Christy wouldn't allow it now. She's married and could even be pregnant."

"Hardly think that would stop her."

Valerie glared at him. "Don't talk about my sister like she's a tramp. For all we know, she only asked for a ride home, and he took advantage of her. Maybe she had an accident in Gordon's truck. That would explain the blood. The way you talk about her, it's a wonder you want to find her."

"Look, Valerie, we're in this together. I want to get Gordon out of jail. You want to find her and be sure she's safe. We need to cooperate."

"Okay, but I don't have to like it."

She didn't have to add, 'or you either.' Her mutinous look said it all. How could Valerie not see her sister as she really was? He frowned. He'd be damned if he'd apologize for speaking the truth. "Look, Valerie. If Christy went away with Buck for a long weekend, and you don't believe they had sex, you're naive."

Valerie shot him a look as dark as the clouds looming ahead and faced the window.

Were they driving into a storm—or perhaps a tornado?

"Stop the car," Valerie said.

Picking up on the urgency in her voice, he braked. "Why?"

She shoved the door open and ran behind a bush with lavender flowers that contrasted with its gray-green foliage.

He pulled the car off the road and strode after her. "Where the hell are you going? Can't you tell it's going to storm?"

"Stay back, dammit," she shouted.

A gust of wind carried the pungent odor, along with sounds of retching. "Hurry up, then," Matt said. "A storm's brewing."

"I need a tissue."

Cursing the delay under his breath, he reminded himself she was sick and needed his help. He pulled a handkerchief from his pocket and strode behind the bush. "Here."

Gently, he wiped her mouth and chin, knowing she must feel awful.

****

Heat rose to her face. She must be a sight. She peeled away few strands of hair plastered to her face by perspiration, grateful for the breeze cooling her skin. "Thanks," she managed to get out. Speaking brought a replay of the sour taste in her mouth. "You're a real gentleman," she whispered. She was sorry he'd sacrificed his handkerchief. And he hadn't even reminded her he told her to eat hot food.

A brisk breeze whipped back her hair as she stepped around the bush. She hoped the smell wouldn't make him gag. She'd been stupid not to take his advice. "I'm sorry to put you through this. I'll buy you some new handkerchiefs."

Matt's face was solemn. "Forget it. The wind's getting stronger. Don't like the look of those clouds." He grasped her wrist. "Get back in the car."

Her stomach roiled. She wrenched her arm loose. "I'm going to be sick again." Damn. Her stomach hurt, as if she'd coughed up everything but her toenails.

He held her hand as she suffered through dry heaves. Her stomach ached. She hoped that was the end. Her mouth tasted like crap. "I think I'm through."

She sighed, feeling washed out.

Rain came, striking her skin like hard pellets and plastering her hair to her head. Matt grabbed her hand. "Come on, hurry to the car." She was tempted to stand there a moment and let the rain wash off her face, but she dropped the soiled handkerchief and ran to the car. Disgusted for being dirty and stinking, she yanked open the door to the backseat.

He pushed it shut. "Get in front."

"I must smell terrible."

"Don't worry about it. Just get in. I need you to navigate."

She climbed in, and Matt got behind the wheel. Now she'd have to ride beside him. He pulled an old towel from the back. "Here, dry yourself off with this."

She did and pulled her wet dress loose from her breasts.

His grin told her he'd liked the view. Her face heated. Raindrops and perspiration still dampened her neck, but she didn't feel cooler. Did she have a fever?

She opened the window a crack and sat close to it. The black cloud hung overhead. Rain slashed at the car. No matter how bad she stank, she had to shut the window.

What must he think of her now? Obviously, he didn't like her sister. Losing her lunch probably disgusted him. Grains of sand irritated her toes. She wished she'd worn something beside sandals. What she wouldn't give for a hot bath. It was a long way to San Antonio. She sighed.

Once they found Christy and things were back to normal, she hoped she wouldn't have to face him at family dinners. That would be too awkward.

His gaze met hers. "Hey, don't be embarrassed. Montezuma's revenge happens to almost everyone who visits Mexico. You should have seen how bad I got it."

"You mean you didn't follow your own advice?"

"Didn't know any better the first time. Had the runs for two days."

"Must have been awful. I don't feel so bad, knowing it happened to you."

"Forget it. Let's concentrate on finding Christy and Buck. Good thing the rain's stopped. They'll be easier to spot." Her stomach still hurt a little, but thank goodness, the nausea hadn't returned.

Opening the window, she strained to see ahead. No cars. Then she glanced behind. "That black pickup seems awfully close. Do you think they're following us?"

Matt stepped on the gas, and his Mustang zoomed ahead. The other vehicle sped up also. Matt slowed. "Let's see if they pass."

The pickup kept a close tail. Valerie craned her neck to see. Two burly-looking men sat in the front. Would they try to run them off the road or shoot at them? Knots formed in her stomach.

Matt's hands gripped the wheel, his knuckles turning white. He glanced in the rearview mirror. "I'm not letting those red-necks get the best of me. I could lose them easily in a town."

Valerie grabbed the map, scoured it for towns. "The only one near is a tiny dot."

Matt made the Mustang shoot ahead. Leaning back, Valerie saw the men gesturing toward them. The truck barreled after them.

Chapter Nine

With a sickening crunch, the pickup rammed the Mustang. Jerked Valerie's head and neck. Gray clouds darkened the sky. She tensed. Not likely a police car would show up on this deserted Mexican highway. Could Matt outrun them?

Gripping the wheel, he scowled. "Damn. They're going to run us off the road."

Holding her breath, she watched the speedometer climb to 85. The rain came back as drizzle. The wet road glistened. At this speed, they could fishtail. Valerie gripped her seatbelt. Stuck her head out the window. Rain wet her face. The pickup closed in again. She gasped.

Metal screeched against metal. The jolt was harder this time. Her shoulder belt strained against her chest, and her heart thumped faster. Would the black truck's grill come through the backseat? Her pulse raced.

Their car jerked to one side, spun crazily, and careened off the road. A lone tree loomed ahead. "Damn." Matt wrestled with the wheel. The Mustang hurtled forward. "Brace yourself."

Their car skidded and shimmied. Valerie held her breath, grabbed the dashboard, and pushed.

Matt wrenched the wheel to the right. The left side of the car scraped the tree. Crunching sounds came from the fenders. Matt groaned. "Ow. That wrenched my arm." Their vehicle rolled to a stop.

From the pickup two husky men in jeans and cotton shirts ran over. They planted themselves, one at each front window. Valerie locked the door and tried to shut the window. The shorter one, his belly bulging his red shirt, gripped it. Forced it to stay open a few inches. "*Dinero*."

The taller one glared through Matt's window. "And jewelry, Carlos," he shouted.

Matt shot Valerie a look. "Stay in the car," he barked.

Would they kill her and Matt? Her heart beat in double time. She clenched her hands into fists. Her nails poked into her palms.

Carlos rubbed grubby fingers over his unshaven chin. "Juan, e*lle es bonita*."

Valerie pulled her damp dress away from her body. Just the thought of either slob touching her made her want to cringe.

Juan stared at her breasts. Looked her up and down. He grinned. "*Si, muy bonita*." He stuck part of his hand through the open window.

She shoved it away. "Back off."

She scowled. They could torture her and Matt, but she wouldn't let them see how scared she was. Matt would fight for her. She was sure of that, but those two men might overpower them. She didn't want to be raped—didn't want to die. Not out here, away from her family and friends. Didn't want her body left for buzzards. What a horrible thought. She shuddered.

Carlos looked stern. "Ain't got much choice, *señora*. Be two of us against your *espouso*. I will be happy to touch you." Carlos grinned and nodded toward the taller man, "He will take care of your man."

That was too much. Valerie reached for the door handle.

"Don't," Matt said.

She turned toward him, whispered, "I can throw him. Can you take the other?"

"My arm hurts. It's useless. I'm getting us out of here." Clamping his lips together, he grabbed the wheel. Gunned the motor. Juan yelled something and fell back. Carlos shook his fist at them, but held onto the window rim until it was pulled from his grasp.

Matt turned the Mustang toward the road. The car bumped and jerked. The motor sounded rough. But on the road, the speed soon rose to ninety. The front end of the car shook, but he kept the speed steady.

Valerie looked back. The truck was way behind. She let out her breath, one she hadn't realized she'd been holding. Matt drove over a hill. She pointed to the left. "There are trees beside that road. We could hide."

"The truck's out of sight. It's worth a try." He jammed on the brakes and careened around the corner. The road got narrow. Ruts glistened from the recent rain.

Valerie gestured. "There's a house. We could pull in like we lived there."

Matt slowed and turned in beside the yellow cinder-block house. He parked behind a red Ford F-350. "Duck. Maybe they'll think the car's empty."

She frowned. "Or maybe they'll sneak up and shoot us."

"You're right. We'll hide behind the house. Get out." He raced around the Mustang and grabbed her hand. "Come on." Together they ran behind the house.

It had a recessed patio with a barbecue grill. A trellis of wood slats intertwined with vines and red bougainvillea flowers shadowed the area.

Matt leaned against the wall of the house and rubbed his left arm. "Think I broke it when we crashed against the tree."

"I hope not." She pressed her fingers to his flesh. "Is it sore?"

"Hurts like hell."

The sound of a door moving alerted Valerie. "Uh-oh. Someone's coming."

A man shoved the door open. "*Que quiere?*"

"Do you speak English?" Valerie asked.

"A little," he said, smoothing his mustache against his dark-skinned cheeks.

"Two bad men, *dos hombres malos*, are chasing us. We need somewhere to hide."

A pregnant brunette with a pretty face edged up behind him. "Pancho, tell them to leave. I don't want any trouble."

The man turned toward the woman. "Do not worry, *querida.* I won't let anyone hurt you."

The brunette clutched his arm. "I don't want you fighting. You might get hurt. Then what would happen to me and our baby?"

Matt pointed to the driveway. "We need to hide ourselves and our car, just for half an hour."

Pancho glanced at their car and scratched his head. "*No es posiblé.*"

"Please," Valerie said. "Could you give us a sheet to cover our Mustang?"

"Get a sheet, *querida*," the man said.

The brunette disappeared and returned with a

striped flat sheet.

Valerie took it. "*Gracias*."

Matt grabbed the sheet, scrambled to the Mustang, and covered the back end. After a quick glance at the road, he returned. "Doesn't cover the front, but maybe they won't recognize it."

"We need to hide," said Valerie.

Pancho pointed to the back of their yard. A few trees with thin leaves, similar to the mesquite trees in Texas but taller, stood behind sparse underbrush.

"We can't hide very well in that," Valerie said.

Pancho's wife said, "Please, just get away from the house."

Matt grabbed Valerie's hand. "Come on. Hurry."

His strong hand held hers. He'd protect her, whatever happened. She ran beside him and squeezed between two scratchy bushes.

He stopped behind another bush. "Get down." Crouching, he worked his way closer to the driveway. "I need to watch the road."

Minutes later, the black pickup jerked to a stop in front of the driveway. Juan stepped down, swaggered to the side door, and pounded on it. Valerie's hand flew to her mouth. Pulse racing, she watched.

A heated discussion ensued. She tried to follow their Spanish. Would Pancho give them away to protect his pregnant wife?

Pancho's voice got louder. "*Vamos mi casa ahora.*"

That she understood. He was telling them to leave. Something behind Valerie rustled. Hearing a rattling sound, she glanced back. Only a foot away lay a snake. She smothered a gasp, hoping the bandits hadn't heard.

The snake slithered closer. Her heart pounded, and her hands shook. Terrified to move, she looked back toward the banditos and held her breath.

The snake's rattle sounded again. The noise grated, like fingernails scratching a blackboard. She froze. Willed the creature to go anywhere but closer to her. Its tongue darted, pointing directly at her. Was it marking her as a target? She watched, barely daring to breathe.

From the house came the sound of a gun cocking. The barrel of a shotgun protruded from the doorway. "Go away, or I shoot," Pancho shouted.

Juan backed off. "Don't shoot. I go now."

Valerie held her breath as Juan edged toward the truck. He climbed in the truck, then stepped out again, holding a gun. He strode toward their sheet-covered car.

More rattling sounds came from behind. Valerie edged closer to the bush, away from the snake. Branches scratched her skin. Her heart pounded, but she didn't dare run. The snake's tongue flicked in and out. Ducking, she inched toward the next bush. Juan approached Matt's car. She hoped he hadn't heard her.

He lifted a corner of the sheet and folded it back. A blast from Pancho's shotgun peppered the ground around his feet. Gravel danced in the air. Fell with a pitter-patter like hail. Juan pointed his gun at the house door. Only the barrel of Pancho's gun showed. Juan shook his fist at Pancho and ran to the truck.

Ducking behind the open door of the pickup, Juan fired. She couldn't see where it went. He faced in her direction. Could he see her behind the bush? A lucky shot could kill her or Matt. But if the snake bit her, she could die before they could get help.

Shivers shaking her, she knelt and kept her head

down. Her cramped muscles ached. Pebbles and damp earth pressed against her knees.

She studied the snake. Had it moved closer? She snatched quick breaths, but couldn't seem to get enough air. How long did it take to die from a snakebite?

Another shot came their way. Matt crouched behind a bush closer to the Mustang. He didn't move. But if he'd been shot, he'd fall.

A blast came from the house. The truck's front window crumpled. Juan cursed and climbed into the truck. He slammed the door. The truck jerked forward and rumbled down the road.

Afraid to move, Valerie kept her eyes on the road, waiting for it to turn around and come back.

Matt hurried toward her. "Those bastards are gone, but they could return."

She held up a hand. "Watch out. There's a rattlesnake nearby."

"Be still. Movement will draw its attention. I'll watch the snake. Move slowly to the next bush."

Matt waited until she stepped behind the next bush. Then he hurried back to his hiding place. Turning to face her, he frowned. "For Pete's sake, get down. They could return any moment."

Valerie knelt. A cool breeze sprung up. Goose bumps pebbled her arms. A bunch of smaller birds pecked at the grass in front of the bushes. A crow's raucous call scattered the flock.

Tiny stones dug into her knees. The snake was still there. She had to get farther away. Valerie edged over to the next bush. Rising up, she brushed off gravel clinging to her skin. She wanted to move farther from the rattler, but the next bush wasn't dense enough. The snake didn't move closer, but it rattled again.

Matt ran toward their car. She clenched her hands, hoping the guys in the pickup wouldn't come back. He crouched behind the Mustang.

Pancho appeared at the side door with the shotgun. "Why you no go?"

Matt stood. "They might come back."

At the sound of a vehicle approaching, Matt ducked. Behind her bush, Valerie scrunched as low as she could. The snake rattled again and came closer. She tensed. Inched a few inches farther in the other direction. Hoped their pursuers couldn't see her.

The black pickup cruised by. Carlos stuck a rifle out the window and fired at the Mustang. Thank goodness he didn't hit Matt. Another shot slammed against the car's back window.

Pancho fired. A bullet clanged against metal, then dropped to the road. Pancho fired again. The truck zoomed away.

Eyes fixed on the snake, Valerie inched away, then ran to Matt. "Are you okay?"

He nodded, fingering his short beard. "We'll wait half an hour, then go. That is if the car's still drivable."

She patted his arm. "Thank goodness you weren't hit."

"Ow." He jerked his arm away. "Don't touch that arm."

"I'm so sorry, I forgot. Let me look at it."

"Can't tell if it's broken or sprained without an X-ray, but I'll wait until I can see a U.S. doctor."

"Pancho put down his gun, but he's staring at us. We need to get out of here."

She walked to the Mustang, snatched the sheet, and

shook it out. "Uh-oh. There's a hole in the back window." The glass hadn't shattered. It had crumpled, leaving a large gaping hole and a widening spider-web pattern of cracks.

She handed the sheet to Pancho. "*Muchas gracias.*"

Matt headed for the car. Valerie walked around to the back of it and stared at the hole in the rear window. What if they'd been inside? A shiver ran down her spine.

As Matt reached for the driver's side door, she ran around the car. "I'd better drive."

Matt shook his head. "It's my car, I'll drive."

"Are you crazy? Your arm's injured." She grasped his shoulder, tried to shove him aside.

"Damn, that hurts. Don't touch me. I can manage. Now get in."

Seated behind the wheel, he hunched his shoulders and flexed his sore arm. "I can drive, but it's going to be a long five hours to San Antonio or Houston. And the air conditioning can't cool us very well with the back window broken."

Matt backed the car slowly. At the sound of a thump, thump of a back wheel, he stopped. "Oh, no. Think another tire's flat. You're going to have to help me change it."

She followed him to the trunk and peered inside. "That donut tire's only supposed to be good for thirty miles, and we already drove fifteen miles on it before we fixed the other tire and put it on. We'd better get a new tire in the next town."

"I looked at the map. It's forty miles to the states. No towns of any size before that. We'll have to chance it."

After getting out the tools, Valerie worked the crossbar wrench on the lug nuts to loosen them. She placed the jack under the Mustang. Matt helped her lever it up. She removed the damaged tire and pushed the donut one into place. Matt helped her tighten the nuts.

Before he could stop her, she got behind the wheel.

He rushed to stand beside the open door. "Get in the passenger seat. I'll drive."

"No way. You might injure your arm even more."

"What if those guys catch up with us again?"

"I'll cross that bridge when we come to it, but I don't think we'll see them any time soon." She started the car before he had time to argue any more. Finally, he got in the passenger side.

An hour later, Matt pointed to a sign. "We're approaching Nuevo Laredo. We have to choose between San Antonio and Houston. Which way do you think they'll go?"

Valerie paused at a stop sign and reached for the map. She gripped it so hard the paper wrinkled, then tried to smooth it out.

Matt rubbed his neck. "If Buck's smart, he'll pick Houston. He's less likely to be noticed."

"She might have asked him to drive her home. I don't think she'd stay away this long of her own free will. Knowing Christy, I think she could persuade him to go to San Antonio, even if he won't take her home." She stepped on the gas, and the car shot forward.

"What if that guy keeps buying her expensive things? She twists my brother around like one of her blonde curls. No woman's going to treat me like that."

Valerie frowned. "You don't understand my sister.

Our family barely scraped by while she was growing up."

"So that's why she's a gold-digger?"

"Don't call her that. She just likes nice things."

"Like a fur cape, which you don't really need in San Antonio."

"Wasn't that a birthday gift from Gordon?"

"Yeah, but I bet it was no surprise. She probably nagged him to get it for her."

"I'm sure your brother loves her and wants her to be happy."

"Look, arguing won't get us anywhere," Matt said. "What's important is to find her and get Gordon out of jail. Keep your eyes peeled for the BAD BOY license. He might be tired of putting up with her by now. If we meet up with them, maybe we can talk him into letting her ride back with us. We can act like we're doing him a favor."

"I think Buck took advantage of her in a weak moment and then wouldn't let her go."

"Yeah, sure. I've watched Christy in action one time when she was drunk. Wouldn't take much of a come on. Bet she didn't give him much resistance. Probably didn't show his darker side until later."

Valerie leaned toward Matt. "I bet she was trying to figure how to get away."

"The road to San Antonio is coming up," Matt said. "We have to choose."

"If they went to Houston, we'd have a hard time finding her because neither of us knows the way around that city. There's the border checkpoint up ahead. I don't have my passport. What am I going to do about that?"

"Stop, and let me drive. When they question us, act natural, but don't mention our stay in El Jardin Bonito's roach motel. If they ask, just say you misplaced your passport and hand them your driver's license."

"Okay." She got out and changed places with Matt. When they reached the checkpoint, Matt stopped and held out his driver's license and passport.

The guard looked them over, and then gave them back. "And you, miss?"

Valerie pretended to be searching through her purse. "I can't seem to find my ID."

The guard looked stern. "How do you expect to enter the U.S. without one?"

Valerie handed him a card. "Here's my health insurance card with my address on it. And here's my driver's license and a credit card with my picture."

"That doesn't prove you're a U.S. citizen."

"My driver's license with my Dallas address is current. I was born in Texas at Parkland Hospital on November 22, 1988, twenty-five years to the day after they took Kennedy there after he was shot."

The stocky guard rubbed his chin and returned her cards. "At least you know your history. What's the state bird and flower of Texas?"

Matt watched her face. She'd better know the answer.

She smiled. "The mockingbird and the blue bonnet."

Matt tried not to grin. They were home free—almost.

The guard's solemn face didn't help Matt's confidence. "Step outside," the man said.

Matt clamped his lips together. "I don't like this

one bit," he whispered.

Valerie didn't either. What were they likely to do to her?

She got out and walked around the car. "You want to know the state's favorite dishes? They're chicken fried steak and barbecue. And the dances are the cotton-eyed Joe and the two-step."

The guard frowned and picked up a phone.

"Valerie, get back inside." Matt crossed his fingers. "Maybe we can make a run for it," he whispered.

The border guard pushed a button on his phone, and then turned to face Valerie. "So," he said, "which Texas soldier survived the fight at the Alamo?"

Behind her, Matt repeated his order to get back in the car. He sounded impatient, but she'd better answer the guard's question first. "No one," she said, "but the first president of the Republic of Texas was Steven Austin."

"Okay, you sound like you're from Texas. Go on."

Valerie let out the breath she'd been holding and scrambled back in the Mustang. "I'm cleared. Drive on."

As Matt started the car, the border guard's phone rang.

Valerie turned to watch. The guard stuck his head out of the booth and beckoned to them. "Keep going," she said. "I sure hope he doesn't have an ICE agent in a car nearby to chase us."

As they left the city, Valerie watched the speedometer climb to eighty-five. "Aren't you afraid we'll get a ticket? If you hadn't been speeding in Mexico, we wouldn't have been slapped into jail."

"Yeah, yeah." He frowned. "We might have been

stopped anyway. Like Dallas cops, they might have a daily quota. We're just lucky we got loose."

She scowled, remembering Ruiz's lecherous looks and grubby fingers on her arm. "Fine for you to say. I was the one who was attacked."

"You were lucky to best him."

She bristled. "I was quick and smart, not lucky." She frowned, remembering Matt's brother, her ex-fiancé. He hadn't given her credit for anything either.

Chapter Ten

Matt stepped on the gas, and they headed into Texas, leaving the border checking station behind. "Valerie, turn forward. Pretend you don't see the guard waving at us. That's what we'll say if someone stops us. Now we have to find Buck and Christy."

Valerie touched Matt's arm. "Look, if we don't stop soon to buy a regular tire to replace that donut one, we won't even get to San Antonio."

"I know, I know, but I won't feel safe until we get farther from the border. I just hope we can find a place to get another tire." Now he regretted he'd insisted on driving. His left arm hurt every time he moved it. He tried to do most of the steering with his right hand.

After an anxious ten minutes checking the rearview mirror, he finally spotted a service station. He pulled off the road and drove into an empty bay. If border patrol was looking for them, he hoped they wouldn't notice his car here. He paced until a mechanic stepped up and agreed to install a new tire and check his other tires. After the worker finished, Matt slapped his credit card on the counter. It seemed to take forever for the computer to print out a receipt.

After they walked out of the service station into bright sunshine, Valerie got behind the wheel before Matt could stop her. "I saw how you babied your arm. I'm stopping at the first doctor's office or hospital I see."

She finally stopped at an emergency clinic on the outskirts of Laredo. Luckily, the place was almost empty, but they still had to wait. Finally, the doctor examined his arm, took an X-ray, and then said it was only sprained and bruised. He put Matt's arm in a sling.

Again, Valerie slid into the driver's seat. "You're not driving until your arm is better. He glared at her, but kept his mouth shut. Finally, they were on their way, maneuvering on through Laredo traffic with a new tire. At least no one was following.

****

A little farther on Route 35, a driver in a red Corvette handed two sacks and a corrugated drink holder tray with two Dr. Peppers to his blonde companion. "Here you go sweetheart," he said and pulled away from the fast food restaurant.

The blonde carefully spread two paper napkins on her lap, pulled out a hamburger, and opened a cardboard box of fried chicken strips. She handed the hamburger and fries to the driver. "You didn't get any honey mustard sauce, like I asked."

"That's tough. Use the sweet and sour sauce." He stepped on the gas.

"Why couldn't we eat inside? It was nice and cool there."

"I don't have time. I need to get back to San Antone and take care of business."

She frowned. "If you're so worried about being followed, why did we stay overnight in Laredo?"

"I was tired. Besides, I figure when the cop stopped that damn brother-in-law and your sister, who were following us, that threw them off our trail. By now, they're either holed up in some Mexican jail or far ahead of us."

"So, that really was Matt and Valerie. Why didn't you tell me then?"

"They're far away now. Just let me know if you see them."

****

Valerie stopped at a service station. When she got out to pump gas, Matt ran around and slid behind the wheel.

"Surely you aren't going to drive with your arm in a sling," Valerie said. "Let me do it."

He shot her a determined look. "My arm doesn't hurt that much. It's my car, and I'm driving."

She clamped her mouth shut. As they left the city, the speedometer climbed to eighty-five. "Aren't you afraid we'll get a ticket? If you hadn't been speeding in Mexico, we wouldn't have been slapped into jail."

"Yeah, yeah. But we finally got released, so stop complaining."

Valerie scowled. "I could have done without being attacked."

Matt's brows furrowed. "Hey, I'm sorry about that. I don't know any woman who could handle a crude police chief the way you did. Just like a man, you gave him what he deserved."

Valerie smiled.

Maybe by now, she'd realize he was different from Gordon and perhaps more of the kind of man she could admire. Matt rubbed his arm. He'd told Valerie it didn't hurt that bad, but it still bothered him. She sat looking out the car window. She was a welcome change from his former girlfriend. Mallory had seemed to be a perfect candidate for an attorney's wife. Gracious and polite, she could help him entertain clients. She dressed nicely, and her face always glowed with a sensuous beauty. Mallory would make a good politician, always siding with whomever she wanted to impress.

Other lawyers in the firm would envy him if he married her. But that was all she had going for her. She was shallow. Why had it taken him so long to see through her?

Unlike Mallory, Valerie didn't hide her feelings or opinions behind polite phrases. She said what she thought without tailoring her opinions for an audience. With Valerie, he knew exactly where he stood. He didn't always agree with her, but he preferred her honesty. After a long quiet ride, they pulled into the outskirts of a small town north of Laredo. Matt drove into a gas station. Valerie touched his shoulder. "Let me fill the tank and check the oil."

He frowned. "I can do it. I'm not a cripple."

"I can do it so much easier. And I don't consider you a cripple. Actually, I think it's miraculous you drove as far as you did with a sprained arm."

Matt hesitated. "Wasn't that bad. But I'll let you pump the gas. Thanks." He handed her his credit card.

While Valerie filled the tank, Matt reached for his cell phone. He dialed his attorney friend. "Got any more info on Buck Robbins yet?"

"Here's what I have." Joe rattled off an address. "He has a cabin in the woods a ways out from San Antonio."

"What's the address?"

"Doesn't have one, but I looked up the legal description. It's in metes and bounds so that should tell you how to find it. I'll e-mail it to you."

Matt got out the map. "Thanks. I'll find the county road it's near."

"Shouldn't you enlist the police?" Joe asked.

"Not yet. I don't have anything concrete to tell them except that Christy's missing." Matt hung up as Valerie handed back his credit card.

She frowned. "The darn pump won't give a receipt. You'll have to go inside to get one." As Matt stepped out, a red Corvette drove by. The top was down, and the woman beside the driver shouted, "Stop." However, the car sped up and zoomed down the road.

Matt ran back to the car and jumped in. "Step on it," he shouted.

Valerie did, but the red Corvette had disappeared around a bend.

Valerie drove eighty and ninety miles an hour, hoping to catch them, but the car had disappeared. After half an hour she touched Matt's shoulder. "We can't catch them. I'd better slow down. I don't want to get arrested for speeding, but at least we're in the States where all I'll get is a fine."

Hungry, she pulled up beside a mom and pop restaurant. Matt lowered his window a crack. "Roll down your window a little so the car won't get so hot." It was after two, and the parking lot held only a few cars.

Inside, pictures of huge red and yellow peppers and gourds were painted on the walls. They ordered food to go, but it seemed to take forever. Finally a peppy teenage waitress brought their order. They wrapped sizzling strips of beef in tortillas with sour cream, guacamole, chopped tomatoes and peppers, grabbed their drinks, and left.

Matt got behind the wheel and took a bite. He glanced in the rearview mirror. A limousine had pulled in back of them, blocking their way. He waved at the driver to move, but the vehicle didn't budge. He was about to get out when two men stepped out of the limo and strode toward his car. Matt sucked in a deep breath. This didn't look good.

The man standing next to the driver's side window strained the seams of his gray suit. The other man, short, but lean, wore a white shirt with a tie and black pants. He headed toward Valerie's side of the car. Knots formed inside Matt's gut. "Valerie, shut the window."

Both men looked Hispanic—not surprising this close to the border. Were they plain-clothes officers looking for information, or maybe ICE men looking for illegal aliens? If so, he and Valerie had nothing to worry about.

Seeing the hard glare of the man facing Valerie, Matt tensed. Sweat beaded on his forehead. He reached for the button to snap the locks. His greasy finger finally connected, but he didn't feel safer. The heavyset man motioned for Matt to roll down the window. Matt obeyed, but only slid it down an inch.

"Don't volunteer anything," he whispered to Valerie. He fingered the passport in his pocket.

The leaner man now stood beside Valerie's window. His hand gripped the window edge, so she couldn't roll it up.

The man facing him pulled at his car door, but it held tight. "Get out. I need to talk to you."

Matt tensed. "Why? I don't know you, and you're

blocking my way."

"I want you to show up in court tomorrow."

"Why? You haven't shown me any badge. Where's your identification?"

He stuck a .357 Magnum through the window opening. "My name's Roberto, and this is my badge."

Matt swallowed. Wished he had a weapon with him. The other man had an identical .357 trained on Valerie. He couldn't gun the motor and zoom off. Could he talk his way out of this?

The larger man spoke in a deep voice. "We want to talk to you, man to man. Please step outside."

The thinner man walked around the hood and stood beside the stocky one. He used a bright yellow handkerchief with black borders and a red stain to blow his nose, sending the aroma of tomato sauce Matt's way before stuffing it back into his pocket.

The pudgy man tapped his cigar against the car, letting ashes drift to the ground. He gestured toward the thinner man. "Be quiet, Felix. I'll do the talking. Mr. Larson, I have need of a good lawyer."

Matt hesitated. This was no random stop. "How'd you know who I am?"

"Let's just say, your reputation travels."

"Why me?" His pulse racing, Matt wracked his brain. The only criminal cases he'd handled had been for burglary and shoplifting in Dallas. But an ex-client could have moved to south Texas. This seemed too well orchestrated for some small-time criminal.

Visions of being shot, execution style, filled his mind. They might hurt Valerie. Time to make use of his prime skill—negotiating.

Roberto wiped his brow with a white handkerchief.

"I know you've represented several men from Dallas with criminal charges."

Great. News must get around. Matt nodded. "So?"

"I need a good U.S. attorney to get my Friday hearing postponed until after next week. I have to make a trip to Mexico this week. I'll make it worth your while."

Matt didn't want him for a client, but it wasn't smart to object too strongly. "What are you charged with?"

"Possession with intent to sell."

"I'm not familiar with any of the judges in this area. Hard to negotiate with one I know nothing about."

"That's good. No one's been in your pocket."

The thinner man spoke up. "Roberto, you don't know nothing about this guy. You need to get someone good, like Louie the Cougar. He could get you off easy and get your bail money back too."

Roberto shoved one hand in his pocket, but kept the gun trained on Matt. "Felix, you idiot, don't you remember? Louie's been suspended for six months by the Texas Bar. Unethical behavior, they claimed."

"Why not hire a good local lawyer?" Matt asked.

"The mayor of Jourdanton has started a campaign to get tough on drug dealers. Talked to three attorneys in town yesterday. They're afraid taking on my case might hurt their chances for the next election. One's running for justice of the peace. The other two want to be on city council."

Matt leaned back in the seat, feigning a nonchalance he didn't feel. "They say I'm good in the courtroom, but what makes you think I'd do any better than say Racehorse Haynes? He got murder suspects off in two sensational cases some years back."

Felix grinned. "You got spirituality. Roberto likes that."

Roberto frowned. "You mean he's got spirit."

Matt said, "I need to get back to San Antonio. My brother's in jail for murdering his wife, but he's innocent. I need to work on his case." He swallowed. Would they let him go?

Roberto took a drag on his cigar. "Getting my case postponed or cleared up shouldn't take long—that is if you're any good."

Felix nodded. "Should be easy. We disappeared their main witness. They've got no evidence." He pointed his weapon at Valerie. "Open the door, Larson, if you don't want the lady getting hurt."

"Hold your horses." Matt unfastened his seat belt. "You should be able to get a lawyer from McAllen or Laredo without much trouble. Why me?"

Roberto seemed to be studying his gun. "Let's just say you're the best pinch hitter I can come up with."

Except Matt was the one being pinched.

Chapter Eleven

Roberto stuck the gun thorough the window's narrow opening. Matt swore. The man rattled off a command in Spanish, and Felix marched over to Valerie's side. People walked back and forth behind the window of restaurant several yards away, but no one looked their way.

The gun rested on the edge of the glass, inches from Matt's head. "I can make good use of you tomorrow at the hearing," Roberto said casually, as if this were a normal business transaction.

Felix pointed his gun at Valerie. Matt kicked himself for not telling her sooner to close the window. He tensed.

Would the guy shoot her? He swallowed. Time for earnest negotiation. He faced Roberto. "If I agree to represent you in court, what do I get?"

Roberto grinned and nodded. "See Felix. I told you he was smart." His gaze focused on Matt. "If you can get my trial date postponed, I'll pay the usual rate: three hundred dollars an hour to plead my case at the hearing. I'll double it if you can get all my bail money back."

"Will we be free to go then?"

"Of course. Do we have a deal?"

Yeah, right. He was good at cross-examining witnesses. He could usually tell when someone was lying, but this time he couldn't be sure. "Doesn't sound like a very good one for me."

Roberto inched the gun barrel into the window. "I'm not releasing the lady unless you agree. Come with me to my hacienda. I have the court notice and a room where you can work on my case."

Felix jammed the muzzle of the gun next to Valerie's window with an ominous click. "You and the lady need to come with us. You ain't got much choice."

Matt opened the door and stuck out one foot. He tried to think what else he to do, but came up short. He didn't want to risk Valerie being hurt. His heart ached, making him realize how much she meant to him. Damn, he'd have to do as they said.

Roberto grabbed Matt's left arm and yanked him from the car. His arm hurt like hell, but he wasn't about to let the crook know.

He and Valerie could run into the restaurant. He might outrun them, but he wasn't sure about Valerie. Besides, they were up against two armed men. They'd be easy targets. He swallowed. Cars whizzed by. Roberto should realize this place was too public to shoot them here, but would he?

If they got in that limo, who knew where Roberto would take them? Maybe to some lonely road. Where he would shoot them. With no one to hear their last words. Or see their bodies slump to the ground. By the time someone found them, they'd be unrecognizable. His stomach cramped. He tightened his hands into fists. He wanted to clobber Roberto, but Felix's gun was tight against Valerie's neck.

He felt as helpless as a trussed up prisoner. Not smart to force their hands. Matt wanted to punch Roberto, but willed his fingers to relax. What if they

killed her first? Made him watch. He smothered a gasp.
To watch her breathe her last—he didn't even want to
think about that.

He shoved his hands into his pockets. Didn't want
them seeing how bad they shook. He took a deep
breath. He had to figure a way out.

Waving his gun, Roberto motioned Matt toward
the rear of the limousine. Behind him the sound of Felix
slamming the Mustang's door echoed in his ears.

Roberto held open the rear door of the black limo;
he tapped his cigar, letting ashes drift to the gravel
parking lot. "You and the woman get in back. She'll be
our insurance you'll do a good job in court. Get my
case dismissed or postponed for a month or two. Then
I'll pay you and let you go...unless you want to
represent me for a longer period of time."

Matt jerked his arm away. "What time does court
begin?"

"Nine in the morning. I was going to skip Friday's
hearing, but fifty thousand for bail is too much to run
out on if it's not necessary. Besides, I need it for some
product I'm buying tomorrow."

Matt stared at Roberto. "Didn't you go through a
bail bondsman?"

Roberto shook his head, his heavy jowls jiggling.
He stepped closer, brushed some invisible lint from his
suit. His strong aftershave mixed with the smell of soap
filtered through the breeze. "Had the cash, didn't want
to stay in that filthy jail a minute longer."

Matt didn't like Roberto's in-your-face tactics, but
didn't step back. Wouldn't do to show fear. Matt
smoothed his mustache. "I can't do your case justice
without researching similar cases. I'd need to go to a

law library."

"Boss, he don't sound too compatible."

Valerie tried to shake off Felix's arm as he walked her at gunpoint toward the limo. "Don't you mean competent?"

"Yeah, what she says." Felix faced Matt. "Shouldn't you know that stuff by heart?"

Matt rubbed his chin. "A good attorney checks out the statute and the prior cases to give his client the best defense he can. I'll definitely need to do some research if I take your case."

"No problem," said Roberto. "We have a laptop with internet access. Whatever you need you can get online."

Matt suppressed a sigh. With his firm's password he could access the regulations on drug possession as well as previous rulings in other cases. Besides, they might hurt Valerie if he didn't agree. Matt gambled Roberto would live up to his word. Even criminals had their own code of honor. While Matt had bet on dice in Vegas, stakes had never been this high. Things might not go as smooth as Roberto claimed. If not, who knew what Roberto would do? What choice did Matt have? "Okay, I'll do it, but—"

Felix grinned. "Now he's talking smart, ain't he, boss?"

Roberto smiled. "I told you he was intelligent."

"I'll represent you only if you don't lay a hand on her or hassle me. Let her stay here at the restaurant while I work on your case. I can't concentrate on representing you if I'm worrying about her."

Roberto shook his head. "She's coming with us."

Matt shook his head. "I won't do it if you take her

there."

Valerie glowered and opened her mouth to speak.

Matt shook his head, glad to see her catch his drift and not say anything.

Roberto pointed to Valerie. "Get in my car, señorita. We're taking you both to my hacienda. Then he'll be sure to keep his promise. Felix will blindfold you until we get there. My housekeeper will take good care of you."

Valerie stood near Matt's car, glaring at Felix.

"Keep the gun on her," Roberto said. Still pointing the gun at Matt, he walked to Valerie. "Step quickly, miss, over by my limo."

Valerie stalked toward the limousine, her body language defiant. But her trembling hands and glistening eyes telegraphed her fear. She gripped her skirt—probably to keep her hands from shaking. Matt wished he could give her some sign or even a hint of a plan. Damn. His brain couldn't come up with anything.

Roberto shoved Valerie closer to Matt.

She glared at Felix. "Take your damn hands off me."

Roberto stared. "Tsk, tsk. Such spirit in a woman is not becoming, my dear."

Valerie planted her feet in a defiant stance, but clamped her mouth shut.

Roberto shifted his gun to her head. Her face paled. "Now, counselor, if you don't want the lady to get hurt, do as I say and get in the backseat."

With Robert's gun still pointed at Valerie's head, Matt's options were zilch. Holding his breath and hoping they wouldn't shoot her, he took a step toward the limo. He was about to slide into the backseat when

Roberto said, "Hold it right there. Blindfold him first, Felix."

Felix slid his gun in his waistband, then pulled out a bright yellow handkerchief, and started to wrap it around Matt's eyes. Matt grabbed for Felix's gun.

Felix shoved his hand away. "Boss, he's trying to get my gun."

Roberto gripped Valerie's arm with one hand and pointed the gun at Matt with the other. "Stop. Don't try anything else. Let Felix blindfold you, or I'll shoot. And I'll keep the lady for myself."

Matt's stomach lurched. He grimaced at the strong garlic smell emanating from Felix. What could he do? He hoped Roberto was on the level about handling his hearing in court...and about letting them go. At least at court they might stand a chance of asking for protection. Surely, they wouldn't allow these two to take their guns inside. On the other hand, Roberto might have no intention of letting them go. His offer might be a complete fabrication, dreamed up on the spur of the moment. Matt didn't know what he could do if that happened. He was so out of his comfort zone he couldn't think straight.

Valerie stood a few feet away, a stoic expression on her face. Matt tried to meet her eyes, to warn her not to start anything. They were in enough trouble as it was. Her lips were still clamped together, probably to keep from blurting out some retort. He had to admire her. Inside she might be quivering like Jell-O, but she was keeping her cool.

Roberto pulled a pristine handkerchief from his pocket. "I want you to blindfold the lady. He slapped the handkerchief in Matt's hand. "Tie it tight around her eyes. I don't want either of you watching where we drive."

Matt tried to keep the blindfold loose, but Roberto elbowed him away and tightened it. He held out his hand. "Your handkerchief, please, Felix."

Roberto tied Felix's handkerchief over Matt's eyes. It smelled of onions and garlic. A damp spot over Matt's nose smelled of salsa. The coarse cotton fabric bound Matt's flesh so tightly he could hardly blink.

Felix grabbed his left arm and shoved him toward the car. "Get in."

Matt's arm hurt. He grimaced, but made no sound. He wouldn't give them the satisfaction of hearing him complain.

After grabbing hold of the car door, Matt did as asked. He heard fabric sliding across the seat. Heard Valerie's rapid breathing next to him. He concentrated on the sound of heavy footsteps, relieved that Roberto seemed to be heading around the car.

Valerie's hand touched his knee. He took hold of it. "Wh-wh..." She sounded breathless. "Where are they taking us?"

"To my hacienda," Roberto said.

Matt hoped to hell that was true. Doors slammed. Sounded as if their captors were settling in up front.

"No talking," came Roberto's voice from the front. "I'll be watching you to see you don't try anything. Drive, Felix, but don't go over the speed limit. We don't need to be apprehended by a cop."

"Hey, boss," Felix said. "What's apprehend mean? How come you have to use such big words?"

"Just drive," barked Roberto.

"Damn. You don't have to poke me with your

elbow. I'll shut up."

Matt felt Valerie's hand tremble in his. He leaned closer and his head bumped hers. Heard her soft "oomph."

"Don't worry," he whispered. "Soon as we get these blindfolds off, and they stop the car there, I'll see what I can do."

"But," she whispered back. "They want you to be Roberto's lawyer. They'll probably keep me locked up at the hacienda."

"I'll insist on them taking both of us to court. Then I can ask the judge for—"

"I said no talking," Roberto said in a quiet but determined voice. "If you do a competent job, I may ask you to appear for me the next time so I can get my case resolved. The threat of incarceration hanging over my head gives me insomnia."

"That something like being incinerated, boss?" asked Felix. "Don't think you'd like that. Might get too hot for you."

"I'm speaking about going to prison. And yes, things could get hot there."

"If you mean doin' time, why didn't you say so?"

Matt's nose itched. He reached up to adjust his blindfold and scratch his nose.

"Don't touch that. I've got my gun pointed at your lady friend," said Roberto in a steely voice.

Matt wished he could see if that were true, but didn't dare touch his blindfold. An itchy nose was the least of his worries. For all he knew, Roberto might be holding the gun on him instead.

After what seemed like half an hour later, the car slowed and then rolled to a stop.

"You can get out now," said Roberto. "I'll lead your lady inside. Don't worry. I won't hurt her...as long as you cooperate." Matt heard car doors open. He held Valerie's hand until she was yanked away. Heavy footsteps were followed by her softer ones. They were leading her somewhere to the right. He didn't like this.

Matt slid across the seat and stepped out. He stretched cramped muscles. He felt along the sides of the limo to guide his way past it. He followed the sound of Roberto's voice.

"Come this way," said Felix as he grabbed Matt's arm and led him along a rough sidewalk. It felt like one of those pebbled ones rather than smooth cement. Matt could smell honeysuckle and petunias. Then he caught the scent of roses and wondered if Roberto took pride in raising them—and if this were indeed his home. Hearing footsteps was better than hearing gunshots.

Up ahead, a door creaked open. Felix shoved him forward. A door slammed behind him. Roberto said, "You may remove your blindfolds now. Welcome to my hacienda."

Some welcome, Matt thought, but kept his mouth shut. He tore Felix's stained handkerchief from his head and looked around. Valerie already had her blindfold off and stood defiant on the earth-colored stone tile. The smell of cinnamon wafted from somewhere beyond the room. A bold ray of sunshine shot through the slit between heavy draperies. Matt strained to adjust to the dim lighting. A red and gold print couch stood against the wall.

Valerie shook off Roberto's arm and stepped away from the man. "How long are you going to hold us here?"

Roberto bowed. "You will be my guests until attorney Larson has either accomplished a dismissal of the charges against me or gotten my hearing postponed."

She put her hands on her hips. "How do we know you'll let us leave then?"

Roberto's expression gave nothing away. "You'll have to take my word for that."

Matt tried to tamp down the knot growing inside. Could he believe this man? Matt had better prepare for anything. "Señor Roberto, I'll do my best, but I can't promise to get all your bond money back." Damn, he shouldn't have brought up the money.

"Get my hearing postponed, and make sure my bond isn't forfeited, and I'll let you loose." Roberto clapped his hands. An older Hispanic woman, short and pudgy, walked into the room. "Maria, get a room ready for the gentleman and his lady. They will be staying for a while."

Matt tried to adopt his courtroom persona, hoping he appeared much more confident than he felt. "I'll need a computer, a printer, and access to the Internet for research." He swallowed. Could he hold Roberto off before their captors shot them or slit their throats?

Chapter Twelve

Valerie sat on the green and rust brocade spread of a four-poster bed in the drug lord's spacious house. She pulled open the matching draperies and cranked open the narrow casement window to let in light and any breeze. Beyond the window roses bloomed in shades of red, pink, white, and yellow, spaced evenly in weed-free beds. Their scent wafted inside. Beyond the flowerbed stood dense woods.

Matt's hunched back blocked her view of the computer on a desk against the wall. She rose and stepped across a green and brown braided rug.

"Matt, do you suppose we could squeeze out that window and escape through the woods?"

He shook his head. "Shhh. Someone may be listening at the door," he whispered. "And besides, I wouldn't fit."

"You're going to appear in court for this guy, aren't you?"

"It's our best chance of getting him to let us go."

"Is he your client now?"

"Technically no. He hasn't given me any money, but he promised me three-hundred an hour when we walk into court, and another three-hundred if I can get his bail returned without any deductions."

"So will you feel obligated to do your best for him and not talk about his upcoming drug deal?"

"I don't have much choice at the moment. If I act as his attorney, I'm honor bound to represent his best interests."

Someone knocked on the door. Valerie tensed. "Who is it?" she asked, hating how weak her voice sounded.

"Señorita, I am Maria. There are iced tea and cookies for you in the front room."

Matt motioned to Valerie to move to one side of the door, away from where it would open. "Just a moment." He took up a position in front of it and pulled it open a crack. He looked, then grasped Valerie's hand. "Come on. We'll check it out."

She held back.

Matt stuck his head out in the hall. "If they were going to shoot us, they'd have done so by now. Besides, they want something from me. And I see a pitcher and a plate of cookies on the glass table in front of the couch."

With halting steps, Valerie followed him across the earth-colored stone tile to the archway into the living room. As if they were ordinary guests, Maria held out the tray with three frosty glasses of lemonade and a plate of cookies. Valerie took a glass and a ball-shaped cookie dusted with sugar and chopped nuts.

They wouldn't die hungry. That was cold comfort. She swallowed. Had to stop thinking like that. Had to trust Matt to get them through this.

Roberto sat in a chair, smoking a cigar. Valerie stopped at the entrance. Matt hesitated too. A handgun lay on the table beside his chair. Its short stainless steel barrel glinted in a ray of sunshine from the window. If Matt saw it, he hadn't let his reaction show.

She swallowed. Their chances of getting out of here alive were slim and none. Somehow, she hadn't figured on dying away from her family and friends. And especially not like this. Knots tightened inside. Not knowing was almost worse than the real thing.

At least he wasn't holding a gun on them now. He smiled. "Come on in. I don't plan on shooting anyone right now, so you needn't worry."

Valerie sat on the edge of the red and gold couch. She didn't feel comfortable leaning back against the gold pillows. Despite what he'd said, she might have to run for her life.

Matt perched on the edge of the couch. He looked more relaxed, but the way his little finger tapped on the cushion beside her revealed his agitation.

Roberto knocked the ashes from his cigar into a ceramic ashtray. A copy of Dan Brown's *DaVinci Code* lay on the table on top of the *Wall Street Journal*. "How are you coming with my case?"

Matt leaned forward. "First, I need to know all the evidence they have against you. They are required to give you copies. I also need to know what else you have been charged with."

After picking up some papers from a desk, Roberto handed them to Matt."

Matt looked over the pages. "Thought you only had one charge against you, not four." Obviously, Matt had his work cut out for him.

Their captor leaned back in his chair. "Possession's the main one."

Matt eased back on the couch cushion. "I see now why you're worried about jail time. Three convictions could mean a life sentence or deportation."

"That's why I need you. I like it here in the U.S."

"But you might be safer from prosecution in Mexico."

Roberto slowly shook his head. "Not with all the rival drug lords staking out their territory. I might be small time, but it's a lot healthier here."

"Did they show a search warrant when you were arrested?"

Roberto nodded. "Only for my car and my house."

"Did they find any illegal drugs on you?"

"No. I was clean."

Matt rose. "Did they search your house? Did they take anything?"

"Just a bag of marijuana, a small amount I had on the kitchen counter. Isn't that rich?" He laughed. "I had a hidden stash of cocaine, but they got me for pot instead."

"Enough for one roach or two?"

"A little more than you'd use for one, but not really enough for two. Does that mean anything?"

"Might be hard for them to prove a charge of possession with intent to sell. They should have had a more encompassing search warrant. I'm going to file a motion to quash to suppress the evidence. Do you have a printer to go with that computer?"

The drug lord nodded. "Felix, bring the printer from my office and set it up in the guest room."

Felix appeared in the hallway. "Sure thing, boss." He turned and headed back the way he'd come.

Roberto picked up the gun and rubbed his fingers along the stainless steel barrel. Valerie tried to keep from flinching.

Roberto set it down. "Sometimes strong persuasion

is necessary." He laid it in his lap, the barrel pointed in Matt's direction.

Valerie leaned forward. "Aren't you afraid you'll shoot someone by accident?"

"Miss, I don't do anything without planning every step of the way. Except being without my usual lawyer has thrown a monkey wrench in my plans. Guess it's what you Americans would call a SNAFU."

Felix appeared in the doorway. "Printer's all set up. What's a SNAFU, boss?"

"It means," Matt answered, "situation normal, all fouled up."

Felix nodded. "Yeah, things are really screwed up now. Roberto almost never goes to court. The lawyer usually talks to the judge and gets it taken care of. Only there's a new judge in town. Guess greasing palms with dough ain't gonna work no more."

Roberto frowned. "Shut up, Felix. We don't want to give our new attorney any ideas."

"You mean he might want more dough too?"

"That's enough, Felix." He picked up the gun and slapped it into his right hand.

Valerie tensed, afraid to say anything. She looked to see if his finger was on the trigger. She'd hate to get shot by accident. Or maybe it wouldn't be an accident. Maybe he was toying with them.

Roberto waved his hand at the plate of cookies. "Help yourself. I promise they aren't poisoned." He grinned, then bent to take one.

Matt didn't touch one until he saw Roberto swallow. Nor did he drink any lemonade until Roberto grabbed a glass and drank some. Valerie followed suit. She'd rather be in his car eating the food they'd taken out, but the cookies would have to do.

Roberto fingered the gun. "Just so we understand each other, Larson, I'm keeping your lady here in the living room while you work on that motion. I want it ready to go when we approach the judge in the morning. So, are you ready to finish working on my case?"

"Yes, sir. Valerie, sit where I can see you if I step in the hall." Matt swallowed the last of the lemonade and rose. "What time are we leaving tomorrow?"

"Eight o'clock. Maria will serve breakfast at seven."

Valerie clamped her lips together. Why did Matt give in so easily? Was he planning something? He couldn't do much while Roberto held a gun on her. She stood. "His notes will need to be typed. Let me go type them up for him."

Roberto's evil grin mocked her. "No, my dear. I watched him work on that laptop. His typing speed is adequate. Might take a little longer, but he doesn't need you. Sit down and keep me company."

Watching Matt leave the room, Valerie suppressed a groan. She'd rather visit the dentist. Roberto would probably keep her alive to force Matt to do his bidding, at least until the hearing was over. But after that, they'd really be at risk.

Roberto leaned back in his chair and blew a smoke ring. The pungent aroma of his cigar nauseated her. And that gun he kept shifting from one hand to the other made her stomach tighten. She felt as if a snake were coiling around inside, waiting to sink its fangs into some tender spot. Would getting shot would hurt for very long, or would Roberto just blast her into oblivion.

A chill shimmied down her spine.

"Tell me, my dear," he said, "how did a nice girl like you get tied up with him?"

"We were trying to catch up with my sister and the man who kidnapped her when you stopped us. Now, we may not be able to find her. Heaven knows what that creep will do to her."

"Too bad. Someone from San Antonio called to let me know you two would come by. Asked if I'd watch out for you. Seeing as I have need of your boyfriend's services, I was only too happy to comply."

This had been planned. Valerie swallowed. Roberto kept picking up the gun and laying it down, making her restless and uneasy. "You aren't exactly what I expected a drug lord to be like."

"I prefer to be thought of as a successful businessman. My operation is small compared to those powerful cartel drug lords south of the border."

"But you seem to be well educated."

"For someone in my business you mean?"

"Well, yes."

"I taught chemistry and English in a university in Mexico for a while...until the beam of opportunity illuminated my way."

"Pushing drugs you mean?"

"I consider myself an entrepreneur. I satisfy a demand for an energizing substance, one that gives the user a sense of greater control over life."

"Cocaine?"

"Some people refer to it that way. I prefer a more appealing term."

"Like what?"

"The great energizer, a way to achieve one's

potential in life. And who knows, if someone's feeling in control, he might just do that."

"I'll bet your main achievement is money, money you gained at other's expense."

"Nothing wrong with being rich."

His disapproving expression worried her. She'd better stop before she put her foot in her mouth. "Do you have any books or magazines you wouldn't mind me looking at?"

Roberto rose and puffed on his cigar, again permeating the air with an unpleasant odor, then laid it on an ashtray beside the gun. "This way, my dear."

If he didn't return to the living room, perhaps she could sneak back and get the gun. However, she felt his hand on her back, urging her forward.

He led her into a paneled library with shelves from floor to ceiling. An antique Greek urn with a raised figure of a woman, her dress appearing to flutter in the breeze, sat on one shelf. Beside it a miniature globe had countries blocked out in various shades of mother-of-pearl.

Leather bound books hinted at first editions. Other traditionally bound hardcovers included works by Shakespeare and St. Augustine. American authors such as Hawthorne, Cooper, Hemingway, Fitzgerald, and Faulkner lined the shelves as well as more current novels by Patricia Cornwell and Patricia Highsmith.

She found it interesting he'd chosen Patricia Highsmith's novels featuring villains who didn't get punished and Cornwell's stories about clues presented by dead bodies. He seemed to have a complete collection of Patricia Cornwell's novels. Was he studying how to avoid getting caught? She shuddered, but picked up a book by Patricia Cornwell and returned to the guest bedroom.

Matt sat hunched over the laptop until supper was served. After eating he worked until eleven. By then, Roberto had allowed her to take a shower and change into a cotton nightgown lent her by Maria. He even let her stay in the bedroom with Matt.

She lay on the bed as a cool breeze washed away the heat of the day. His broad shoulders and the cute way his dark hair curled into two whorls on either side of his neck drew her attention. His full lips were clamped together, a sign of his concentration.

She remembered the warmth and comfort of his body beside hers when they'd shared the narrow cot in the Mexican jail. She'd been touched by his offer to kiss her goodbye when he thought they might face a firing squad, but he hadn't offered again. However, she'd caught his gaze on her more than once. He'd held her hand and protected her at every turn and even complimented her. She knew she could trust him to keep her from harm. She remembered his kiss on her mouth in jail. What would it feel like to taste those sensuous lips again, to feel his mouth on hers in a kiss when he wasn't rushed or desperate like they'd been in jail?

Roberto obviously expected them to sleep together. She wished she had on something sexy instead of this prim cotton gown, but neither of them needed to be distracted. They should be figuring out a backup plan for escape. Except, she couldn't help looking forward to being held in his arms again, to feel that marvelous warmth. And if he didn't kiss her goodnight, well, she'd kiss him. She could hardly wait to show him how much she appreciated his support, and how much she wanted to taste his lips, really taste them. She could only hope he wanted that too.

"Matt."

"What?" He turned to face her, his look serious from concentration.

"He did promise he'd let us go after you appear for him in court, didn't he?"

"Yes, but I plan to stay in the courtroom until I feel it's safe for us to leave."

"And then we'll take a cab to that restaurant, pick up your car and burn rubber getting away from here, right."

"Yes, that's my plan. Now don't talk to me. I need to get back to work on this presentation so he can't complain I didn't do a good job."

He sounded annoyed with her for interrupting. She clamped her mouth shut.

She lay in bed watching him. It was getting late, and she could hardly keep her eyes open. When he finished at the computer and got ready for bed, what would he expect? She'd seen his picture in the paper with a gorgeous socialite. No doubt he had women seek him out—he probably chose the best-looking, sexy ones to take to bed. Valerie hoped his jerk of a brother hadn't repeated what he'd said about her—that she had about as much sex appeal as an old maid's teakettle covered with a flowered cotton cozy.

She'd liked her flowing, flowered dress of cotton voile because it was cool and feminine—until Gordon said that. Afterward, it hung unworn in her closet until she gave it to Goodwill.

If sex appeal was what it took to win Matt's

attention, she should give up now. She couldn't see herself sending come-hither glances and making flirtatious comments like Christy. After all, even in a well fitting bathing suit, her average figure hadn't attracted attention.

So why was she even thinking about Matt expecting sex tonight? If she could win Matt's admiration for helping to find Christy, and for being a good person, that was all she could hope for. And once they were free, he might give her a hearty hug—except that wasn't all she really wanted.

She snuggled under the sheet. Unbidden, those memories of his body next to hers on that narrow cot, with his arm around her waist warmed her heart. Even though she'd fought off Ruiz, she'd felt warm and safe in Matt's arms, just knowing he was there to protect her.

****

Sometime during the night, she felt Matt's body against hers. Damn, she'd fallen asleep without trying for a goodnight kiss. But Matt's hand was cupping her breast, sending wild tremors through her. Her pulse raced. Was he trying to rouse her for a midnight tryst? Heart pounding, she opened her eyes. His head rested against her shoulder, a lock of hair dangling on his forehead. He snuggled closer. She smiled, loving the feel of his chest against her. Then cool breaths flowed across her cheek, and the slow rhythm convinced her he was sleeping. Darn.

"Ummm, feels good," he murmured. She caught her breath. Had she been mistaken? Then he muttered, "No, Mallory," turned away from her and began to snore softly.

He and Gordon didn't have a sister. Who was Mallory? Frowning, Valerie scooted away from him. She wouldn't be a substitute for another woman. What had she been thinking letting herself get close to Gordon's brother of all people?

The next morning Valerie rushed around, dressing in the small adjoining bathroom, still wondering about Mallory. A few minutes later, Valerie sat down to a breakfast of sausage, scrambled eggs, and pancakes served with individual sauce dishes of boysenberry jam and raspberry jam. Two jars of jam stood on the counter beside a coffee maker, a mixer, and a food processor. Next to those stood a blender, beneath a board with pegs hung with various keys.

Back in the guest room after they'd eaten breakfast, Matt stood in the doorway to the hall, holding a sheaf of papers and the laptop.

She picked up her purse, hoping they'd let her go with them. Seconds later, Roberto and Felix came down the hall and stood by the front door. Roberto nodded to Matt. "Ready?"

"Ready as I'll ever be." Matt cleared his throat.

That might have been a stock phrase he tossed off, but Valerie guessed he was wishing he hadn't revealed so much.

Roberto frowned. "You'd better be. I don't intend to stay in that filthy jail. Now come along." He put a hand on Matt's back, urging him toward the front door.

Valerie moved to follow, but Felix barred her way.

"Excuse me," she said, "please let me pass?"

Felix grabbed the doorknob and laid a hand on her shoulder. "Step back, miss."

She shoved his hand away. "But I'm a paralegal.

He might need help in court."

"You will wait here."

"You mean until after the hearing?"

"You will stay in the guest bedroom until Roberto agrees you can come out." Felix picked up the .357 from the table beside Roberto's chair. "Do you need to be persuaded?"

She swallowed. "No, I don't." She marched toward the bedroom. He followed and shut the door behind her. Feeling frustrated, she plopped down on the bed.

A click near the doorknob sounded ominous. A quick pull on the knob confirmed her fear. The door wouldn't open.

Chapter Thirteen

Valerie pounded on the bedroom door. "Let me out! Roberto promised we could leave after Matt attended the hearing."

The only noises came from water swishing in a dishwasher and a power mower outside. Birds chirped in the trees outside the window. A hint of cinnamon lingered in the air from the cookies Maria baked. They weren't going to let her out, and she didn't trust Roberto to let her go after the hearing in court. She had to escape.

She found a crank that opened the narrow casement window. The scents of honeysuckle and roses wafted in. Now if she could just slip outside without Felix or Maria noticing and get to a car. But she'd need the keys.

Off to one side of the spacious yard past the rose bushes, Maria hung out some rugs and started beating them. If Valerie could squeeze through the window without making any noise, she could hide behind the bushes while she planned what to do next.

Getting one leg out was easy, but her foot didn't reach the ground. She'd have to balance on the sill until she got through and then jump. Holding onto the frame, she lifted her other leg and stuck it out. But then, her rump wouldn't fit through the narrow space. If she were built like one of those super models, with 38C breasts, a tiny butt and no stomach, she bet Matt would have awakened her before going to sleep. No time to think about that now. She pulled her left leg back inside and turned sideways. She leaned out the window as far as she could without letting go of the frame. Her toe just barely touched the ground.

Putting her weight on that toe, she leaned farther out the window until she could stand on the ball of her left foot. Grabbing hold of a finger-sized branch of a nearby bush, she held her breath and squeezed her hips through. Careful not to make any noise, she pulled her other leg free.

Now for the car keys. She had to sneak past Maria into the kitchen, get the keys, and make it to the car before anyone noticed. She walked around to the front door, ducking under windows on the way.

Valerie punched the doorbell and ran like hell around the house. Maria was still in the back yard, beating rugs, and still in sight of the back door. Felix shouted, "Maria, there's no one at the door." The door snapped shut. Damn, she'd have to try again.

This time she hid where she could see both Maria and the front door. After Valerie rang the bell and hid, Maria stepped out the front door. Valerie raced to the back door, ran into the kitchen, and grabbed some car keys. Damn, another set hung right next to them. Not sure which one she needed, she took both.

She dashed out the back door. Ran toward the PT Cruiser in the driveway. After jumping in, she turned the key and jammed her foot on the accelerator. The key worked, thank heaven.

Behind her Maria and Felix yelled, "Stop."

Heart pounding, she gunned the motor and zoomed

out of the driveway. She tossed the other keys on the seat beside her and hoped she could find the courthouse before the hearing was over.

On a hunch she turned right at the stop sign. If she didn't see any signs telling her which way the town was, she could always turn around and go the other way. Luckily, she hadn't seen any other car for Felix to follow her.

Tall grass lined the highway, its musty dry grass smell telling her the area needed rain. Up front appeared a sign saying four miles to Jourdanton. She let out her breath. This was the right road.

At last she reached the main street of the town and was glad to find the courthouse and a parking space. After locking the car, she tiptoed inside and slid into a rear seat at the back of the courtroom. Thank goodness Roberto was facing the judge and didn't turn around.

Matt presented his case to the judge. His honor ruled he'd hold the final hearing in a month, and bail money would stay in the registry of the court until then. Roberto stalked out of the courtroom, and Matt followed. Valerie kept her face turned away until Roberto passed. Then she touched Matt's arm.

He stared at her and opened his mouth to speak. She placed a finger over her lips. Matt nodded.

Roberto turned and argued with Matt. "You need to file for a change of venue. Get this moved out of this municipal court and into a county one with a judge who knows the law.

"Sir, I can't do that. Not until you have a trial in this court, and the judge has ruled.

"B-but..." Roberto turned, and his gaze met Valerie's. His face reddened. "What the hell are you doing here?"

Valerie swallowed, then rose. She grasped the back of the bench in front to still her trembling hand. Keeping her voice calm, she tried to adapt a matter of fact tone. "I came to watch Matt at work. Now, if you'll excuse us, I need to talk with him."

The judge banged his gavel. "Order in the court. Please move your discussion outside. Counselor Larson. Tell your client he'll be charged with contempt of court if he doesn't leave the courtroom immediately."

Roberto stood with feet apart and his hands clenched into fists.

Valerie stepped into the aisle. "Your honor, his client is likely to cause trouble for his attorney and me. Might we have an escort to my car?

The judge frowned. "Counselor, is this true?"

Matt faced the judge. "I believe so, your honor.

The judge rose. "Bailiff, escort these two to their vehicle."

As Matt and Valerie walked down the hall beside the bailiff, Roberto stalked toward them, gesturing wildly. "How dare you? I'll report you to the bar for unethical behavior and have you disciplined. And you'd better watch your back in San Antonio, or wherever you practice."

The bailiff patted his holstered gun. "Stand back."

As the bailiff ushered them outside, Matt said, "What's your name? If I file charges against him, I may have to call you as a witness."

"Yes, sir, my name's John Duncan."

Duncan stood guard while Valerie motioned Matt to the PT Cruiser.

"But that's not—"

"Shut up and get in. I'll explain later." She climbed inside, glad the car was black and hoped Roberto wouldn't recognize it. Roberto stepped to his black limousine and started to unlock the door. Then he turned toward them, his face red. "They've stolen my car. Stop them." He took a step toward them.

The bailiff barred his way. "I'll have to ask you to wait here until they leave."

Roberto scowled. "But that's my car."

The bailiff grabbed hold of his arm. "Your car is over there. I watched you arrive in it."

"The PT Cruiser is my car also. She stole it from my house."

"I cannot take your word for that."

Duncan pulled out his gun. "Step aside, sir, if you please."

Roberto's face turned purple. "Don't threaten me. I'll report you for conduct unbecoming an officer of the court."

Duncan stepped closer to Roberto. "I said, step aside."

Roberto glared at him for a moment, and then walked toward his limousine.

Valerie shoved the pedal to the floor and zoomed away from the courthouse. Matt stared at her. "How on earth did you get away with this? Is it his?"

As she drove out of town, Valerie explained how she'd escaped with the car. "Of course," she added, "I plan to trade it for your Mustang if I can remember where that restaurant is."

Matt patted her arm and grinned. "You're something else. Glad to have you for a partner. Now if we can only find Christy."

Valerie basked in his admiration. It would be nice if he could see her as a desirable woman as well as a partner in his search for Christy.

They switched cars at the restaurant. Matt gave the keys to the manager and asked him to call and leave a message at Roberto's house.

****

Hours later, Matt and Valerie approached San Antonio. Matt called his attorney friend, Joe, who'd managed to dig up more complete directions for Buck's cabin and recommend somewhere Matt could buy a gun.

Later, while Matt rubbed his sore arm and waited for the gun dealer to do a background check, he studied the map and located the farm-to-market county road Joe mentioned. Then, with his new gun stashed in the glove compartment, he headed east as Valerie drifted into a fitful sleep.

Ten minutes later Matt shook Valerie's arm. "Wake up. I need your help. We're on the county road Joe mentioned, but I haven't seen anything leading off from it. We're fifty miles from the city limit."

She yawned. "Shouldn't we have found the cabin by now?

"Yes, dammit. I need you to help look for it."

"We must have gone too far. Turn around and go back to the highway. And slow down. You're going too fast for a country road that's full of ruts. If we had a carton of whipping cream, it would be shaken into butter by now."

Matt frowned. "Hold your horses. I'll turn around." Where did she get off telling him what to do? Gritting his teeth, he admitted to himself she was probably right.

135

The road was too narrow for a U-turn, but he managed to jockey the Mustang until it was facing back toward the main road.

As he pulled onto the highway, Valerie asked, "How far from town is the cabin?"

"Thirty miles from the city limit."

"Why did you go fifty miles before turning around? That wasn't smart."

He shot her a glare. "I don't need you to tell me that. "

"Okay, okay. How about if I keep my eyes peeled for it."

And your mouth shut, he wanted to say, but didn't.

Fifteen minutes later, she grabbed at his arm. "Back up. I see a road. Is the distance right?"

He braked and pulled over to the shoulder. "Close enough." Slowly he backed past low mesquite trees whose lacy-leafed branches almost hid the dirt road. "You have keen eyes."

After he drove about two miles, the road diminished into two ruts with weeds in between. Soon weeds filled the ruts, and the car crawled.

He turned off the engine. "Do you see anything?"

She pointed toward a path leading through the trees to a cabin built of weathered boards. Off to one side stood a rusty green pickup.

He leaned over and opened his glove compartment. He pulled out the small caliber gun he'd bought earlier. "I'll sneak up on the house. You stay in the car." He opened the door and stepped out. She did the same.

Patting the gun stuck in the back of his waistband, he frowned. "I told you to stay put."

"I'm coming with you. I'll be careful."

"But you'll make me vulnerable."

"No one will see me."

He frowned. "Guess you'll do it anyway. Okay, sneak around the right, and I'll go on the left. Look inside the windows."

Matt crept through the underbrush on the left side of the road, while Valerie moved along the other side. He stepped on a twig, making a noise. He froze, his gaze glued on the window and front porch. Nothing happened. He started up again. His footsteps sounded louder than the rustle of the leaves waving in the wind. Ragweed, with its rough smell also swayed in the breeze. He stopped to listen, but heard only the ever-changing call of a mockingbird.

Sounds from the other side of the cabin could mean Valerie was getting ahead of him. Not good. Hurrying to catch up, he tripped on a root and fell against a prickly pear cactus. Scores of tiny stickers imbedded themselves in his leg. Damn, he should have worn long pants. Later, he'd have to pull those suckers out one by one.

Rising, he saw she was way ahead. He ignored all the stings deviling his leg. Good thing the underbrush grew close to the building. He could almost see into the window from here.

A sickening odor assailed him. Smelled like blood and death. He felt like gagging. Oh Lord, what if they found Christy's body inside?

****

On the other side of the cabin Valerie inched closer, careful to avoid the prickly pear cactus. What was that awful odor? Smelled like something dead. Oh no, not Christy. Surely, Buck wouldn't—he'd seemed to like her. It was scary to think she and Christy might have actually come in contact with a psychopath.

Valerie scrunched down to pass under the window. The rotten odor intensified, reminding Valerie of the time she'd been to a morgue. Crossing her fingers, she hoped against hope something other than Christy's body was causing that familiar stench.

She wanted to see inside, but no bushes grew near the window. Someone inside might see her. And she had no weapon. If she stood off to one side, she could look in the window. A bed with the covers heaped in the middle stood against the nearest wall. The smell was overpowering. Did a body lie beneath the quilt?

Valerie had to let Matt know what she'd seen. Still unsure if Buck or someone else were inside, she crept round the back. No windows here, thank goodness. Matt was barely visible through the trees and underbrush. After she beckoned to him, it seemed to take forever before he worked his way to her.

"Seen anyone?" he whispered.

"Not exactly."

"What does that mean?"

"I thought I saw—" She swallowed. "I thought I saw a body in that bed. The smell is terrible. I couldn't tell."

"You don't think it's—"

"Don't say it. I can't believe Buck would actually kill her."

"See anyone moving inside?"

She shook her head.

"I'm going in."

She grabbed his arm. "Don't. It could be dangerous."

"I have a gun. You stay here. I'll knock, then stand aside."

"What if you get shot?"

"Call 9-1-1. Now stay back." He crept toward the front. She followed, staying a few paces back. Just before reaching the window, he rose up to peek inside.

"Don't expose yourself."

He turned and frowned. "I'm not, dammit."

"Do you see anything?"

"Not much, it's dark in there," he whispered and ducked to pass the window.

Valerie followed. Leaves crunched underfoot. Dirt wedged its way between her toes and her sandal soles. At least tonight she'd be free to take a shower.

Matt mounted the steps. She crouched beside the wooden porch, keeping her gaze on Matt. He knocked. A dank odor from outside—skunk cabbage maybe, entwined with the smell of death. Somewhere in the distance a frog croaked.

A crow cawed, startling her. Flapping its wings, it took off from a nearby tree.

Matt knocked again. He glanced at her. "I told you to stay back. Why can't you follow orders?"

She frowned and ducked beside the porch until only her head and shoulders rose above it. "Is anyone coming?"

He shook his head. "Anyone home?" he called.

Silence. Even the little birds in nearby trees stopped their chatter.

"Open up. I'm looking for Christy," he called loudly. Still no one answered.

Matt glared at Valerie. "Stay back, so you won't be a target."

Valerie frowned, but backed up. Did he think she was brainless? She could still see him, but it would be hard for anyone to shoot her from the doorway. Matt acted as if he were invincible. She hoped he wouldn't be shot.

Holding his gun ready, Matt grabbed the doorknob; he pushed. The door creaked then gave way. No one else showed at the doorway, but an awful smell permeated the air. Matt disappeared inside. She scrambled up on the porch.

Matt's footsteps echoed. Sounded like a wooden floor.

She heard no other noises and peeked inside. The smell grew stronger. Against the wall stood a bed with a hump in the middle.

She swallowed. "Is-is somebody here?"

"No one's here."

Holding her breath, she hurried inside. The smell was stronger. Christy couldn't be dead. She just couldn't.

Holding her nose, Valerie stepped close to the bed. She grabbed the edge of a faded quilt and yanked it back.

Chapter Fourteen

Standing in the deserted cottage, Valerie feared the worst. She yanked the quilt all the way down. No body. Nothing there but a heap of blankets. Thank goodness. Her breath whooshed out in a sigh of relief. She plopped down on the bed. "It's not Christy. I was so afraid."

Matt walked closer to the bed. "You must be relieved. It would be awful to see your sister dead. I'm glad you don't have to." He bent down and kicked something out from under the bed. Here's what's making the smell—a dead raccoon.

"Don't touch it. It might have had rabies."

The smell was becoming more bearable, especially now that she knew what caused it. She walked around, looking for a bathroom. There was none. Why would anyone build a cabin without a bathroom? "I need to go, and there's not even a toilet."

"Too bad you're not a guy. You could just find a tree."

"Yeah, right. Guess I need to find a bush. Don't come out. I'll manage." She hurried around back. Several yards through the trees sat a ramshackle, leaning outhouse. As she got closer, the smell about bowled her over. Hadn't whoever stayed here heard of Pine-Sol?

A sagging door hung from one rusty hinge,

revealing a splintery board seat. The rough-hewn hole was smeared with feces. Buzzing flies darted in and out. No way would she use it. Stepping closer to the cabin, she was about to lift her skirt when something poked her back. She reached behind to brush the branch away. Feeling cold steel against her, she froze, her heart in her throat.

"Don't move," said a gruff voice. He sounded older. Definitely not Buck. "You're trespassin'. Unless you want your drawers full of buckshot, get the hell off'n my property. That clear?"

"Uh, yes sir. If you'd just point that gun down, I'll leave immediately." She spoke loudly, hoping Matt would hear.

The metal object against her back was removed. She turned to face a wiry man wearing overalls and holding a shotgun.

Steely black eyes above a grizzled beard sent shivers down her core. "Sorry, I didn't know this was your cabin. I thought it belonged to Buck Robbins."

"Well, you got the wrong place. His is on the next road. I sold it to him. You better skedaddle pronto."

"Uh, sure. We'll be out of your hair in a jiffy." Oh no, now she'd alerted him to Matt's presence.

He frowned. "Someone else here with you?"

"A friend. We're looking for my sister. We think she's with Buck."

"Well, I ain't seen no couple prowling 'round here. They're probably a bit smarter than you folks, if'n they stay away from where they's not wanted."

She stepped back, keeping her eyes on his shotgun. Damn, she still had to go. She hoped she could hold it until they got away.

"Matt," she called. "This man says we're trespassing. We have to leave."

Matt emerged from behind the corner of the house. Had he been listening? Probably not. Knowing Matt, if he had, he'd have rushed over to protect her.

Backing toward the car, she kept her eyes on the older man. Out of the corner of her eye, she saw Matt holding his gun ready.

"I wouldn't try anything if I were you," Matt said in a stern voice. "Keep that shotgun pointed down, and we'll leave. Valerie, get in the car."

Trusting him to hold the man off, Valerie ran. Dry weeds scratched her legs. Stumbling, she turned her ankle. It hurt like the dickens, but she ran the rest of the way. She scrambled inside and slammed the door.

A few seconds later, Matt climbed behind the wheel. "Let's go before he changes his mind about shooting us."

Matt backed to a place where he could turn around. Not until they reached the highway did Valerie heave a sigh of relief. She crossed her fingers, hoping Matt wouldn't remind her she'd picked this road.

Back on the road she kept her eyes peeled. "There." She pointed to a road on the right. "That must be the one."

Matt turned in. This road wound through scrubby mesquite trees and was even more rutted than the other. After they'd gone about a mile, the road petered out into a small clearing around a cabin. No car or truck stood near. A twin trail of flattened weeds leading to the cabin showed a vehicle had been there recently.

Valerie's pulse quickened. She crossed her fingers, hoping this time they'd find Christy. This place was larger and in better condition. Built close to the ground, it had no porch or doorsteps, only a wood door with peeling red paint.

Matt held his gun ready and strode toward the door.

Valerie hurried after him, trying not to limp, but her ankle hurt. "Do you think it's wise to brandish a gun like that? The owner might shoot first and talk later."

"Maybe you're right." He shoved the gun into his waistband and knocked.

They waited. A crow cawed, but no sounds came from behind the door.

Valerie peeked through the dusty window, making out vague outlines of a couch and a day bed. She was glad to see the bed didn't have a heap of blankets on it. A breeze ruffled her hair and stirred the leaves on nearby mesquite trees. Thank goodness this cabin didn't smell of death.

Matt tried the door. It wouldn't budge. "I'll check the windows and see if I can get in that way."

Valerie walked a few paces behind, staying alert for any ominous sounds.

Matt tried one window. His muscles bulged, but the window didn't move. He dropped his arms and beckoned her to follow.

Around back, he tried a tiny window. After a few grunts, he raised it halfway. "Won't open any more." He stuck his head inside. "Anyone home?"

No one answered.

Valerie twisted a lock of hair. "Do you suppose Christy might be tied and gagged inside?"

"I hope not. I'm too big to climb in. You want to

try?"

At least he was asking, not ordering. "Sure."

He gripped his hands together to make a foothold. She held onto his shoulder and managed to get a knee on the windowsill.

Wriggling through the narrow space into the tiny bathroom was awkward. The bottom of the window scraped her back. Slowly she worked her way inside, then managed to steady one foot on the top of the toilet seat.

Seconds later, with both feet on the floor, she listened carefully. "I'll check out the place, then let you in."

Matt frowned. "Better let me in first. We don't know who or what you'll find."

He was right, dammit. She hurried past a porcelain sink set in a wooden counter and through the living room past a sagging couch to let him in.

He looked around. "Doesn't seem to be anyone here."

"There's only this room and the bathroom, unless that door leads to another room."

Matt yanked the door open. "It's a utility closet."

A black vinyl couch stood against the knotty pine wall. "That's Christy's black sweater. She's been here, but I don't know where he's taken her." Valerie tried not to think about what he might be doing to her sister.

"How can you tell it's hers?"

"It has tiny black beads arranged in a fancy design. I gave it to her for her birthday. Excuse me. I need to use the bathroom." She limped toward the tiny room.

"Wait a minute, Valerie. Did you hurt your ankle?"

She nodded. "I think I just twisted it, but it should

be okay after a while."

"You need to take it easy. Let me know if I can help."

She shut the door and lifted the top to the toilet seat. A smear of blood stained the rim of the seat. She gasped and flung open the door. "Matt, come here."

His large form filled the doorway. "What's the matter?"

"There's blood on the toilet seat."

"We don't know if it's Christy's."

"But she's been here."

Valerie bent down. "Here's a spot on the floor."

Matt backed up. "And another by the door."

Valerie swallowed. "You don't think it's enough to—"

"Enough to show she's been killed?" He shook his head. "There'd have to be a lot more for that."

"Think we should call the police?"

"We don't have much to go on. They'd give us a hard time if we got them out here just for this."

"Do you suppose Buck will bring her back here?"

"I don't know. You want to wait around? He might return and shoot at us."

At the noisy sound of a vehicle Valerie froze. Matt ran outside.

Valerie paused on the threshold of the open door. She gasped. "That truck—it's the same one we saw at the other cabin."

The rusty pickup, obviously needing a new muffler, jerked to a stop behind Matt's Mustang.

Still dressed in coveralls, the man who'd threatened them at the other place, climbed out. He reached into the truck and pulled out a shotgun.

Grasping it under his arm, he marched through the weeds toward them. The look on his face and the cool breeze fanning her skin gave her chill bumps. Valerie stepped next to Matt, glad to be in the warm sun. She nudged Matt. "What's he doing here?"

Matt slid his gun from the holster and held it ready. "Not sure. Stay back." He pushed her behind his body.

Valerie tensed. The shotgun was pointed at the ground, but it wouldn't take much to shift it toward them.

The man spoke. "Didya find that fellow Buck or your sister?"

She shook her head. "Doesn't seem to be anyone here."

"Best you leave then. Next time I see the fella, I'll say you're lookin' for them. Got a phone number I kin give him?"

Matt shoved his gun into his waistband, pulled a business card from his wallet, and held it out.

The man tucked it in a pocket in the bib of his overalls, then stepped closer. Creases appeared between his eyebrows. "If'n nobody's here, why you folks still hangin' 'round?"

"Thought he might come back soon," Matt said.

"On a weekday? Ain't never seen him here 'cept on the weekends and during huntin' season."

"We thought he might bring my sister here. Did you see a woman with him?" Valerie asked.

The old man rubbed the back of his neck. "Don't reckon I did. Place ain't nice enough for bringin' anyone but a slut to shack up with."

Where did he get off referring to Christy as a slut? Valerie opened her mouth to object. Matt shot her a stern look and held a finger to his lips.

The man pointed to the house. "You kin see that red car of his ain't here. Ain't no reason for you to stay. Plenty room round my truck so you folks kin get out." He shifted the shotgun to a horizontal position.

Valerie's pulse raced. Would he shoot?

Matt grabbed her hand. "We were just leaving."

Valerie pulled her hand loose. "But," she whispered, "we haven't looked for any more blood or signs of a struggle."

"Later," he whispered. "Come on." He supported her elbow all the way to his car.

As they turned onto the highway, a rustic sign Valerie hadn't noticed before said Ridge Road. Valerie twisted sweaty hands in her lap. "Now what do we do?"

"We wait a while for him to go away, then go back. He can't have much reason to stay there after we leave."

"Why would he sell a place better than his and stay in the other one?"

"Maybe he grew up there, and the other one feels more like home."

"With that stinking outhouse?"

Matt zoomed into the parking lot of a Dairy Queen. "We'll wait here."

Valerie marched into the restaurant. "Order me a Dr. Pepper, please. I'm going to use the bathroom," she called over her shoulder.

****

Matt paid for the drinks, picked them up, and eased into a booth. She sure was direct. His much younger secretary was very polite and always asked his opinion before she did anything. Valerie seemed to have a good head on her shoulders. Maybe he ought to give her some slack and ask her opinion before announcing what they would do next.

The hard plastic seat was hell on his bare legs with those prickly pear spines jabbing into his skin. Leaning over, he tried to pull one out, but it wouldn't give. Other prickers poked his fingers.

When Valerie returned, she gave him a quick smile and slid into the booth across from him. "Thanks for the drink."

He leaned forward. "Do you have any tweezers in your purse?"

"Why?"

"I tripped over a prickly pear plant and got stickers in my legs."

"Oh, no. Does it hurt bad?"

"Do politicians straddle the fence?"

"I'm sorry. You should have told me. We'll have to buy some tweezers. How long should we wait before going back to the cabin?"

Legs on fire, he shifted in his seat. That didn't help. He took a swallow of Dr. Pepper, hoping the irritations would lessen soon. "Half an hour should be enough."

They finished their drinks, and Matt drove to a drugstore where Valerie purchased some tweezers. After asking her preferences, Matt bought two ice cream cones and pointed to the door to a patio with tables and chairs. "Let's sit out there. The sun is warm, and you can remove some of the prickers."

"I've gotten a few myself. You must be pretty uncomfortable." She licked the strawberry one.

"I can hold yours while you do it."

"Wait a minute. You'll probably lick most of it to

keep it from dripping."

He grinned. "And if you feel slighted, I'll buy you another one. Is it a deal?"

She laughed. "Sure." She took a lick. "It's melting, and you're getting most of it, but that's okay. I'll hold you to another."

"Fine." He rested his leg on a chair while she bent over and pulled out spines, one by one.

He loved the touch of her soft fingers. Soon she'd gotten most of them out, and he felt much better.

When she was done, he sighed in relief. "I really appreciate this."

Twenty minutes later, his skin now pricker free, thanks to Valerie, he rose and headed back to the counter. "One hot fudge sundae to go, please."

"And another strawberry cone," she said.

"You want both?"

She put her hands on her hips. "I thought the sundae was for you."

"No. You've earned it a hundred times over. You like nuts?"

She nodded. He turned to the pimply teenage boy behind the counter. "Lots of nuts, please." He put four one-dollar bills on the counter. "Keep the change."

Matt handed her the ice cream confection with a flourish. "Sweets for my sweet."

She smiled. "Would you like a bite?"

"Just one." He took a spoonful and handed the empty plastic spoon back to her. "It should be safe to return to the cottage now. Hopefully, that guy won't be there."

Chapter Fifteen

As Valerie ate her sundae, Matt drove back down the rutted road. Thank goodness, the green truck wasn't there, but neither was the Corvette. Still, he held his gun ready as he stepped out into dry, scratchy weeds, glad it was his left arm that hurt. "Stay in the car," he ordered, making his voice sterner than usual. He shot her a determined look, hoping to intimidate her enough to obey. He didn't want her getting hurt.

Instead she reached for the door handle.

He frowned. "Look, we don't know who might be there. I have the gun so it's better I go first. Trust me on this...please?" He waited.

Several seconds later, her hand dropped to her lap. "Okay, but if no one's there, I'm coming in. I want to see if there are any more clues that Christy's alive or..." The tension in her voice caught at his heart.

"Don't worry yet. She's probably still alive." He hoped that made Valerie feel better.

After easing the car door open quietly, he tiptoed toward the cabin, peered through a dirty window, and saw nothing.

He straightened, then took another step toward the front door. He tensed when a twig crackled underfoot. He thought he saw someone's shadow inside. Then clouds dimmed what little light shone through the panes. He leaned closer to get a better look.

A shot rang out. The sound whistled past. He ducked. Almost deafened by the noise, he wasn't sure from which direction it had come. He ran back to the car. He scrambled inside, suddenly conscious of a burning pain in his arm.

Valerie looked shocked. "You're bleeding."

His arm hurt like hell. He hoped it was only a flesh wound. He needed all his strength to get them out of here. Glad the sun had come out again, he backed the car as fast as he dared. More shots spurred him on. "See if you can get a glimpse of the shooter."

"I see a man standing beside the cabin."

"Is it Buck or the old man?"

"Can't tell. The sun's in my eyes."

"Well, is he old or young?"

"Can't tell that either."

"Does he have a beard?"

"Yes, but I can't tell if it's gray or blond."

Matt spun the car around, barely missing a tree. "Keep looking. Is he following?"

"Yes, but he's on foot. Speed up."

"Dammit. I'm going as fast as I dare. I don't want to break something underneath."

More shots rang out. One pinged against the side window right behind him. Far as Matt could tell, the tires hadn't been hit. He held his breath until he turned onto the highway.

Jamming down on the gas pedal, Matt glanced in the rearview mirror, watching for a green truck or a red Corvette. "Could you tell if the man was skinny or stocky?"

"He was slim, but so was Buck the last time I saw him."

"Did you see a car or truck near the cabin?"

Valerie shook her head. But he could have hidden it in back."

"Buck wouldn't hide a Corvette. Guys with sports cars want everyone to notice."

"Maybe he recognized me, didn't want me to suspect he has Christy."

"I don't buy that. He shot at me. Must be that old codger trying to frighten us away."

"Look, we need to get to town and take care of your arm. I don't want you losing a lot of blood."

The red blotch on his sleeve was getting bigger. The pain made him wince. "I'm glad I made you stay in the car."

"You didn't make me."

"But you stayed put. I want you to trust me to keep you safe."

Her gaze met his. "I do."

He hoped she'd continue to trust him. He didn't want her hurt. His left arm throbbed. "Keep your eyes peeled for a doctor's office or clinic."

Five minutes later she grabbed his right arm. He flinched. "Don't do that. You'll cause an accident."

She pointed. "There's a doctor's office up ahead."

"But it's a chiropractor."

"I'm sure they can treat flesh wounds. They may not be allowed to write prescriptions, but surely their medical training includes more than manipulation of muscles and tissues."

Matt pulled over and parked. Feeling tired and a little weak, he followed Valerie inside.

After one glance at his blood-soaked sleeve, the receptionist grabbed the phone.

The air conditioning intensified the chill. He wanted to pull the sleeve away from his arm, but worried it would stick to his skin.

"Dr. Smith," the receptionist said, "you'd better see this man right away. He's bleeding."

"Be right there." The doctor's voice sounded from the speakerphone.

A tall man in a white coat appeared in the doorway. He adjusted his glasses. "Follow me."

Feeling faint, Matt obeyed, barely conscious of Valerie's footsteps behind him. Inside a small examining room, Matt slumped into a chair.

"Get on the table and take off your shirt," directed the doctor. The nurse hustled around, laying out supplies.

It was all Matt could do to climb up on the examining table. The nurse helped him peel his sleeve from his skin. That hurt even more.

"What happened?" Doctor Smith asked.

Matt felt cold. Was he going into shock?

Valerie spoke up. "He was shot at."

The doctor stared at her. "How come?"

"We drove up to a cabin on Ridge Road a ways out from town. We were looking for my sister. When Matt stepped out of the car, some guy shot at us."

The doctor looked puzzled. "Were you trespassing?"

"I suppose so," Valerie said, "but we were only checking to see if my sister was there."

"Hmmm. And someone didn't wait to find out why you came, just shot at you?"

"That's right," Valerie said.

The nurse swabbed something on Matt's left arm.

The odor of disinfectant hung all around him. Matt flinched and clamped his lips shut. Blood kept flowing out.

The doctor took hold of Matt's arm. "I can't tell much without an X-ray, but it's obvious he has a bullet wound." He placed a gauze pad on the wound and pressed. After a few seconds, he turned to the nurse. "Give him some Tylenol, and clean it up. We're not licensed to do surgery. He needs to go to the hospital."

After the nurse finished, and Matt swallowed the pills, he slid off the table. Valerie supported him as they walked down the hall. He hated to lean on her, but he was afraid he'd pass out. He held his arm against his stomach. It hurt less that way.

Valerie seemed almost as worried about him as she had about Christy's possible pregnancy. He wasn't sure he ever wanted to put a woman through that.

The nurse patted his good arm. "You can get up now and return to your car."

He let Valerie help him to his feet. Then he focused on putting one foot in front of the other. His arm was oozing blood again. He was getting fuzzy. He shook his head to clear it, but that didn't help.

Valerie urged him to keep walking. Back in the waiting room, he barely made it to a chair before collapsing. Then everything went black.

Something strong smelling was shoved under his nose. He struggled to move away, but the nurse kept a grip on his shoulder.

"Take a good whiff. We need you conscious before you leave here." She turned to Valerie. "You need to take him to the emergency room and get the bullet taken out."

****

Valerie's heart beat faster. She stepped closer. "Is it serious?" Just thinking about Matt possibly dying made her realize how empty she'd feel without him. They'd been a good team while hunting Christy. She'd enjoyed his sense of humor and his optimism. When had he come to be so important that life without his friendly grin wouldn't be nearly as enjoyable?

Matt could hardly stand up long enough to sign the credit card receipt, but he did manage to stumble to the car. Valerie asked for directions to the hospital and then drove them there.

Four hours later in Matt's hospital room, Valerie looked up as Matt opened his eyes and sat up. He glanced down at the dressing on his arm, then faced Valerie. "I don't remember much beyond lying on an operating table and breathing in anesthetic. At least I don't feel any pain."

She rose from her chair. "I bought you a shirt. Let me help you put it on."

Helping him struggle into the shirt was awkward. "Your hands feel cool on my skin. Does that mean I have a fever?"

A stern-faced nurse strode briskly into the room, her white nylon uniform rustling faintly. "I need to check your vital signs before the doctor will okay your leaving." She marched over, took his blood pressure, and stuck a thermometer in his mouth. "Ninety-nine point eight. You'd better remain here overnight."

He frowned. "But I can't stay. I have to help Valerie find her sister. She's been missing for several weeks now."

"You're our patient," said the nurse. "You

shouldn't leave until the doctor says so. If you leave before he okays it, you'll have to sign the AMA form. That stands for Against Medical Advice."

Valerie studied Matt's face. It had taken on a red cast, probably from his slight fever. "Do bullet wounds often cause infections?"

"Sometimes," the nurse said.

That didn't make Valerie feel any better. She squeezed her eyes shut and wondered if such infections were life-threatening. She grasped his hand and squeezed. Tried to smile. Wouldn't do for Matt to see how much she worried.

"I feel so tired." His weak voice sent a wave of guilt through her. She should have been the one to take the bullet. Christy was her sister, not his.

Valerie glanced at the nurse's face. The woman's solemn expression didn't tell her anything. She let go of Matt's hand and stepped closer. In a whisper she asked, "If he gets an infection from this wound, could it be fatal?"

The nurse frowned and held a finger to her lips. "Mustn't upset my patient. If you won't cooperate, I'll have to ask you to leave. I can have security escort you out."

"I'm not leaving." Valerie put all the determination she could muster into her voice.

"Then you'd better guard your tongue. And by the way, we reported the bullet wound to the police. We're required to do that, you know."

Annoyed, Valerie clamped her lips shut. She pasted a smile on her face and walked back to Matt. "You're going to be fine."

The sound of footsteps told her the nurse was

leaving.

Matt's eyes were shut. He seemed relaxed. She hoped he was asleep. That should help him heal better. However, she couldn't resist leaning down to listen to him breathe. She couldn't hear anything. Her heart caught in her throat. He couldn't die, just like that, could he? She grasped his wrist. Felt for a pulse.

Chapter Sixteen

Matt's eyes were closed. He lay without moving in the hospital bed. It had been at least ten seconds since he'd taken a breath. Worried, Valerie touched his hand. It was still warm. Should she push the call button?

A loud speaker blared. "Doctor Smith, please report to the nurses' station on third floor." Footsteps sounded outside the room, and the smell of bleach wafted inside. She'd hate to look foolish. But his life could be at stake. She pressed the button.

Just then, Matt took a deep rasping breath. "Thank you, God," she whispered and sank back into the chair beside his bed. She didn't know whether to rejoice in his noisy breathing or be alarmed.

Hearing a whisper of fabric, Valerie looked up. A stern-faced nurse stood just inside the doorway. You pressed the call button. Why?" the nurse asked. Her hushed tones sounded more like an accusation than a question.

"He wasn't breathing, but he is now. I was worried." Seeing the woman's annoyed look, Valerie felt stupid. "I was afraid he was dying."

Without a sound, the woman strode to the side of the bed. Her disapproving look swept over Valerie. She checked his pulse. Her eyes bored into Valerie. "With your limited knowledge, you did the right thing."

The nurse pivoted on sensible white shoes and left,

the rustle of her nylon uniform the only sound. Valerie frowned. The woman would make a great spy or perhaps a good inquisitor. Bet she starched her underwear.

Valerie touched his forehead. Very warm. Had his temperature risen? She couldn't tell, but she'd be darned if she'd press that button.

Valerie paced the floor, then sank back down in the chair and watched Matt sleep. He just had to be okay.

Outside, the sun finally set, streaking the clouds with gold, which changed to bright pink, then faded into a dusky pink and finally gray.

Gray was how she felt. Anxious about Matt. Worried about Christy. Why hadn't she paid more attention to Buck earlier? Was he a psychopath? Was he raping or torturing Christy?

Valerie had stayed in the car and trusted Matt to do the right thing at that cabin. Now she wondered if that had been smart. Maybe if she'd been the one to approach the door of the cabin, she could have reasoned with the shooter.

Had Buck drugged her sister? Had she been trying to get away? Valerie couldn't imagine Christy not trying to escape. But then again, she wouldn't risk injury to an unborn child.

An hour later Matt finally opened his eyes. "You still here?"

"Of course. I've been worried about you."

He smiled. "Nice to know that."

"Do you feel any better?"

His expression solemn, he said, "It's like I've been dragged through a knothole and got stuck halfway."

"Does it still hurt bad?"

"Not as much. They must have given me something for pain."

The nurse knocked softly, then strode in. Her no-nonsense shoes made no sound as she took his temperature and checked his blood pressure. "The doctor said you could leave since your vital signs are okay. I'll order a wheelchair. You can check out at the front desk, but first, an officer is waiting to talk to you."

Half an hour later, after the police officer left, Valerie brought Matt's car around and parked beside the curb. A nurse pushed Matt in a wheelchair to the car's front passenger side. A slight breeze teased his hair. "Do you need any help getting in?" the nurse asked.

He shook his head, but stayed in the chair until the nurse headed back inside. Valerie walked around the car and stood in front of the wheelchair, ready to help him in.

"Push me around to the other side," Matt said. "I'll drive."

She glared at him. "Who do you think you are, Superman?" She opened the passenger door. "Now get in. You're too heavy for me to lift." Ignoring his grumbling, she practically pushed him in before returning to the driver's side.

****

Sometime later, Valerie slammed the car door, waking Matt. Where were they? He felt fuzzy. Blinking, he looked around. The car sat beneath the portico of a Spanish style building with an orange tile roof. MasterCard and Visa logos showed in the window. Looked like a motel.

The motel office door opened, and Valerie came to

the car window. "You're awake. How do you feel now?"

"Groggy. Where are we?"

"We're still in San Antonio. You need rest. I got us a motel room."

"What time is it?"

"Nine o'clock. We were lucky to find a vacancy. It looks like a nice place." She drove around the building and into a courtyard, paved with cobblestones. In the center a fountain tinkled. Droplets sparkled in the light from wrought iron lamps. Flowers ringed the small pool, their fragrance drifting into the warm night air.

She parked the car and came around to open the door. He struggled to rise. Her arm around his waist steadied him as he took halting steps.

He liked the warmth, although he hated leaning on her. This was ridiculous. He shook off her arm. "I can make it."

"Are you sure?"

He nodded and took a step forward, then wished he hadn't. He felt dizzy.

She sprang into action, putting a hand under his arm. That helped. Garnering all his strength, he finally made it to the sidewalk. He leaned against the wall while she unlocked the door, then stepped inside and headed for the bed.

After sinking down on the soft mattress, he looked around. "Only one bed?"

She nodded. "It's king size, but you're in no shape to do anything more than sleep, so don't get any ideas."

He grinned. "But if I felt better…"

"Forget it," she said, but he caught her grin. "Let me get you into bed."

He sighed. "I'd rather be getting you into bed."

She helped him pull off his shirt and pants, leaving him in only his briefs. Her hands felt cool and smooth on his skin, making him wish he were in better shape. He'd love to feel her hands sliding slowly over his skin, touching him everywhere.

He wondered if she minded taking care of him as much as he hated having to depend on her. She must be anxious about finding Christy, but she hadn't said a word about that since they'd left the doctor's office.

He met her gaze. She seemed worried about him.

She pulled the covers over him. "I'm sure you'll be in good shape after a few days. Not that your shape isn't—well, awesome, but you know what I mean."

He grinned, enjoying the compliment. Glancing at her face, he sensed she was embarrassed to admit that. Other women had fawned over him until he wasn't sure what to believe. They seemed to bask in his attention with some kind of hero worship. They never really saw past his looks and position as a successful attorney to see the real Matt. Valerie treated him like an equal. He found that refreshing.

"Do you want to sleep now or watch TV or talk?" she asked.

"I'm not sleepy anymore, and I don't want to watch TV." After he gradually worked himself into a sitting position, he leaned against the headboard. Might be interesting to draw her out, get to know her a little better. "Who's your favorite author?"

She looked surprised. "I don't know. I like so many."

"What kind of books do you like to read?"

"Romances, mysteries, action adventure."

"Some women won't admit they read romances."

"Well, I haven't read many lately, haven't been in the mood since Gordon and… Guess I might as well say it—since Gordon dumped me."

"Oh. I thought it was a mutual understanding, that you weren't right for each other…" Guessing that wasn't likely the case, he hesitated, not wanting to hurt her feelings.

Valerie looked glum. "He said that if I were going to be the fiancée of a candidate for office—guess he was thinking of running for mayor even then—I'd need to dress more stylishly. He didn't like my pinstripe suits, said they were too mannish—didn't show off my figure. Whenever we went out to eat, and he saw a woman who was really stacked, he'd stare until she passed by."

"But, you're a paralegal. You're supposed to look professional, not sexy when you're working."

She rubbed the back of her neck. Her voice dropped to a whisper. "You know what, he had the nerve to add, 'what little figure you've got.' He was talking about my boobs, damn him." She looked down, probably hating to admit Gordon told her that.

Matt's glance shifted to her chest. "They look nice to me…what I can see of them." He grinned.

A smile graced her lips.

Matt rubbed the back of his neck. "Surely, he didn't say that when you…"

"Were in bed you mean?"

Now he wished he hadn't brought that up, but knowing Gordon, he would have taken her to bed. Matt didn't like to think of his brother with Valerie. How could Gordon miss seeing how adorable Valerie was?

"You don't have to answer that if you don't want to."

"Hey, I'm over him. It's not like it matters anymore. But if you must know, he said I could have been more uh…sexy in bed."

Her face had that woebegone look. Matt wanted to stand and pull her into his arms, but he wasn't sure he was strong enough to do that. He settled for taking her hand and squeezing it. "I can't believe Gordon was that crass. He's a politician, dammit. Should know how to be diplomatic. Why the hell didn't he let you down gently?"

Valerie shrugged and sat on the bed. "Guess he was tired of me and didn't care what I thought."

Summoning all his strength, he reached for her. "He must have been blind not to see what a jewel you are." He pulled her closer. She felt surprisingly soft for someone so strong.

One look at her face and the tear sliding down her check, and he was lost. He wanted to kiss her until she smiled again.

He pulled her against his chest and kissed her. Her lips melded to his as if they'd been made to fit. She tasted. She nibbled. She rained kisses on his cheeks. He felt adored like never before, like she understood who he was and cared about him. He felt as if he were soaring above the clouds and risking the dangerous heat of the sun before plummeting back to earth with her glorious smile shining on him.

He cradled her adorable face in his hands. He couldn't stop kissing her. And she responded as if she couldn't get enough. She wasn't just wanting comfort. She wanted him, all of him. That thrilled him to no end, but dammit, he wasn't up to anything more.

Swept away, he rode a wave of yearning to the crest, then savored the reality. Her arms were still holding him tight. He'd never felt like this before. If this was love, it was wonderful beyond words.

Finally, he raised them both to a sitting position and dropped his arms. "I wish I could, but…"

She kissed him gently, and stood. It's enough just to know that…"

"That I want you?"

She nodded. As soon as he was better, he'd take her up on that. But for now, he'd better change the subject. "I want you to know how much I appreciate your willingness to help me research Gordon's case and testify in court."

"I don't believe your brother would murder Christy. He dotes on her, buys her anything she desires. I can't count all the necklaces, rings, and new clothes he's bought her. I could definitely testify to that."

Gordon had shown Matt some of the gifts he'd bought for Christy, but never mentioned anything he'd gotten for Valerie during their engagement. And unlike with Christy, his brother had never brought Valerie to meet him. Gordon was apparently still a sore subject with Valerie.

Matt didn't want to think about his ex-girlfriend either. Mallory was beautiful, always dressed nicely. Like his mother, Mallory had a pair of shoes to match everything she wore.

The only time he'd seen her without makeup, she'd pushed him away. Standing beside the pool at a swim party at his friend's house, she'd looked so cute in that bikini. He'd picked her up and tossed her into the pool. Surfacing, she looked fresh and innocent with her makeup washed off. She'd shrieked and called him a bastard. He'd jumped in after her, meaning to kiss and apologize. Scowling, she climbed out of the pool and shouted that he'd made her look ugly. She raced into the house. He tried to follow, to tell her she didn't look bad, but she slammed the bathroom door in his face. When she appeared half an hour later, her face perfectly made up, she insisted he take her home. On the way she barely spoke to him and sat sullen as he drove.

He'd asked, "Why make such a big deal about getting wet? You had your bathing suit on."

"You let everyone see how ugly I look without makeup. My hideous birthmark takes forever to cover."

"I never noticed it."

"Don't know how you could miss it. And now, none of the men at that party will ever ask me out."

"So, you went with me to get some other man's attention?"

"You're not the only fish in the sea. Just because you work for a prestigious law firm, you think that makes you special?"

Lost for words, he'd clamped his mouth shut. He walked her to her door and waited while she unlocked it. "See you around," he said, not sure if he ever wanted to.

"Not if I can help it." She slammed the door in his face. Looking back, he realized it was mostly his pride that was hurt. Valerie must have felt much worse when Gordon dumped her. He hoped she really was over him.

Now, he smoothed a silky lock of hair from Valerie's face. "Do you like science fiction and thrillers? Those are my favorites."

"Oh, yes. I read those too. I prefer the ones that

dwell more on the characters and the culture than the technology. I like C.J. Cherryh and Catherine Spangler. Who do you like?"

"Heinlein, Crichton, Tolkien, and of course, Grisham. I like to see action and read about situations where there's a lot at stake."

"Do you see much action in divorce cases?"

"Oh, yeah." He clenched his fists. "Especially when a battered woman tries to divorce her husband. Sometimes I feel like getting one of those bastards alone in a deserted alley and giving him some of his own treatment. But of course I can't."

"But you get the wives a fair share and a chance for a new life. That's helping them a lot."

"I try." He rubbed the back of his neck.

"Does that hurt?" she asked.

He nodded.

"Roll over. I'll massage it."

Her hands, cool and smooth, worked on his back and neck, relaxing his muscles. Melting under her hands, he couldn't help wondering what it would be like to have her touching him in other places. And no matter what his brother said, she had pretty breasts. Even as weak as he was, he felt himself hardening.

Damn. And now he couldn't even manage a cold shower by himself.

Chapter Seventeen

Inside a rustic motel cabin, Buck wiped perspiration from his forehead. Christy lifted blonde hair off her neck. She must be just as hot. She stretched. Her lush breasts strained against the fabric of her blouse. He was getting hard again.

He picked up the phone and called the front desk. The air conditioning's not working in number seven. Send a fan, please. He waited at the door until a man came with a fan. He set it up to face her. "That should cool you off. I know this motel cabin's crummy. Only place I could find on short notice."

She let the fan blow over her, then met his gaze, her pouty lips pulling at his senses. "Why are you treating me like this? Why won't you let me call my husband or my sister? When you found me, I only wanted a ride home, not a wild trip all over kingdom come."

"You didn't object when I said I'd take you to Monterrey."

"I don't remember that. Must have been after you took me to the clinic. Guess I was pretty well out of it then."

He patted her shoulder. "You're so much better now." He wanted to kiss her, but something in her eyes told him he'd better go slow. "I'll take you out to dinner at a nice air conditioned place."

Fingering a lock of her blonde hair, he let it slide through his fingers. "Your hair's like silk."

Her brief smile warmed him. He bent to kiss her.

She leaned away. "Don't, Buck. I'm better now, and I just want to go home."

"But Christy." His voice low, he smoothed his fingers over the back of her hand. It felt so soft. She didn't move away this time. He squeezed her hand. "Christy, sweetheart, we were so good together." Holding her gaze, he stroked her ear. "We could be again."

"Please, don't," she whispered, her voice quivering. She pulled her hand from his, but didn't look away.

His jeans were unbearably tight. Christy was the gold at the end of the rainbow. For her he could be patient. She was worth waiting for and so hot he might even give up his quick trips to Dallas. If he could have her all to himself, that was. He just had to make her see that staying with him would be tons better than returning to that stuffy, bean-counter husband.

Until now, everything he really wanted had slid from his grasp. The BB gun he'd pulled the corner of the wrapping off days before Christmas was for his older brother. The job at the private eye firm went to someone with a college degree. And then there was Christy. Beautiful, fun-loving Christy, whom he'd wanted since he'd first seen her.

He grasped her hand again. "Your mother was wrong to forbid you to date me after that first time. I might have been a little wild in high school, but I've changed."

"You were pretty wild that last night we were

together."

He grinned. "So were you. Really hot that night."

She giggled. "I was already dating Gordon, but I couldn't resist being with you one more time—except I didn't mean to go so far." She blushed. "Or so many times in one night."

He squeezed her hand. "You were fantastic." He pushed back the thought that he'd been her one last fling. He preferred to believe she only married Gordon for security and would have chosen him if only he'd had a steady well-paying job then. Now his new job paid well, but it required him to travel a lot.

The minute he had gotten back to San Antonio, he called Christy. Shocked to hear she was going to marry Gordon, he'd gotten her new address by saying he wanted to send a wedding present.

Oh he'd taken one to the church all right. A pair of crystal wineglasses. Unable to resist, he'd engaged the bride in a long passionate kiss before she pushed him away. Then that damn brother-in-law had ejected him from the wedding. Buck had drowned his disappointment at a local bar in a glass less elegant. How good it had felt to kiss her then. Just remembering the feel of her cool lips beneath his had spurred him to hope he could be with her again. And now he was.

The day after the wedding he'd had to go out of town on business, but when he returned two weeks later, he still missed her. He'd tried to stay away, but he couldn't stop thinking about her. He bet she and Gordon hadn't used those glasses yet. After picking up a bottle of champagne, he'd driven to her house, hoping Gordon wouldn't be home from work yet.

A woman who'd been so hot and willing before she

got married should be glad to see him even if only to share a drink in her fancy new wine goblets.

Christy moved closer to the fan. "This only helps a little." Tears ran down Christy's cheek. "Please take me back to Gordon. I want to go home."

He took her hand in his and squeezed it. "That's not what you told your husband and that prick of a brother-in-law the day you left. Heard you clear as day. You said, 'If you won't take me to Monterrey, I'll find someone who will.'"

Her jaw dropped. "How do you know about that?"

"Drove by your place and parked across the street."

"Whatever for?"

"Been out of town. Brought a bottle of champagne. Thought you might share a drink with me. Just for old time's sake. Couldn't help hearing you shout at Gordon and his legal eagle brother. Then you jumped into that truck and drove off."

Christy planted her fists on her hip. "You followed me to that bar, didn't you?"

"So what if I did?" He'd figured then she was ripe for the taking. "I've wanted you ever since the first time I saw you walking out from a high school dance with some dude. That night when you danced with me at that bar I figured you might as well be with me instead of some guy who might spike your drink with knock out drops."

She frowned. "I didn't think anyone there would do that."

"You can't be sure." He smiled and smoothed a finger over her soft cheek. "I can tell when a woman needs comforting. I'm good at that."

Christy backed away. "All I wanted was to get

away, have a few drinks, maybe dance a little."

He grinned. "And you were great, Sugar. Those guys in the bar were cock-eyed jealous of me."

She walked to the window and glanced out before turning to face him. "I hadn't realized I was pregnant. If I'd known I was, and that drinking and dancing could cause a miscarriage, I never would have gone out." She brushed a tear from her eye.

He stepped closer and took her hand, but the look in her face said he'd better not try anything more just yet. "Hey, maybe it was gonna happen anyway—you know, could have been something wrong with the baby."

Christy scrubbed tears from her eyes. "If I'd carried the baby a little longer, a doctor could have told whether it was a boy or a girl. Now I'll never know. I wanted that baby."

"Sure you did." He pulled her against him. He could feel her hot face through his thin T-shirt. But the doc at the clinic said you're young and healthy. Said he was sure you can have another."

Tears ran down her cheek. He pulled out a handkerchief and dabbed at her face. Her tears got to him, the way no other woman's could.

Her voice broke. "Thanks for waiting at the clinic. Must have been several hours."

"Only a little more than two. Couldn't leave you there alone."

"After that, why didn't you call my husband to come and get me? Why drag me to Mexico? I wouldn't have thought you'd want to play nursemaid to me while I was getting over a miscarriage, especially in Mexico."

"It was so hot and muggy that evening. Thought

I'd drive through the countryside to cool you off."

She frowned. "Then you kept on going. You never intended to take me back to Gordon, did you?"

"Hey, baby, I lost you once to him. Figured it was time I got another chance."

"But I'm married now, and I was pregnant. Doesn't that mean anything to you?"

"You didn't act like it at that bar. You were drinkin' and dancin' up a storm. Shot those come-on glances right at me. I wasn't letting it pass without— without taking you up on a chance to get lucky."

"Well, you wouldn't have. Sorry if I gave you the wrong impression. I care enough for my husband not to give in. You're good looking enough to tempt any women. Go find someone else."

He grinned. "But, baby, you're the one who lights my fire." He wouldn't tell her what he'd been hoping— that she and Gordon might break up so he could be with her again. She was so much fun to be with when she was in good humor."

Except he hadn't seen the fun side of Christy since that night at the bar. She'd finally recovered some of her old spirit, but she hadn't stopped begging him to take her back to Gordon. He wouldn't give up. He'd try his charm on her again. Show her life could be tons more interesting with him than that stuffy bean-counter she'd married.

Christy walked into the tiny bathroom. He held her gaze as he walked toward her and pried the lipstick from her hands. He placed a gentle kiss on her forehead. She backed away. "Don't."

"Would you feel better if you took a nap?"

She nodded. "You won't try anything while I sleep,

will you?"

Except for refusing to take her back home as she'd asked, or letting her use the phone, he'd treated her well. Ordered from room service the whole week they stayed at a hotel in Monterrey, except she hadn't eaten much. She'd been pretty lethargic. But she'd liked that back rub he'd given her last night—until he couldn't resist letting his hands creep around to her breasts.

"Stop," she'd said and moved away. "I have a bad headache, and my stomach is crampy again. Remember I've just had a miscarriage."

She made her way to the bed, lay down, and closed her eyes. She still looked washed out. If she got away, she'd call Gordon collect. He couldn't let her try that.

While she slept, he made a phone call and read a magazine.

Two hours later he was getting antsy. He sat on the bed, hoping she'd wake soon.

Finally, she opened her eyes and met his gaze.

"Feel better now?"

She nodded. "I need to get up and comb my hair."

"Don't. I like to see it spread out on the pillow like that."

"Gordon wants me to get it cut. Says I'll look more sophisticated as a candidate's wife. And he says it gets in the way when we make love." She was blushing. Probably hadn't meant to reveal something so personal.

He smiled at her. "I'd never say that." He twisted a lock around his finger, then smoothed it from her face as he bent to kiss her.

She leaned away. He'd tried to be helpful and understanding when she'd lost the baby. But he wouldn't give up now.

175

She looked at him with sorrowful eyes. I have to go to the bathroom to freshen up.

"Baby, you look great to me." He loved her rumpled from sleep look, wished it had been from making love to him. She didn't say anything, just walked inside the tiny motel bathroom and shut the door.

He must be moving too fast. He wished she'd let him kiss her again. The first time he'd kissed her had nearly blown him away. Buck remembered as if it were yesterday. She'd been still in high school. Her lips were warm and he'd wanted more when she'd let him fondle her breasts. They'd been full and firm, just the way he liked. They still looked that way. He ached to touch them again.

Back then her admiring glances had made him feel so good, like it didn't matter that he was only a mechanic. Before she'd realized what he was up to, he'd undone the top button of her blouse. He'd gotten her so excited that she stuttered when she tried to tell him to stop.

She'd had to say no twice before he got the message, but he hadn't tried to force her. Good thing too, since they were parked in the driveway, and her mom was waiting up. The porch light had blinked then. He'd savored one last kiss and caressed her breasts again before she straightened her clothes and fled into the house.

When he called her the next day, she'd said her mom had a threatened to ground her for three months if she went out with him again.

And she hadn't, except for a couple of times when she'd snuck out to meet him, and once, years later after she'd moved to San Antonio.

After five years, he thought by now he would have gotten over her. But every woman he'd been with during that time paled next to Christy. He told himself if he could only have sex with her once more, he could get her out of his thoughts, out of his dreams, out of his mind, but he knew in his heart he'd never have enough of Christy.

He hadn't believed his luck when he'd called three months ago and asked her out, and she'd accepted. He remembered every minute of that night, how she'd clung to him, how she'd moaned in ecstasy. He'd been riding so high that by the next morning he'd called and asked her out again.

She'd given him some lame excuse about being in a fashion show at Neiman Marcus. And then he had to go out of town several weeks for his job. He'd gotten back the day before she married Gordon Larson. It was hell watching the accountant prick marry her at that fancy wedding.

He guessed she'd married Gordon for security. But now he made enough to offer her that, too.

She marched out of the bathroom, her blond hair smooth and shining, and her lips so rosy he ached from wanting to kiss her and hold her. "Please you've got to take me home. It will look bad for Gordon to appear in public without me at his side."

"Sure, Sugar, but how about you and me getting together, just this once?" He hoped he could pull her under his spell again.

"I still don't feel very good. Please just take me home."

"You're better now. Please? Just once, for old

time's sake?" He couldn't believe he was begging. He never had before.

She shook her head, but her eyes spoke of longing, perhaps for acceptance and love. Was her husband too busy campaigning to give her any attention? Buck felt sorry for her, but he couldn't let that sway him to take her home. She pulled away and sat on the edge of the bed.

He took hold of her hand, but she pulled it back. "Now you're being a tease, just like you were that night I took you home, and your mother flashed the lights."

"I wasn't being a tease then. I didn't want my mother to catch me half dressed."

"But all evening you acted as if you wanted me. Teased me unmercifully, and then you wouldn't let me into your pants. Bet you let Gordon on your first date."

"I did not. He was nice."

He frowned. "And I wasn't. Wasn't that what turned you on, a ride on the wild side—someone more mature than tame high school guys?"

She stood and brushed past him and walked to the window. Leaning against the sill, she looked him in the eye. "What if it was? That doesn't matter now."

"You enjoyed rebelling against your parents." He smirked. "Like you did that Friday night, only then it was Gordon's authority you flouted."

"That's not true. Besides, who are you to spout off about psychology?"

"Hey, I went to college."

"Yeah, but did you graduate?"

"Hell, no. They kicked me out for smoking pot in the dorm. Who needs college anyhow?"

"So why didn't you go somewhere else?"

He walked to the window and looked out. "Didn't have the money."

Christy sat on the bed. "Why didn't you swallow your pride and ask your parents?"

"My father's dead. Social security wasn't enough to support my mother and my younger brother. I had to help out with the bills."

"Oh, that's too bad about your father. Couldn't you have worked and gone to college part time? You'd be able to get a better job now."

He frowned and marched over to stand in front of her. "I make good money now as a pharmaceutical salesman. You want good times and nice things. I can give you that."

"You've got brains, and you're persuasive. You could make something more of yourself."

"Right now, I got a line on something that pays a whole lot better."

"Is it legal?"

He caught her hand, pulled her up from the bed. "Never mind. You don't need to know."

He tangled his hands in her long blonde hair. He caught her around the waist and tried to kiss her.

She turned her head and pushed his hands away. He jammed her against the wall, pressed his body against hers. He could feel her breasts against his chest, feel the hard nubs of her nipples poking against him. Was he imagining it or were her breasts throbbing in response to his holding her? He was getting hard.

She swallowed, leaned her head away from his. "I can't. I won't do this to Gordon." She shoved him away.

He scowled. "I'm not good enough for you

anymore. Is that it?"

"It's not that. I'm married now."

"But you were already going with Gordon that last time I saw you. That didn't stop you then."

She backed away. "I wasn't sure he'd ask me to marry him."

"But you slept with me when you thought I was still working as a mechanic, said you thought I was a hottie. I hoped then you meant it. He took hold of her hand.

Gently, she pulled her hand away, then stepped to the window and raised it as if she thought fresh air might cool his determination. She turned back to face him. "Please, pretty please, would you take me back to my place, mine and Gordon's? My husband, my mom, and my sister must be awfully worried by now."

"Look. You're already back in San Antonio. Why not have some fun before I take you home? I'll take you out for dinner and dancing." And hopefully, he could persuade her to have sex if she got mellow enough.

He dug his cell phone from his pocket. "Go ahead and call Gordon. Tell him you'll be home tomorrow." Gordon was still in jail, so he wouldn't answer.

Christy dialed, then pulled the phone from her ear. She looked disappointed. He's not home. I'll call Valerie at her apartment. She tapped the number and listened. "She didn't answer. I'll call Mom. She'll be worried."

Buck shook his head and pulled the phone from her grasp. "Battery's too low for a long talk. You can call her later. It needs charging, and I don't have the charger with me."

She flipped her long hair over her shoulder. "I'll

use the motel phone to call Mom."

"They don't allow long distance calls." He laid his cell on the dresser, then led her to the closet. He pulled the red dress he'd bought her from the hanger. "Put this on. You look great in that blouse, but it's too tight. Don't want all the other guys staring at my woman's boobs."

Christy pulled out of his grasp. "I'm not your woman. I'm Gordon's wife, and since he's running for mayor. I can't be seen out in public with another man."

He scowled. "With me you mean. There you go again, saying I'm not good enough for you."

Christy looked away. After a minute, she turned to face him. "It's not that. I've made my choice, and I'm married. Look, it was nice of you to take me to Monterrey. But I'm afraid I was too groggy and sick to realize where you were taking me."

"You should have thought of that sooner, sugar, before you went to that bar, danced like a whirling gypsy and drank too much."

"I must have fainted after I stopped Gordon's truck on that lonely road."

He rubbed the back of his neck. "When I saw all that blood, I nearly passed out. It was all I could manage to carry you to my car. You might have died right there if I hadn't come by. Why the hell did you drink so much if you weren't feeling well?"

"I only had one drink."

"Yeah, baby, but you can't handle your liquor. That was a double you had."

"When I figured out what was happening, all I wanted was to save the baby, but the pain was so bad I must have passed out."

He tossed the red dress on the bed. "So why didn't you insist on going to the hospital right away? I could have taken you there immediately instead of that clinic."

"I was so groggy, I only wanted the nearest doctor."

"And after I took you from that clinic and said I was taking you to Monterrey, you didn't tell me to stop."

"I don't remember that. I was so torn up about losing my baby. Must not have been thinking clearly." She brushed tears from her cheeks. She headed for the bathroom. "I have to wash my face."

Buck grasped her arm, stopping her. "Wait a minute. You hadn't been married very long. That was my baby, wasn't it? Why the hell didn't you tell me?"

Chapter Eighteen

Buck stared at Christy, waiting for her answer. She brushed tears from her eyes and shook her head. She stood in the bathroom doorway, her hand gripping the doorknob. "I couldn't have been pregnant with your baby. Gordon and I had been married almost three months by then. I didn't even realize I was pregnant until I had the miscarriage."

Buck scowled and grabbed her shoulders. He pushed her up against the bathroom door. "You're lying."

Christy met his gaze. "No, I'm not. Now leave me alone." Her soft hands gripped his arms. She pushed him out of the bathroom and slammed the door behind him.

Someone knocked on the motel room door. "Who's there?" Buck called.

"Pierce."

Buck opened the door a crack. "Make it short. Christy's in the bathroom."

"Come outside, then."

Buck stepped out, leaving the door partly open behind him. Hot, humid air enveloped him. Must be one hundred degrees. San Antonio was great in the spring and fall, but summers sure took the starch out of a person.

Buck looked the short stocky man in the eye. Guy

needed a haircut and a shave. "What's up, Pierce?"

"Hiding the woman isn't enough. That damn lawyer, Matt Larson, is in town to defend his brother, and that son of a bitch lawyer sounds too good in court.

"How'd you find that out?"

"I was waitin' for my case to come up in district court in Dallas, an' Larson was arguing with the judge. Held his own, he did. Don't think he's handled any murder cases, but I read in the paper where his law firm won a bunch of them. Gordon Larson might walk, might even win voters' sympathy. Carter don't want that happening."

"What do you want me to do?"

"What if that broad you've got with you is delivered to him in a crate at that office he's using during the trial? Should mess with his confidence." Pierce grinned.

Buck rubbed the back of his neck. "Carter must be desperate to try a stunt like that. That could throw any man for a loop."

"Can you handle it? For an extra five grand?"

Buck swallowed. "What if she runs out of air and dies?"

Pierce shrugged. "So much the better. Or..."His eyes sparked with a steely glint. You could make sure she's dead. And if that's too much of a job for a weenie like you, we can handle it."

Buck glared at Pierce. "Hey, I'm tough enough. I just don't like risking jail time." The sinister tones in the man's voice made Buck's blood run cold.

A chill snaked down Buck's spine. He gripped the doorjamb so hard his knuckles turned white. No way would he let them take Christy.

Buck strived to appear nonchalant. "No need to kill her. Stop worrying. I'll keep her out of sight 'til after the election."

Pierce's dark eyes bored into Buck's. "What's the matter? Got a thing for that broad?"

"Hell, no. I already have a record. I'm not risking a murder rap." He clenched and unclenched his hands, but kept them in his pockets. Now he wished he'd never agreed to keep Christy hidden. He'd been glad to take money to keep her by his side, but what if they demanded he give her up? Knots tangled inside.

Pierce's gritty laugh grated on Buck's ears. "You're too soft. Hand her over. We can make sure she don't surface till after the election and maybe not then." His ugly laugh curdled Buck's blood.

Pierce's heart—if he had one—must be made of granite. Buck clenched his fists even tighter. If he let them take Christy, she'd die. He couldn't risk that.

He backed against the door and planted his feet firmly on the floor. If Pierce tried to snatch her, Buck would kill him. With his bare hands, if necessary. But if he got caught with Christy, and the cops forced him to give a DNA sample for a state database, he'd be dead meat. Buck crossed his fingers, hoping it wouldn't come to that. He straightened his back and planted both feet firmly. "Forget that. She's mine to deal with. I'll keep her out of sight."

"Okay. We can do Larson's broad instead. Can you lure her here?"

Buck rubbed the back of his neck. "That's risky too. Don't want to be nailed for conspiracy in a kidnapping either."

"What if I raise your share to ten grand? Will you

help us then?"

Buck ran his fingers through his hair. Couldn't risk the Dallas police getting a lead on him. "No."

"What's the matter? You yellow?"

"Hell no. I'll need to stay here and keep this broad out of sight. If you want the sister grabbed, you take care of it. One stubborn broad to keep an eye on is enough."

"You're a friggin' coward. Carter ain't gonna like this." He turned on one heel and strode down the sidewalk. Buck stalked inside and slammed the door. Time to check on Christy and make sure she hadn't tried to climb out that tiny bathroom window.

She stood in the bathroom doorway, fists clenched and tears running down her cheeks. "You bastard," she shouted. "I wouldn't believe you'd stoop so low if I hadn't heard you."

Buck's stomach knotted. She could queer everything if she got loose. "What did you hear?"

"Enough. Thought you were obsessed with me, but all you care about is the money. You even discussed killing me."

"That's not true. I care about you. And I won't let them take you."

"What if they take me by force, and you can't stop them? They'll either kill me or kidnap Valerie...or maybe both." Her mouth formed a tight line, and her hands shook. She glared at him. "Then they'll kill you. Well, I'm not standing around waiting for that to happen." She tried to push past him and reach the door.

"No." He grabbed her wrists. "You're not going anywhere."

****

Two days later, near the San Antonio Riverwalk with the morning sun filtering through the motel room curtains, Valerie yawned and sat up. A glance at the other bed showed Matt wasn't there. It was ten a.m. She checked the bathroom. Not there either. The pages he'd been working on were gone too. She found the note he'd left for her. It said that he'd gone to Joe's office to work on the case. He'd only left the hospital yesterday. She hoped he felt good enough to tackle that.

Matt had told her they were choosing the jury today. He said the attorney from his firm who was helping him, was busy on a case in Dallas. She'd awakened at four a.m. and saw Matt scribbling. Looked like he was poring over cases he'd copied from the Southwest Reporter. Seeing his furrowed brow, she was afraid he didn't feel ready to defend Gordon. He must feel anxious. She wished she could do something to help.

A knock sounded at the door. Matt must have come back. Smiling, she shrugged into her dress and called, "Who's there."

"Maintenance. Manager got a complaint about the air conditioner. I need to come in and check it. "

Disappointed it wasn't Matt, she opened the door a crack, but kept the chain fastened. A short stocky man in need of a shave stood there. Dressed in jeans and a clean shirt, he held a wrench in his hands. She undid the chain.

The man shoved the wrench in his pocket. He grabbed both her wrists. She kicked him and tried to break loose. A taller man, one she hadn't seen before, shoved a cloth at her face. It smelled sickly sweet like some kind of chemical.

She couldn't break the heavyset man's iron grip on her shoulder. She opened her mouth to scream, but the cloth muffled her protest. She turned her face to the side and drew in a breath of fresh air, but the other man shoved that cloth right back over her face.

She tried to kick him in the crotch, but couldn't seem to make her legs obey.

The rangy man shoved her leg down. She tried to scratch his face, but couldn't muster enough strength to do more than rake her fingernails over his cheek. He slapped her face. "Dammit bitch, don't try anything else, or I'll break your neck."

Valerie gasped and felt herself blacking out.

"Pierce," the tall man barked. "Hold this bitch still long enough for me to tie her up."

Strong arms wrapped around her, making it hard to breathe anything but the chemicals in the cloth pressed against her nose. She turned her face every which way trying to avoid that sweet smelling rag. That made her neck ache. Beating against his chest with her fists, she struggled to remain conscious.

"That's enough, Slim Jim," the stocky man said. We need her alive for now." He twisted her arm behind her back.

The pain made her yelp. The cloth dropped away. She gulped in fresh air. "What do you want?" she asked, hating that her voice sounded weak.

Pierce flashed her an evil grin. "We're taking you to see—"

"My sister? Is that what this is about?"

"Not your sister. I mean your boyfriend, Matt."

Valerie twisted her neck and managed to pull a few inches back from the suffocating cloth. "Have you got my sister, too?"

"Hey, we ain't got nothing to do with your sister. Some other dude—"

"Shut up," Slim Jim said. "She don't need to know nothing, 'cept what we tell her." He grabbed her arm and yanked her toward the door.

She didn't want to leave, but she didn't have much choice. She grabbed her purse. Maybe if she went willingly, she'd be able to scream when they got outside. She hoped they hadn't gotten Matt too.

They dragged her over the threshold, still holding that cloth over her face. Before they'd taken her more than a few steps, she blacked out.

****

Seated in the reception area of his friend, Joe's, office, Matt looked up from his notes. It was almost ten o'clock. Time to call Valerie. She'd been sleeping so soundly he hadn't wanted to wake her.

The phone rang and rang. Maybe she'd gone out for breakfast. At ten-thirty he dialed again. Still no answer. When she didn't pick up the phone at eleven, he called the manager. Damn, he wasn't in. Matt left a message.

It seemed to take forever for the manager to call back. When the phone rang, Matt snatched it.

"Mr. Larson, I found the door to the unit open and no sign of your Valerie or her purse."

A haunting sense of dread filled Matt. "Were any of her things there?"

"Didn't see much."

Matt remembered they hadn't brought much to the motel.

The manager continued. "I thought maybe she

went to wash clothes or get some food. I checked both the restaurant and the laundromat next door and asked around, but no one's seen her. Does she have a cell phone? You could call her on that."

"Thanks, I'll do that." Matt hung up. He dialed her number again. No answer. Maybe her battery was dead.

Matt rubbed the back of his neck. He'd planned to take Valerie somewhere for breakfast before returning to study the questionnaires filled out by the jury panel, but he'd lost track of time. Now he feared something had happened to her.

He straightened his papers and copies of case summaries on the credenza, intending to rush from the suite, but the phone rang.

"Joe Morales' office, Larson speaking," he answered.

"Matt, it's Hal returning your phone call. Look, I know Dick begged off on helping you and suggested you call me. I'm sorry I can't get away today either. One of our biggest clients was arrested on suspicion of murdering his wife, and I'm the one who's worked with that client. I just can't leave Dallas now. Can't you get a postponement?"

"Afraid not. We've gotten two already. The judge is under pressure from the mayor and the police to get it over with."

"I see. Tough luck. Wish you the best."

"But—" Damn, he hung up. Matt slammed down the phone.

With a heavy heart, he rode the elevator down and strode across the lobby. Inside his car, he turned on the radio to see if they would report any shootings or kidnappings. I'm being paranoid, he thought. She probably just went out for breakfast, and the wind blew the door open. Or maybe the maid didn't shut it tight when she came to clean.

As he waited for the red light to change, a knot in his stomach insisted his worries were justified. A throbbing headache made it hard to concentrate.

The light changed. His car shot ahead. Finally, he pulled to a stop in the parking lot in front of number 27.

The door was shut. Maybe she was back. He tried the doorknob. Locked. He pounded on the door. No answer. He called her name. Heard nothing but the raucous calls of a crow and the beep, beep of a road repair machine backing up down the street.

Jiggling his key in the stubborn lock, he caught the faint smell of chlorine. Inside, the bed was made. The maid must have come.

Visions of her body, bleeding and limp in the tub, propelled him into the bathroom. It was bare except for a comb and lipstick sitting on the counter.

He picked up the phone. Called the desk. "I'm looking for my girlfriend, Valerie Trumbull. She's tall and has reddish blonde hair. Has anyone there seen or talked to her this morning?"

"No, sir. And there's no one else here in the lobby except our maintenance man."

Matt gripped the phone. "Let me talk to him."

Matt described Valerie, asked the man if he'd seen her.

"No. I just came in. I haven't started on my list of rooms to check, but I'll be on the lookout for her."

"Thanks." Matt was grateful the man hadn't said, for her body. He marched into the lobby, spoke to the receptionist, then scribbled his cell phone number on his business card, and handed it to the clerk. "If you see her or talk to her, call me immediately."

Then he stepped outside to call the police and tell them what he knew. The sun beat down on him as he waited for them to answer.

"Sorry, sir," said the officer on duty. "Unless you find evidence of foul play such as blood, or a ransacked room, we don't do anything except take your name and number. After she's been missing twenty-four hours, call us back, and we'll see what we can do."

"Damn." Matt stuck the phone in his pocket and punched the wood post that supported the overhanging motel roof. He walked around the motel calling Valerie's name. A couple of occupants opened doors and stared, but said nothing. His sick feeling grew. The air was already hot. Perspiration dripped from his forehead and ran down his cheeks.

His cell phone rang. Hoping it was Valerie, he snatched it up. "Hello."

"Matt," said his brother, "It's me. Have you found Christy yet?"

Matt paced beside his car. "No. When the phone rang, I was hoping it was Valerie. Now she's missing, and we haven't found Christy, but we've been hot on her trail. Valerie doesn't think the guy she's with will hurt her. He used to date her years ago."

"I've been worried sick wondering what some depraved man will do to her. Thanks for taking the time to hunt for her. What's that guy's name? Christy might have mentioned him."

"Valerie calls him Buck, says he's a wild card."

Gordon groaned. "You've got to get me out of here. I want to help look for her. It's a bad scene here.

My cellmate's one tough son of a bitch. Rumor is he's in for murdering his girlfriend. He knew who I was."

"That's what comes from being in the public eye." Recalling his sharp tones, Matt wished he could call his words back. Gordon was probably feeling guilty about Christy's disappearance. Matt ran his fingers through his hair. He had no business taking his frustration out on his brother. After all, Matt had left Valerie alone and unprotected.

Damn. What he wouldn't give to go back and live this morning over. He'd wake Valerie with a kiss, take her to breakfast and drive her to Joe's office with him, where she'd be safe. And he'd camp on the judge's doorstep—well beside his office—until he could get Gordon's case postponed and until he could get assistance from his firm. Then he'd take Valerie to stroll with him down San Antonio's famous River Walk with all the flowers, shops, and nice places to eat, where he'd be right beside her to protect her.

His brother's voice pulled Matt back to the present and his brother's situation. "My cell mate claims I figured his taxes wrong two years ago and cost him his refund. His insults are bad enough, but I can't sleep wondering if he'll slit my throat."

"Gordon, I'm doing what I can to get you out of there."

"I'll let you go so you can work on my case. I'll see you in court this afternoon."

"Yeah, right." Matt clenched his hand into a fist. He had to get Gordon out of there. He wouldn't tell his brother his associates at Smith, Brown, and Hackberry were too busy to help with the defense at this afternoon's hearing. Gordon would find out soon enough. Matt could ask Joe here in San Antonio to assist as co-attorney, but Joe didn't handle many criminal cases. Besides, his secretary had said he'd be tied up all day.

Matt dialed Valerie's number again.

"Hello," a man said.

"I must have the wrong number," Matt said.

"Caller ID says you're that attorney, Matt Larson. Lookin' for your lady friend?"

Matt's stomach lurched. "What are you talking about?"

"That broad you left in that motel room—"

A hot breeze flashed over him. A dark cloud moved in front of the sun, but didn't cool the air. Matt's gut tightened. "What about her?"

"You'd better do what we say if you want to see her sweet ass again."

Matt gulped. Gripped the phone tighter. "What do you want?"

"Justice," said the guy. Any man that kills his wife should get fried or at least get a long sentence. Gordon Larson doesn't need to be mayor of our good city, right, Slim?"

Another voice sounded in the background. "You got that right, Pierce."

Matt swallowed the lump in his throat. "The verdict is up to the jury. Murder trials can last for weeks. I'm not waiting that long to get her back."

"If you want to see her alive again," said Pierce, "just see that your brother doesn't walk the streets until after the election."

"Is Valerie all right? Have you…have you hurt her?"

"Looked pretty good to me, don't you think so, Slim?"

"Yeah, she's got great knockers," said the other guy, barely loud enough for Matt to hear. A sinking feeling came over him. They could rape her. And he couldn't do a damn thing to stop it. "If you guys hurt her, I'll find you and—"

"And what? We ain't hurt her, not yet anyhow. Had to tie her up to keep her from kicking us."

Valerie must have put up a fight. He hoped she'd connected with at least one of their dicks. While he tried to decide what to say next, they broke the connection. Damn.

If she was tied up and the police couldn't find her or Christy before Gordon's trial was over, what was he going to do? Damn his associates for getting involved in so many Dallas trials. According to the office manager, no one except Hal was free enough to come to San Antonio to help with a poor case, but Hal had begged off. Matt put in a call for Bob and crossed his fingers that he'd call back soon.

Sick with worry, he marched inside the motel office, grabbed the phone book, and called the police again.

****

When Valerie came to, she lay on a hard floor in what looked like a warehouse. Stacks of empty wooden pallets stood against a wall. Dust motes fluttered in a slim shaft of sunlight from a window. They'd tied her hands behind her back, and a rope bound her ankles. She shifted her position on the cold cement floor. Her neck ached.

Vaguely, she recalled being driven a few miles

before being dumped here. She must still be in San Antonio, but where, she had no idea. Her purse lay open three feet away.

Scuttling over to it, she worked it to one side so she could search for her phone. Her numb wrists slowly came to prickling life. Her phone and wallet were gone. Damn. And so was her nail file and anything else she could use as a weapon.

Had they dragged Matt here, too? She called his name, but no one answered. They must have lied when they said they were taking her to him. They must not have Christy here either. She hoped her sister was with Buck. She didn't think he'd hurt her, but he most likely was keeping her a prisoner. For Christy's sake and Gordon's, she hoped her sister hadn't gone with Buck willingly.

She had to escape before they came back. She didn't want to think about what they'd do to her if she didn't.

Squirming her way toward the shaft of light, she finally managed to crawl around the second stack of pallets. There was a window all right. Damn, as high as it was, she'd never be able to reach it, much less climb out, and drop to the ground without getting hurt. She needed to find the door, see if it were locked. Sliding across the dirty floor, she inched close to the nearest stack of pallets and pulled herself up.

As she rose to her knees, she discovered more aches and pains. It would help if her hands were free, but try as she might, she only succeeded in making her wrists raw.

By steadying herself against the stack of wooden pallet boards, she finally managed to stand. Now she could see another room, maybe an office with a phone.

Moving a few inches at a time, she made it to the archway. A few more feet, and she could see out the glass window. She inched over to it. No wonder they hadn't taped her mouth. This building stood on a gravel road facing a field of overgrown weeds and two short mesquite trees. Nothing else was in sight. She could yell until her voice gave out. And it wouldn't do a bit of good.

She tried the door to the outside. Locked of course.

A phone sat on the desk. Hooray. She could call 9-1-1.

It was awkward, trying to sit on the desk with her hands and ankles bound, but she managed to get close enough to reach the phone buttons from behind her back. She knocked the receiver loose. No dial tone sounded. Craning her neck, she punched in the numbers anyway. Nothing happened.

Again she tried to wriggle her hands loose. She wished her hands had been tied in front so she could chew at the twine. Seeing a drop of blood on the desk, she gave up.

Wait. Maybe there were scissors in the desk. Jumping down, she backed up against the front of the desk and tried to open the drawer. It was locked. Damn.

She'd just have to make it outside and run—no make that hobble—and hope she could find someone to help.

The crunch of tires on gravel sounded outside. Were her captors returning? What would they do with her?

A black pickup pulled to a stop. The two men who'd left her unloaded a large wooden crate from the back. They settled it on their shoulders. Were they smuggling designer clothes or handbags?

It was just the right size to hold a body. Was there one in there—or she drew in a ragged breath—or did they intend it for her? She scuttled back into the other room, as quickly as she could. She had to hide fast.

She inched between a stack of pallets and the wall. The rough edge of the top one stuck into her neck, making it hard to breathe. She nudged it with her chin, intending to duck down beneath it.

It wouldn't budge. Ducking lower, she shoved it with her head. It stuck. She pushed harder. It moved, making a noise. Loud footsteps followed. Her heart beat faster.

"So, there you are. Playing hide and seek? Forget it, sister. You're not getting away," said the lanky man called Slim.

Pierce grabbed her arm and yanked her from behind the stack of pallets, knocking her against his protruding belly. Recoiling from his underarm odor, she bumped into the stack of wood pallets. The rough edges scraped against her arms and back. "Don't you ever take a bath?"

Pierce slapped her face. "Shut up, slut."

Her face stung, but she wouldn't let him get away with that. "I'm no slut, but you're a bastard."

"You bitch." Pierce punched her nose. It hurt. Sticky blood ran down her face. It dripped on her dress, which was probably filthy by now.

"Slim, come hold this hellcat," he ordered.

His partner grabbed her wrists and pulled them both up behind her back until she couldn't help but cry out. "Ow." She clenched her lips together. She wouldn't give them any more satisfaction.

He pointed to the wooden box. "That's what you're gonna get for being bad."

She stared. "You're not putting me in that." It didn't look very sturdy. If they did, she'd wait until they left her alone, and then she'd punch and kick her way out.

Slim grabbed some duct tape. "First we need to shut her up. Don't we, Pierce?"

"Yeah, don't need no screaming broad alerting anybody outside."

Trying to dodge Slim, Valerie hoped that meant there was someone near enough to hear her scream. However, with Slim holding her arms in an iron grip, she couldn't do much but squirm and mumble. Soon they had her mouth taped.

Then to her horror, despite her struggles, Pierce wound duct tape around her arms and chest.

Her heart beat faster. Would they tape her nose? She'd die from suffocation.

When Slim stood back to look and cut another piece of tape, she let out the breath she'd been holding. She snatched another breath, hoping it wouldn't be her last. Pierce shook his head. Put tape round her ears. She doesn't need to hear us talking about what we're going to do.

"Right." Slim wound the strip over her ears, then continued up to her forehead, blocking her vision. Pierce managed to hold her still despite her struggles. She wished her mouth were free so she could bite his arm.

Pulse racing, she waited for them to tape her nose, but they didn't. Oh my gosh—they were lifting her.

Going to put her in that crate. Take her goodness knew where. She gasped. Her heart beat frantically. She wriggled. Hoped they'd drop her on the floor. At least she could roll around then unless she had broken a bone.

"Be still, bitch," one of them barked.

She tried to shove her knee against the man who was holding her legs, but he just clamped them closer to his body so she couldn't knock him where it hurt.

She felt them lower her, probably down into that crate. The surface felt more like wood than concrete. At least it wasn't cold.

The pounding of a hammer penetrated the tape over her ears—her heartbeat echoed each blow. They were closing it. Would she run out of air? Would they bury her alive? She shuddered. How could they expect to get away with this?

She took in a deep breath—desperately hoping this box wasn't airtight and her struggles wouldn't use up precious oxygen. Already, it seemed harder to breathe. She couldn't be sure until she started running out of air. What would it be like? Would she gasp and feel weak? Would her chest hurt? Would she get nauseated like in altitude sickness? Or maybe she'd just black out and never wake up? She didn't want to think about that.

The hammering stopped. "That should hold her," said one of them.

Footsteps getting fainter told her they were walking away. Then a door slammed.

Were they going to leave her here in this deserted warehouse until she died?

Chapter Nineteen

Matt looked out the motel office window and rubbed the back of his neck. Somewhere out there, kidnappers had Valerie. His stomach tightened. He wouldn't give in to their demands and make his brother accept a plea bargain for a crime he hadn't committed. Matt had told the police about the call from the kidnappers. All the officer said was he'd contact that division, and someone would call Matt.

After half an hour, an officer called back. "We sent a man out to that motel to question the employees. No one saw or heard anything. There's nothing else we can do right now."

Matt hung up. He pounded one fist on the motel coffee table so hard that magazines and papers jumped. He was helpless. Damn, he should never have left her alone.

He wanted to rush to rescue her, but where could he go? San Antonio covered miles of territory. He buried his head in his hands. He could only pray they'd let her go before they killed her.

He had her cell phone number. Maybe the police could negotiate with those bastards. He called the station again, asked to speak to a hostage negotiator. They gave him directions to the police station and said he could come talk to a detective in person.

His notes for Gordon's trial lay spread out in Joe's

office. Matt felt guilty for taking time away from that, but Gordon should understand. Matt wanted to be there when the cop talked to Valerie's kidnappers.

Green tile decorated the police station inside and out. They ushered him down a hall and into a cubicle with chest high partitions. Behind the desk sat a man of medium build wearing a light blue shirt, a tie, and a navy blazer. "I'm Detective Richard Knox, what can I do for you?" He adjusted his glasses over his protruding ears and listened. Matt told him what he knew.

Officer Knox called in a short, pudgy technician with a receding hairline, who set up a laptop. "We'll record the conversation and attempt to trace the call. I'll put this on speakerphone, so you can start the conversation, but it's imperative you don't say anything after I start talking. Can you do that?"

Matt nodded. "Here's the number." He scribbled it on a piece of paper and laid it on the counter.

Detective Knox called a technician and explained the situation. He also summoned a uniformed officer dressed in a light blue shirt and navy pants. Leading Matt and the officer to a small room with two chairs, Knox motioned for Matt to sit and told the officer to close the door. "As soon as we get a fix on the location, send the nearest patrol cars there."

"Understood," the tall, thin officer said and stood motionless at the door, which had a window.

Matt handed Detective Knox the slip of paper with Valerie's number. He punched some buttons on Knox's phone. The ringing sound filled the area, jarring Matt's nerves.

A gruff voice answered. "Who's this?"

Matt leaned closer to the speaker. "It's Matt

Larson. What are you doing with Valerie?" He heard a muffled moan.

"She's okay. I hear noise in the background. Where the hell are you?"

Matt swallowed. "I'm in someone's office, and I put the phone on speaker mode so I can hear you better. Now cut the crap, and let me talk to Valerie."

"You can't."

"Dammit, put her on the phone."

"She's not here."

"You're lying. I heard her moaning," Matt said.

"Uh, must have been the wind blowing you heard."

"Where have you taken her? Is she all right?"

"I don't have to tell you anything."

Matt tensed. Detective Knox held a finger to his lips, then waved at Matt to continue talking.

"Can't you at least tell me if she's alive?"

"Your voice sounds funny. Sure you ain't recording this or something?"

"What if I am? I want to be able to play it in court when the cops catch you."

Detective Knox shook his head and reached for the phone.

"Fat chance," claimed the gloating voice. "What if your broad is dead by then? Revenge won't be so sweet, will it?"

Matt gulped. Clenched his hands into tight fists.

The technician appeared at the door and signaled with his thumb and index finger that he'd gotten a fix. A dot appeared on the map on the computer screen. Detective Knox pointed to a uniformed officer standing nearby and mouthed, "Go." The officer looked at the map and rushed from the room. Another followed.

Knox grabbed the phone. "This is Detective Knox of the San Antonio Police. If you release your hostage alive, we can offer you leniency, and a plea you can live with."

"I'll think about it if you find us. Don't think you can. Goodbye."

"Wait," called Detective Knox, but only a low buzz came from the speakerphone. He pointed to a chair. "I'll follow them. You wait here."

"No. I need to be there."

Knox shook his head. "No way. You'll slow me down and perhaps mess things up."

"But if she's been shot and near death—I want to be there to hold her."

"She'll need paramedics then."

"You can't stop me from following you," Matt said.

Knox glared at him. "I can charge you with interfering with police action."

"I don't care. I'm going."

Know blew out a breath. "Might as well have you where I can control your actions. You can ride with me, but only if you stay in the backseat. Don't get out unless I say you can."

Matt frowned, but said, "Okay," and strode after the officer.

Minutes later, he slid into the backseat of Knox's unmarked Crown Victoria. Unlike the Mexican police car, this one was thoroughly equipped. A computer monitor listed the information they had on the kidnapping and that four squad cars were responding. From the radio came comments from the cops in the car ahead. The plastic seat underneath him felt hard and uncomfortable. Probably easier to hose the backseat down after transporting dirty prisoners. He caught a faint odor of urine. There were no door handles. Damn. Like a prisoner, he couldn't get out, even if he wanted to.

Detective Knox sped up the ramp to the freeway and whipped around cars so fast Matt wondered how he avoided scraping the sides of some.

Matt gripped the edge of the seat, his insides knotting. He hoped Valerie was okay, that they hadn't roughed her up. Knowing her, she wouldn't take much without a fight. He'd enjoyed traveling with her. Although she'd argued at times, she had been helpful and sympathized with his situation at the law firm. She'd defended her sister, even though Christy must have been a fool to go out alone that night. However, she did offer to help him free his brother from a jail sentence. Buildings and houses rushed by. His brother was in jail, but getting Valerie back safely was more important now. Detective Knox exited the freeway, drove down a busy street. Businesses flashed by and changed from posh offices to shabby ones and then to run-down pawnshops and convenience stores. Traffic dwindled.

Knox turned down a street, and soon the stores petered out. Occasional warehouses stood by the roadside. Almost in the country, he pulled up behind four white patrol cars with gold and blue logos, in front of a squatty cinder block building with a large glass window.

Inside a sat desk with a phone. No one was visible. Four uniformed officers burst from the other cars. Three crept around the sides of the building. Another,

Parker—Matt read his name on the badge—held a device to his ear. Parker pointed to Detective Knox and nodded. "Your show now," he whispered.

Knox grabbed a megaphone from the front seat, stepped away from the patrol car and shouted. "Police. Come out with your hands up."

No one answered.

Detective Knox shouted again. A breeze rustling leaves in the trees across the street made the only sounds.

Another cop rounded the side of the warehouse building. "Looked in a window. Place appears deserted. Found a "For Rent" sign lying under some bushes."

Knox motioned to two of the officers. "Johnson and Levi, see if you can get in."

Johnson, the taller man, tried the door. "It's not locked."

"Be careful. We'll back you up," Knox said. He and the remaining cops drew their guns and moved closer.

Johnson and Levi disappeared into the building. Minutes later they returned. Johnson shook his head. "Nobody inside."

Impatient, Matt yelled, "You sure she's not in there?"

"No sign of anyone. No body either."

Matt flexed his fingers and drew a sigh of relief. At least she wasn't dead, not yet anyhow. He shut his eyes. After a second, he opened them. He wouldn't think about that. She had to be okay.

He banged on the window. "Let me out. I need to see for myself that they haven't left her tied up in a closet or something."

Knox walked to the squad car and opened the back door. Matt rushed inside with Johnson and Parker behind him. Only a few papers lay on the dusty desk. A drop of blood lay by the phone. Had she tried to call for help? He pointed that out to the nearest officer, then followed him through the door to the back. Except for a shaft of light from the lone window, the back section was dim. It smelled musty. Matt walked to an eight-foot-high stack of pallets just past the window and looked behind. Nothing there. The rest of the warehouse room held nothing of note.

In front of the pallets lay a few splinters. He waved Officer Johnson over. "Look at this."

"So. Probably came from those pallets."

"But the wood's different. There are marks on the floor, as if some kind of crate were dragged across it." Matt bent down to look closer. He swallowed. "Do you suppose they killed her, put her body in a crate, and dragged it across the floor?"

Officer Johnson shrugged. "Can't tell anything from that. Those marks could have been made at any time." Matt followed the tracks to the front room. Similar scratches marked that floor.

Outside Johnson reported what they'd found to headquarters. Knox said, "Looks like a dead end."

Matt cringed at the use of the word dead, but followed the officer to his vehicle. Knox waved toward the front. "You can ride up here now."

On the way back to the station, Matt's shoulders sagged. He'd left questionnaires from potential jurors spread out in Joe's office. He should go over them and work on the opening statement for Gordon's trial. He needed to get the judge to agree to a postponement, but all he could think about was Valerie.

Were they torturing her? He squeezed his hands into fists. Was she even still alive? She wouldn't give up without a fight. He shut his eyes, imagined her vivacious smile wiped from her face, the spark gone from her eyes. How could he have left her to face that? Again, he kicked himself for not taking her with him this morning.

At the station, he stepped out of the Crown Victoria and looked around for his car. As if in a fog, he heard Detective Knox telling him not to worry. Saying they'd find Valerie and call him as soon as they did. Matt scribbled Joe's phone number and his cell phone number on a card and handed it to Knox.

His stomach knotted, and his shoulders hunched as he trudged toward his car. He wanted to stay and wait for news, but he had to talk to the judge and ask for a continuance to a later date.

At Joe's office, Matt glanced at his notes spread out on the credenza. Gordon was rotting in jail. Matt needed to get him out.

He plugged in his cell phone to be sure it was charged in case the police called with news. It just sat on Joe's desk without a peep. A couple of times he called the police station. No news. Not knowing if she were alive or dead cut him to pieces. How would he face it if they killed her? He'd feel as if his heart were cut out. She might die, and he hadn't even told her he cared about her, or how she made his life so much brighter, made it worth getting up each day.

Frank Carter had to be behind Valerie's kidnapping. How did the man think he could get away with it and still be elected mayor? Even if Valerie were returned safe, Matt vowed to do what he could to expose the scumbag.

Joe's secretary had been there since nine. After saying, "Hello, my name is Becky," the thin woman with silver gray curls retreated into the reception area and made no sounds except for the faint clacking of computer keys.

He'd already tried to put in a call to the judge's office, but the line stayed busy. From the front office he heard Becky fielding a few calls, telling them Joe was at court.

Now he wished he hadn't filed that motion for a speedy trial. Gordon had wanted to get it over so there'd be more time to let unfavorable publicity die down. After all, he was innocent and expected to be exonerated. Matt hoped with all his heart that he could pull it off. But right now, all he could think of was Valerie.

****

She was hot. And stiff. Valerie's arms and knees ached. Her shoulders felt as if she'd slept on granite. Her wrists felt raw, and she couldn't pull her arms in front of her. She couldn't see. Something was tied tightly around her head and over her ears, too. She couldn't hear anything.

They'd beaten her. Her cheek and her arm still hurt. They'd bound her with duct tape. They'd drugged her too. She could breathe, but she couldn't pull any tape loose with her hands tied behind her back.

She tried to wriggle out of the ropes around her wrists. That only tore at her skin. Not knowing what they'd do next made her heart pound. She had to get away. Then she felt the vibration. She must be on some kind of truck. Now she was even more scared.

Where the hell were they taking her? She hoped it wasn't the city dump. No one would ever find her in time. Tossed there by her kidnappers, she'd take her last breath, permeated with foul odors from the rotting discards of the city. And with more stuff piled on top, her body might never be found.

Matt and her family would never know what happened. Tears filled her eyes, trapped by the duct tape. It was bad enough that she had to die alone and scared. She hated causing pain to those she cared about.

Maybe she could pull her feet through her arms so she could get her hands in front of her. She tried, but her knees came up against hard wood.

She turned her head, felt something soft. Smelled like that rag they'd held to her face. She moved her face away as best she could, but already she felt as if she were losing consciousness. She fought against it, but the blackness took over.

Chapter Twenty

Sitting in his friend, Joe's, San Antonio office, Matt studied his notes. His vision blurred. What did he expect after being up all night, then running around looking for Valerie? The police had to find her soon. But what if they couldn't find her before, before—

"Mr. Larson," Joe's secretary stood in the inner office doorway. "National Parcel Service Delivery. Sign here." She held out an electronic receipt device.

Matt waved her away. "Can't you sign it?"

"It has your name on it. The man insisted you do it."

Frowning, Matt took the special pen. Who on earth would send him something here? He scribbled his name, and handed the pen and the device to Becky. Maybe his associate back in Dallas had sent him copies of research to help him in the trial. It was after noon. He barely had time to look them over. He tried the judge's office again. Still busy.

Becky's heels tapped on the hardwood floor as she left the inner office. "Just set it down over there," Becky said.

Matt heard the package hit the floor. It sounded heavy. He stepped into the outer office and stared at a huge crate, almost as big as he was. The sturdy deliveryman headed for the door.

"Wait," he called. "Who sent this?"

"Can't read the writing except for where it says to deliver personally to you." The man hurried out into the hall.

Matt stared at the six-foot wooden crate. Becky, Joe's secretary did too. "Oh my gosh. Is that from your firm? The box is big enough for your computer and a whole bunch of law books."

"Don't know why they'd send those here. It smells funny, like some kind of chemical might have been spilled on the outside of the box. Surely, no one would put a bomb in this large a box." His pulse raced. But they could put a body in it. He felt empty inside. They couldn't—they wouldn't kill Valerie and send her body to him.

With hesitant steps he approached. The box lay on the gold carpet, its rough edges out of place beside the sleek dark wooden end tables and gray upholstered chairs. The closer he got, the stronger the smell. A sense of foreboding chilled him. Made his spine tingle.

He backed off and shook his head. "I'm not sure it's safe to open it." He knelt beside it and listened. "I don't hear anything ticking. Is there a screwdriver around so I can pry this open?"

She edged away from the box. "No."

"How about scissors?"

"Yes, but I don't think they'll be strong enough."

"Bring them."

He glared at the box. He rubbed the back of his neck. What if it were Christy in there—alive or maybe dead? His stomach lurched. Or could it be Valerie? Watching Becky approach, he held out his hand. If Valerie or Christy were inside and unconscious, delay could mean her death. He swallowed. Suddenly, he felt sick. He knelt beside the crate.

Becky slapped the scissors into his outstretched fingers. "Scalpel, forceps, doc?"

"Not funny," he snapped. "Someone could be inside and die for lack of air."

"Oh, no. Can I help?" asked Becky.

"Not unless you have a crowbar in your desk."

He tapped the crate. "Valerie. Are you in there?"

Joe's secretary gasped. "You really think someone's inside?"

He put his ear against the box. Listened. No sounds pierced the dead silence. Even Becky seemed to be holding her breath.

He needed that box open.

Now.

Using the scissors, he pried one edge loose about half an inch.

Bending down, he tried to see inside. Looked for a bomb. It was too dark inside. He couldn't make out anything.

Taking a chance he wouldn't set anything off, he stuck his fingers in. Tried to pull the top up. It wouldn't budge. Wedging the handle of the scissors inside, he finally managed to separate the top from the side.

He peeked inside. Saw hair. Couldn't tell if it were Christy's blonde locks or Valerie's strawberry blonde ones. Then he saw cloth. Brown like the dress Valerie was wearing yesterday. A lump formed in his throat. He stuck his arm inside, felt flesh under the cloth. Flesh, slightly warm, thank goodness. "Valerie, talk to me." She didn't answer.

Heart pounding, he said her name again, louder.

He held his breath. She had to answer, had to be

alive.

No sound came from inside. His heart sank. She couldn't be dead. She just couldn't. "Becky, call 9-1-1."

He shoved his arm in further. He wanted to shake her shoulder, but couldn't reach it. He nudged her. "Come on, Valerie, wake up."

What if those bastards had put a bomb in there with her? His pulse raced. Frantic now, he grabbed the top of the crate and yanked. The thin board creaked and splintered, but didn't come loose all the way. He ran around the box and wedged the scissors in between the top and the other side. He leaned over, saw it had been nailed shut with long nails.

He straddled the box and grabbed the board with both hands. Jerked the top free. Got a splinter in his hand, but he ignored it. The strong odor coming from inside made his eyes water. Valerie lay there, not moving. But at least there was no sign of a bomb.

He stepped around the box so he could look at her face. He bent over her. "Please, Valerie, I don't want you to die."

Tape wrapped around her head covered her eyes. Dried blood was caked on her lips. The sight made his stomach jolt. He clenched his fists. What crazy bastard would do something like this? He wanted to kill whoever did this.

He held his breath. Bent closer to see if she were breathing. Damn, he couldn't tell. She had a bruise on her cheek and winced when he touched it gently.

He let out his breath. She'd winced. Dead bodies didn't move like that. He grabbed the scissors again, slipped a tip under the tape and cut through it. He pulled it away from her face. She moaned.

Remembering a CPR class he'd taken, he reached down to press her neck just under the ear. At first he couldn't feel any pulse. His heart raced. She had to be alive. He couldn't face it if she weren't.

He felt a faint throbbing against his finger. His heart pounded in staccato beats. "Call 9-1-1," he shouted, then realized Becky was already dialing. Thank goodness. He probably couldn't get the facts straight or give out the address.

About to raise Valerie to a sitting position, he stopped. She could be injured as well as unconscious. Shouldn't move her.

Was that a groan he heard? The sound was so faint he couldn't be sure. He leaned closer. "Valerie." His voice came out hoarse. "It's Matt. Talk to me." He grasped her arm. It was cold. He rubbed her skin, trying to warm her.

She moaned. Damn. Her hands were tied behind her back. He grabbed the scissors, pulled her arm to one side, and struggled to cut through the rope.

"Ow. Hurts."

Finally, he managed to sever the rope and free her hands. "What hurts, dear?"

"Every…" She spoke in a hoarse whisper. "Everything."

"Becky," he called. "Did you get through to 9-1-1?"

"They're on the way."

"They'd better get here soon," he said. Valerie's mouth lay partly open, as if she were too weak to shut it. She looked pale. Her breaths came in fits and starts. He shut his eyes. "God, just let her be okay." He opened his eyes. "Hang in there. Help's on the way."

215

"So tired." She shifted slightly, as if she were lying in bed trying to get comfortable. She moved slowly as if it was all she could manage to move anything.

He shook his fist. If he ever got hold of the insane person who did this—

Her eyes drifted shut.

"No. Don't go to sleep. Stay awake until the medics get here."

"Sleepy."

He pulled at the tape caught in her hair.

"Ouch. Hurts."

He grabbed the scissors, cut some of the tape away from her hair. He was afraid to pull it from her skin. That might hurt. "I'll let the paramedics cut the rest off. Stay awake and talk to me."

"Hurts…to talk."

He had to keep her conscious. "Tell me. Who did this to you? Did they beat you?"

"Ohhh," she groaned. "Hit me. Put in box—moved in truck."

The box must have slid around on the delivery truck floor. She could be bruised where he couldn't see.

"Got splinter. In my arm."

He hoped that was all that was wrong, but in his heart, he feared she was much worse. No telling what injuries she'd suffered. He clenched his fists. "Those bastards." He hoped to hell she could describe them well enough for the police to nail them. He squeezed her arm. "The medics—they'll take you to a hospital and put you on a nice soft bed."

"Th-thank goodness." She sighed.

He leaned closer. The smell was stronger now. "Did they drug you?"

"Chloro-chloroform, I think."

He leaned closer and found a rag under her hair. Something he hadn't noticed earlier. He pulled it out. Holding it up, he sniffed. The odor was strong. He tossed it away from him. "Open a window and the door, Becky. We need fresh air in here."

Valerie couldn't die, not now. She'd insisted on driving when his arm had been injured, sat by his bed after he'd been shot, and massaged his body with caring hands. He didn't know how he'd manage without her.

Even though he'd only taken a quick sniff, he found it hard to concentrate. He wanted to throw the rag as far as he could down the hall, but the medics would need it to know how to treat her. He draped it over the end of the crate. "Becky, can you put this in a plastic bag?"

She scurried away and returned with one.

"Don't breathe that stuff." Holding her nose and averting her head, Becky held the bag while he dropped the cloth in inside. Then she wrapped a rubber band around the top.

Again he kicked himself for not insisting Valerie come with him this morning. Of course, he'd had no idea someone was targeting her. This had to be connected to Christy's disappearance. It didn't matter now. What did was getting Valerie medical attention.

He hadn't been able to get through to the judge to get Gordon's trial postponed. If he showed up in court this afternoon, would another box be delivered with Christy's body in it—or maybe her dead body? He shivered, then clenched his fists. The police had better catch those thugs. He'd focus on seeing Valerie to the hospital. That was all he cared about now.

He caressed her hand. "Valerie, talk to me."

A moan was all he heard. "Becky, did they say how long they'd be?"

"No. Just that they'd send someone as soon as possible. Seems they have a lot of calls right now."

"Hang in there, Val. Help is on the way." He hoped to hell they'd get there soon. Her hand felt warmer now, or was he imagining it? Dammit, where were those medics?

As if in answer, a siren sounded. It had better be coming here.

Suddenly, the siren stopped. "Becky, look out the window for an emergency vehicle."

"It won't do any good. The window looks out back, not onto the street."

Minutes dragged. Finally he heard them coming down the hall. Matt sighed in relief. He patted her arm. "Just hold on. The medics will be here in a minute."

A paramedic appeared in the doorway. He looked puzzled. Matt pointed to the crate. "Over here."

The paramedic beckoned to someone behind him. "Bring that in." Then he rushed to Valerie.

Matt backed up. "She was delivered in this box a little while ago."

The paramedic's name badge said, "Robert." He touched Valerie's shoulder. "Can you breathe all right?"

Valerie moaned. "Yes," she finally got out.

Then Matt remembered the chemical soaked cloth. "She was drugged. Maybe chloroform." He held out the plastic bag. "Here's the rag they used. The box came by special delivery."

Robert sniffed, then backed away. "You're right.

She was drugged." He felt the back of her neck, then felt her arms and legs. "Ma'am, do you think you have any broken bones?"

"Don't know. Head hurts."

"Not surprising." He touched her face. "Nothing's bleeding now, but you have an abrasion from the tape." He turned to a female paramedic wheeling a gurney inside the door. "Lower it, Margie."

She positioned the gurney beside the crate. Matt tugged the side of the box loose. Gently, the paramedics fastened a neck brace on her, then lifted Valerie onto the gurney and raised it up. Margie grabbed the scissors and cut the tape binding Valerie's ankles, then gently pulled it from her skin. "We're taking her to Southwest General Hospital. That's the closest one."

Matt stepped closer. Looked at Margie. "Don't I know you? Margie Kleghorn, isn't it?"

Margie nodded. "It's Margie Marston now. We went to high school together."

"I want to ride in the ambulance with her."

"We don't usually allow that. Are you her fiancé?" asked Margie.

Matt took hold of Valerie's hand and squeezed it. "Not yet, but I care about her, and I'm worried." All he could think of now was would she be all right? Time enough later to think about what their future might hold.

"Okay, I'll allow it," said Margie. "Follow us."

On his way out, Matt turned toward Becky. "Call the judge. Tell him what's happened, and get him to postpone the hearing if you can."

Inside the ambulance, Margie locked the cot into place, so it wouldn't move, Matt guessed. Turning to

Matt, she pointed to a bench near the back of the vehicle. "Sit," she ordered in no nonsense tones. She spread a blanket over her patient's still form. Then she stuck a needle in Valerie's arm and attached it to a tube, probably an IV. She attached something else to Valerie's chest and kept checking a monitor screen.

The vehicle lurched around a corner and rolled over something bumpy. Feeling the vibrations, Matt guessed it to be railroad tracks. The gurney and the monitor jiggled slightly. Margie shook a fist in the air, muttered under her breath, "Bump again, Robert, and you'll be sorry."

Grabbing hold of the bench to steady himself, Matt wondered how many bumps Valerie had suffered through on the ride in the delivery truck to Joe's office. It was a wonder she didn't have a goose egg on her head.

"This is going to hurt, ma'am." Gently, Margie cut and pulled most of the tape from Valerie's face. Her patient's moans, barely audible over the sounds of traffic, tore at Matt's heart. He wanted to beat that bastard bloody.

Sitting on the bench, Matt wanted to reach out and take her hand. He didn't dare disobey Marge's order and get closer. "You've got to live," he muttered. He felt like telling her, I want to be with you for the rest of my life, but did he mean that?

Since Mallory, he hadn't thought about anyone like that, hadn't dated anyone more than a few times. Now he wondered if the sour taste she'd left had poisoned his attitude toward all women.

He glanced at Valerie, lying so pale and still. She might get mad and yell at him, but she wouldn't just refuse to see him again. He'd give a lot, just to hear her shout at him. He'd love to hear the sound of her voice, no matter what she said.

He'd never developed any kind of friendship or trust with Mallory—not like he had with Valerie. He'd never felt this with anyone else. Perhaps all he'd felt for Mallory had been lust. When he'd caught a glimpse of the person beneath the veneer, he hadn't found much substance. Valerie however, was her own person, vibrant, persistent, a woman who was going somewhere, and heaven help the person who tried to stop her.

He rubbed the back of his neck. Would Valerie be all right? She just had to be.

Valerie had been with him all the way, helping him hunt for Christy. He'd heard the pain in her voice when she'd told him how his brother had treated her. But she'd also said she didn't believe Gordon would kill her sister.

He was sure Valerie loved Christy and hoped to find her alive, despite the fact that Gordon had dropped Valerie for her sister. Matt hoped he and Valerie hadn't been on a wild goose chase.

He worried too, about saving his brother from a murder charge if they didn't find Christy. He hoped no one would find Christy's body lying bruised and broken somewhere.

Maybe Christy really was dead. And maybe Valerie was in danger of dying. Knots twisted inside. Things couldn't get much worse.

He watched closely. Listened carefully. Couldn't hear her breathing. Couldn't see her chest move. The heart monitor's continuing beep seemed ominous, whereas before it had been comforting.

She looked so pale. Holding his breath, he gazed at her chest, waiting for it to rise and fall again. Valerie just lay there. So still. So quiet.

The paramedic was taking Valerie's pulse. It had been too long since Matt had he'd seen her chest move. He held his breath and listened. "Why can't I hear her breathing?"

Chapter Twenty-One

Valerie lay still, her skin pale, like the sheets of the ambulance cot. Matt rushed from his seat. He stood beside the paramedic, hardly daring to breathe. Margie adjusted the IV and stared at the flat line on the monitor. "Shit, her heart's not beating," she muttered.

"Dammit. Do something," Matt insisted, his stomach twisting painfully. She couldn't die, she just couldn't.

Margie glared at him. "Cool it, Matt. Get out of my face and let me work." She told the driver Valerie was crashing and to go faster.

As Matt eased back onto the bench, the siren changed tone, became louder and more insistent. Margie added something to the IV and began CPR. Her movements seemed steady. But she'd clamped her lips together. Furrows lined her forehead.

Perched on the edge of his seat, Matt felt like pacing. Couldn't in the small space. He shifted on the hard bench. His stomach churned. If only he could get his hands on the men who'd done this—he'd flatten them like he'd stomp on cardboard boxes.

Another attorney might defend those men and force the DA to prove them guilty. After that it was up to a jury to decide the punishment. Matt swore he'd unearth as much evidence as he could to put them behind bars for a long time.

Margie counted, one, two, three, and all the way to fifteen. Then she pressed hard on Valerie's chest. She did it again and again. He watched for signs of tiring, ready to offer to take over, but the paramedic seemed to be holding up okay.

In fact, she appeared a whole lot calmer than he felt. Valerie looked even calmer—no not calm, make that lifeless. He leaned forward, twisting his hands in his lap. He'd rather have her alert and arguing—even shouting at him—than silent like this.

Margie's back blocked his vision of Valerie's face. With the siren screaming as the ambulance raced through the streets, he couldn't even hear his own breathing.

Finally, the monitor line started moving again.

"Gotcha," Margie murmured.

He gripped the edge of the bench until his knuckles turned white. Valerie would be all right. She just had to be. And as soon as they allowed, he'd sit by her bed, hold her hand, and tell her how much he wanted her to be all right.

Margie was still leaning over Valerie when the ambulance came to a stop in front of the emergency entrance. The back doors swept open. Margie and Robert lowered the gurney and wheeled it toward the entrance. Margie trotted along beside, holding Valerie's wrist, apparently checking her pulse.

Matt jumped out of the ambulance and hurried to catch up. "How's she doing?"

"Can't tell much yet, but we got her back," Margie said.

Inside the hospital, a nurse in scrubs and a doctor stood waiting in the hall. "Room three," the nurse said and grabbed hold of the gurney.

"Give me the bullet," demanded the doctor.

Margie said, "She coded on the way here. Gave her a dose of epinephrine and started CPR. Had her IV's wide open. She was already on 100 percent oxygen. We got her back in under two minutes. Heart rate is 60, respirations are 8, and blood pressure is 76 over 48."

As they pushed the gurney down the hall, Matt started to follow, but Margie blocked his way." You can't stay with her." She pointed back to the row of chairs facing the attendant's desk. "Tell the clerk as much information as you can. After she's stabilized, the doctor will come talk to you."

Matt walked back to the attendant with a heavy heart. He told her what he knew, then slumped into one of the empty chairs.

Leaning over, he rubbed the back of his neck for a few minutes, and then straightened. He didn't need a crick in his neck. He had to stay in good shape to encourage Valerie, and make her want to live if she were on the verge of giving up. He might even tell her he needed her. The thought surprised him. It wasn't like him to admit he needed anyone, but he didn't want to think about being without her for the rest of his life.

Valerie seemed to appreciate him for who he was. Unlike Mallory, she wouldn't push him to make partner in his law firm unless he really wanted that. She'd probably feel the same no matter what he did for a living, as long as it was honest and made enough money to live on.

Shit. How could he bear to sit where he couldn't see her? He couldn't hold her hand and tell her to hang in there, that he wanted a life with her—if she wanted to share it with him. He'd been let down when Mallory threw him over, but that had felt nothing like this. It was as if his heart were being ripped from him. His life would be meaningless without Valerie. It wouldn't matter how much money he made or even if he made partner or not. Without her to share in any successes, they'd seem hollow.

He paced the short space between the row of wooden chairs and the Formica counter in front of the attendant. The attendant glared at him, then turned back to her computer.

"Sorry if I'm disturbing you," he muttered and plopped down on a hard seat.

As soon as he knew she'd be all right, he wanted to tell her how much she meant to him. That ought to make her smile.

What if she only thought of him as a good friend and a help in finding her sister? She wasn't indifferent to him he was sure. But what if she didn't feel the same way he did? What if she'd been so hurt by Gordon's rejection that she couldn't trust any man, and especially not Gordon's brother.

He'd listened to her brief explanation of why she and Gordon had broken their engagement before they'd even set a date. The pain in her voice spoke more eloquently than words. He'd wanted to throttle his brother for being so cavalier, but she'd said to let it be.

He didn't know if she'd really forgiven Gordon for ditching her for Christy. However, one thing he was sure of. Valerie still hadn't gotten over the disappointment. Maybe she felt she wasn't desirable. As soon as she got better, he'd set her straight on that. For now, he just prayed she'd be all right.

When they finally let him see her, she was sleeping. Not wanting to disturb her, he slipped quietly into a chair.

A nurse walked in, her white rubber-soled shoes leaving only subdued sounds. After glancing at her patient and the monitor, the nurse made notes on a portable computer. Stepping close to Matt, she whispered. "Let her rest. I suggest you come back in the morning with some fresh clothes for her."

"Her clothes are all in Dallas," Matt said in low tones.

"Hold on." The nurse examined the clothes Valerie had been wearing, and wrote something down. She handed Matt a piece of paper. "Here are her sizes. There's a Walmart nearby. Pick up some clothes and underwear. Don't forget shoes. She didn't have any when she arrived."

Matt frowned. Should have thought of that. "Thanks." He left the room and headed for the desk to ask directions. He could get some of Christy's clothes, but they might not be the same size, and worse than that, seeing her missing sister's clothes might make Valerie depressed.

Half an hour later he stood in a Walmart. What would be comfortable? Maybe a sweat pants set. He picked out a pair with flowers embroidered on the top. Now for the underwear. After hunting for several minutes, he finally swallowed his embarrassment and found that section.

He hadn't realized how many types of bras there were. Seeing some women picking over the selection, he backed away into another area. He didn't want them watching while he chose something. Should he get sexy or something cotton?

After the women left, he fingered one with a lacy covering over sturdier material. What was that stiff curved thing inside? It felt like a wire. Did women really wear those things? Some bras had padding. He'd supposed some women wore that to make their breasts look bigger. He didn't think Valerie did.

He chose a white cotton bra, and put it down. She'd probably like something sexier. He picked a lacy one that looked firm enough to hold her breasts.

Now to get some panties. There were some on sale laid out on a table.

White ones, red ones, pink ones, black, blue, and even kelly green ones. But they were all different. Some were full size, some were like bikini bottoms, and some were no more than thin slivers of flimsy material with a tiny triangle in the middle. He picked white ones of each style except the skimpiest one.

A clerk eyed him with a strange look. "Need some help?"

He held up the smallest scrap of material. "What do they call this?"

The clerk seemed to be stifling a snicker. "That's a thong panty. Do you need help with sizes?"

He shook his head, dropped the thong panty, and hurried off sure his face was red as a delicious apple. Seeing nightgowns nearby, he picked up a white silk one with lace on top, and paid for everything. Now for shoes. Drat, he didn't have her size. Maybe slippers would do. After all, she might take a while to recuperate. He could get shoes later.

There wasn't much selection. The only pair that looked like it might fit was furry and shaped like a gorilla. Somehow, it fit her—she hadn't taken any nonsense from that police chief in Mexico. Must have taken both thugs to stuff her in that box. If there were only one, he'd have come off bloodier than Valerie.

Matt took his selections to the register. The clerk, a lanky teenage boy with spiked blond hair stared at him. "These for you?" His look made it clear what he thought.

Matt slammed some bills on the counter. "No. Just ring it up. I'm in a hurry."

Later, after grabbing a toothbrush, a comb, and some lipstick, Matt hurried back to Valerie.

****

The next day Valerie looked up at Matt from her hospital bed.

His brown eyes looked anxious. "How are you feeling?"

She took a deep breath. "I hurt in lots of places, but I'm okay. Being cooped up in that box was creepy. I hated not being able to see. Guess that's what it would be like to be buried alive." She shuddered, not wanting to think about it anymore. It had been bad enough answering all the questions from the police. She thought she'd given a good description of Pierce and Slim, but they still hadn't found them.

Matt smiled and took her hand. Then he kissed her. His mouth was soft and gentle and hinted at wanting more. His hands gripped her shoulders. His thumbs caressed her skin. Relief and adoration shone in his eyes. She put her arm around his neck and kissed him back, throwing her heart into it.

He deepened the kiss, then nibbled on her ear, giving her a warm glow inside. "You don't know how glad I am to see you, to know you're going to be okay."

She frowned. She'd seen the yellow-green tinge around her eyes, the mottled bruise beneath her left cheek. Yet, he was smiling at her as if she looked pretty good.

"They told me you could go home now."

"That's the best news I've heard since I got here. Flying back to Dallas by myself would have seemed lonesome without you." Without a reason to be with him every day, she'd really miss him. She hoped and prayed he'd call as soon as he returned, and they'd spend more time together.

Valerie grasped his hand. "By tomorrow or the next day I should feel up to helping you look for Christy again. We'll find her alive. I know we will."

"Let's see how you feel then. I want you to get well before you go anywhere. By the way, I bought you some clothes." He pulled lavender sweats, a white silk nightgown, a lacy bra and three pairs of panties in assorted styles and colors from a shopping bag. "I wasn't sure what you'd like, but I think I got the sizes right. The nurse wrote them down for me."

"You didn't need to get all that, but thanks. I sure can use these." She glanced at the sweats he laid out on the hospital bed. "They look like they'll fit just fine."

"You're welcome." In another bag she found a toothbrush, a comb, and some orange lipstick. At the bottom was a pair of fuzzy gorilla slippers. Her kidnappers had taken her shoes. She'd have to wear the slippers.

Matt squeezed her hand. "I'll be back in ten minutes. Think you can be ready by then?" Valerie nodded, and he left the room, shutting the door on his way out.

****

Driving her to Gordon's house, Matt couldn't help smiling. Knowing she'd miss him made him feel warm all over. "You're not flying to Dallas yet. I'm taking you to Gordon's house. He offered it for a few days. Unfortunately, he won't be there since I still can't manage to get him out on bail."

"I see," was all she said.

She'd insisted she could walk to his car, but the nurse suggested riding the wheelchair would keep her slippers clean. As soon as they reached his car, she stood and took a deep breath. She seemed a little shaky as she climbed into his front seat. He hoped she'd be all right soon.

He was really looking forward to having Valerie there with him for several days. He wanted to enjoy her company for much longer. Not about to rush her, he wasn't sure how long he could last without doing more than kissing her. Lord, as strong as his feelings were, as soon as she got better, he wanted to make love to her, but didn't know how she'd feel about that. It would be a hard blow if she turned him down. His mother had once said, "A faint heart never won a fair lady." He wasn't about to give up. She was worth waiting for.

He was glad to see her face had more color. The orange lipstick he'd chosen looked a bit odd above lavender sweats with the pink embroidered flowers, and the gorilla slippers didn't seem to go with the rest of her outfit, but she didn't say a word.

When he parked in front of Gordon and Christy's house and shut off the engine, Valerie pushed the car door open on her side.

"Wait." He got out and ran around the car. "Sure you're up to walking? I can carry you." He wanted a good excuse to hold her close. If she snuggled against his chest, that might let him know how she felt about him.

Stepping out, she shook her head. "Thanks, but I'm sure I can make it."

He put his arm around her shoulder to steady her. "You okay with staying in Gordon and Christy's house? After all, he—"

"I'm fine. Staying here doesn't bother me—not anymore."

Matt shot a glance at her. "You sure?"

She nodded. "Christy's the kind of wife he needs, one who can entertain with style and mix with important people. I'd feel uncomfortable doing that. I'd rather Gordon remain ancient history, but guess I'm stuck with him for a brother-in-law…at least at family gatherings. I imagine Christy appeals to him in a way I couldn't." She blinked a couple of times.

He wanted to erase any leftover hurt. "Any guy who says you aren't appealing must be blind."

He took her hand and squeezed it. He hoped the look in his eyes said she was more than just appealing. She smiled. He wanted to blot out the sting from Gordon's rejection and bury it deep in the past. Matt hoped that would be easy now she had him as a friend. Dare he hope for more?

Matt turned from unlocking the door. "Gordon was an idiot. Couldn't see the true gold for all of Christy's glitter."

She met his gaze as if unsure he were sincere. "Somehow, while growing up I always felt she overshadowed me. Especially when Mom kept saying how pretty she was."

Matt held the door open. "Hey, it's the same with my dad and Gordon. He can do no wrong. It's as if I don't exist. And Mother can't stop talking about how proud she is since he's running for mayor."

****

Valerie stepped inside Gordon and Christy's house. He must know how she felt. They were two of a kind, almost like they shared a kinship.

"How did your mother react when he was arrested for murdering Christy?"

"She was crushed. But let's not talk about them. I just want to tuck you in bed. So you can rest, that is."

Valerie wrinkled her brow. From his intent gaze, which wandered from her eyes over her breasts down to her hips and waist, she was picking up vibes. Now that she was twenty-seven, it was time she stopped letting her mother make her feel as if she were lacking in anything. Matt didn't seem to think so. Why should she?

Recalling that kiss he'd started, the one she'd thrown herself into, set her pulse racing. Just remembering, she couldn't help licking her lips.

Matt pushed the door shut. His brown eyes glowed as he grasped her hands and pulled her closer to his strong muscled body. His spicy lime aftershave teased her senses. "Welcome home. I know this isn't your home, but you could use some good memories."

Desire glowed in his eyes. He was going to kiss her. Suddenly feeling much stronger, she met his gaze and stepped into his arms. She needed to forget how his brother had hurt her. Matt was different, and he found her appealing. Dare she take the risk? *Carpe diem*, said her heart as she met his mouth with hers.

No matter that she was in Gordon and Christy's house, she felt as if she'd come home at last, home to the arms of someone who liked her as she was. Home to someone she could care for. She reveled in the feel of those masculine lips ravishing hers. His tongue pushed inside, exploring, thrusting, and plundering. She cradled his face in her hands, slid her tongue into his mouth, and roved its depths with wild abandon.

Matt pulled away just enough to look into her eyes. "Wow. You're some kisser. Don't know how any man could say you're not sexy. Hell, you're temptation in the flesh."

Her heart beat faster. The glow from his words warmed her like sunshine on a January day. How could any woman resist him?

He took a deep breath. "We need to get you in bed. You should take a nap."

"I'm not sleepy."

"How about a game of chess then?"

She grinned. "You're on. If I win, you have to bring me a great big bowl of ice cream."

"If I win, you have to feed me the whole bowl with a spoon." His tongue swiped his lower lip.

"Don't bother licking your lips. I'm going to beat you."

"Fat chance. Sit on the couch. I'm sure Gordon's got a set around here somewhere. Would you like some coffee or tea?"

"Coffee with milk and Sweet'n Low."

He disappeared into the kitchen. About five minutes later, he brought her a steaming cup full and some powdered creamer. "Couldn't find any milk, but I'll get some later. Here are some ginger snaps."

Valerie sipped the coffee. "This is fresh brewed. I didn't realize you knew your way around a kitchen."

"A bachelor has to learn a few things to survive. And a Mr. Coffee helps."

However, when she tried to bite a cookie, it was hard. "These might work as miniature hockey pucks."

"Sorry, I didn't realize they were stale."

Valerie won the first game. Matt insisted on a rematch, which he won. They played a third, and she beat him. Then he told her to lie down while he went shopping.

She awoke to the smell of pizza, hot from the oven, on a tray. After they demolished that, Matt brought in a huge bowl of strawberry ice cream, some fresh cookies, and a spoon.

When he held a spoon to her lips she grabbed his hand. "I was kidding about feeding me."

"You won, so I'll feed you. Open up."

He ate a few spoonsful, but fed her most of it. When she opened her mouth for the last one, he held it away from her. "Your lips must be cold. I need to warm them."

Before she could say anything else, his lips were on hers, warm, willing, and hungry. She was too, but not for ice cream. The spoon clattered to the dish, which fell to the carpet with a soft thud.

His hands cradled her face, as if she were a rare blossom. His next kiss was gentle and roving. His hands dropped to her shoulders and caressed them. "You're sweeter than ice cream and much warmer."

Glowing inside, she wrapped her hands around his

neck. Kissed his mouth. Fire zinged through her. She'd felt sparks between them before, but wow. This was electrifying. Too mesmerized to pull away, she let him stretch it out into a long, lingering, mind-blowing mating of their mouths.

Dazed, she moved back just enough to see his beaming face, thrilled to realize he felt the same attraction as she did.

Then he pulled away. Chilled and apprehensive, she wondered if he were merely carried away by the moment.

"You need to rest," he said. I've made up the guest room for you. It's the one next to the bathroom." He turned and left the room.

Was she assuming too much? She made her way into the bedroom. Lying down, she pulled the covers over her shoulders and scrunched her eyes shut. She wasn't sleepy, dammit. Why had he left her so abruptly?

After tossing and turning for half an hour, she finally fell asleep. Later, a soft knock on the door awakened her. Glancing out the window, she could tell it was twilight. She must have been more tired than she thought. "Come in."

Matt stuck his face inside the barely opened door. "Do you like Chinese food?"

"Sure."

"Be right back."

And twenty minutes later, he was. "Do you feel up to eating in the dining room?"

She nodded. Minutes later, sitting at the table, she breathed in the aroma of tangy soy sauce and savored the smell of deep-pink sweet and sour sauce mixed with the aroma of fried chicken.

Leaning over to pick up a piece of meat, she noticed he was gazing at her breasts. Her nipples hardened in response. "This top fits a little tight. Maybe I should exchange it for a larger size."

He grinned. "Don't. You look great the way you are. Just don't go outside like that. I don't want the neighbors to enjoy the view like I am."

She started to get up, but he came around and touched her shoulders. "You feel tense. Lie down, and let me rub your shoulders."

"What about your arm. Doesn't it hurt too much to do that?"

"It still bothers me, but I'll mostly use my right arm and hand."

Soon he had her so relaxed she almost forgot to eat. When he nibbled the back of her neck and pulled her up to face him, she barely had time to wipe her fingers on a napkin.

His lips met hers in a kiss so hungry she forgot about food. Grabbed his shoulders, hugged him, and kissed him back.

After a heart-stopping kiss, he released her. "After supper, you probably had better go to bed and get a good night's sleep, unless…"

"I'm sick of lying in bed." She met his gaze. "Unless what?"

He smiled. "Unless you'd rather do something else." His hands caressed her breasts, sending shivers of delight through her.

She looked away, then back at his face. "You're going to make me say it, aren't you?"

He pretended to look innocent. "Say what?" He

slid one arm around her waist and pulled her close. His other hand slid inside her shirt to fondle her breast, making it tingle. His intent brown eyes met hers, intent and inviting.

She swallowed. "You know."

A thousand watt gleam illuminated his face. "You think I have plans to seduce you?"

She felt herself blushing. "I think you're already doing that."

Grinning, he picked her up and carried her toward the bedrooms. She nestled her head on his shoulder. That felt every bit as good as she had imagined it.

She hoped he knew that she wouldn't want to be in Gordon and Christy's master bedroom. Sure enough, he took her to the guest bedroom and set her down. Barely inside, he reached for her.

They had all night to explore each other, but she couldn't wait. He pulled the lavender top over her head. Realizing he felt the same urgency swept her exhilaration to new heights, like reaching the crest on a roller coaster. She could hardly wait.

As he tossed her shirt aside, her breasts strained against the lace bra. Her heart beat furiously. His quick work with the clasp freed her breasts. He caressed them with warm hands, and then pressed a kiss on each one, making her feel adored.

He looked at her as if she were more precious than diamonds and more intoxicating than champagne. She felt like swirling into space, but seeing Matt's broad smile made her want to stay close and enjoy the ride with him. She welcomed him into her arms and her heart. She hugged him, loving the feel of his sturdy warm chest pressed against her bare breasts.

Backing off, she managed to unfasten the buttons of his shirt. He rained kisses on her neck and shoulders. She explored the firm flesh of his bare chest with her fingers, hoping she could set him aflame like he was doing to her, like a roaring fire on a cold winter's night. She hadn't felt this warm or this wonderful for—she couldn't remember how long—perhaps never. And from the look in his eyes, things could only get better.

He eased her down on the bed. His fingers smoothed over her breasts as if they were made of the choicest marble. "So beautiful. Made to be touched." He grinned as he squeezed and fondled them. "I like touching a real flesh and blood woman, one who doesn't worry about getting her hair or her makeup messed up."

"I don't have any on except lipstick."

His smile spread even broader. "By the time I'm through, you won't have any." He leaned down and gave her a long satisfying kiss, melting her heart.

She uttered a faint, "Oh," then grasped his shoulders to pull him close. She kissed him again, then tugged at his shirt. She couldn't wait any longer to get him completely bare.

"Let's not rush. We have all night. And I came prepared—just in case." He pulled a handful of condoms in rainbow colors from his pocket and set them on the bedside table. "Now choose. In the order you'd like me to use them." He grinned.

Just the thought of spending the rest of the night in bed set her heart beating faster. She laid out a red, a yellow, and a blue one, and hoped she would feel up to it.

He bent his head to taste a breast and suckled until

she writhed with delight. Anticipation stirred within, heating her to a fever pitch. He kissed her other breast, then teased her nipple with his teeth, his brown eyes intent on her face.

He took her breast in his mouth, drawing on it. She couldn't help arching toward him. She'd take all the attention he'd give her. By the time he drew away, she was wet, willing, and aching for more.

As she reached for his belt, he squeezed her breasts and gave her a long, languorous kiss. He backed away just enough so she could see the shine of admiration in his eyes, then his mouth descended on hers. His lips ravished hers, demanding a response she was only too happy to give. She couldn't help but respond. Currents of longing cascaded through her body, made her fumble with his zipper.

Pulling it down, she marveled at the enormous bulge in his briefs.

He grasped her by the waist and pulled her off the bed. "Too many clothes." He slid off her sweat pants as she pushed his trousers over muscled thighs.

Panties and briefs gone, she moved into his arms, then tumbled with him onto the sheets. The feel of warm skin and hard flesh against her bareness was heady. Pure male dominance shone in his eyes.

He kissed her, and then smoothed his fingers over her shoulders. "Do you know how much I want you?" His eyes told her he wanted her so badly he'd be devastated if she refused—not that she would.

She smiled. "For today, in this bed, I'm yours. Yours to kiss, yours to make love to, yours to do what feels good."

His eyes lit up. He leaned toward her. His fingers

slid between her thighs, touching, caressing, exciting her even more than she'd thought possible, until she finally said, "Please. I can't wait any longer."

Joined together, she thrilled to the intensity of his thrusts. He'd hurtle to great depths, pull back then rush inside, like torrents over the rocky ledge of a waterfall.

He rose up. "Do you hurt anywhere? I can stop now if—"

"Don't you dare." She grasped his face, pulled him close for a deep kiss.

Grinning broadly, he plunged deep into her depths, making her feel as if they'd never been fully explored before. He carried her to new pinnacles of delight.

She'd never thought of her shoulders as sexy, but his flurry of kisses made her feel they were.

He rose up, looked into her eyes. "I use lots of words in court, but I've only got two for you."

"I'm almost afraid to ask."

He smiled. "Special and sexy."

Her heart spun in a new rhythm. She felt sexy and desired as never before. She took a deep breath and smiled. It was like celebrating Christmas, Easter, and the Fourth of July all at the same time.

His rhythm thrilled her. She kept up with every stroke, shoving her hips to meet him just as vigorously. She loved giving him her all. Made her glad to be a woman, glad to have such a wonderful man taking her on a thrilling ride.

"Oh, Matt, you're marvelous." She hugged him tightly as he climbed right along with her to the stars, whirling to another galaxy, where time and space stood still, and only the two of them existed.

Drifting back to earth and satin sheets, his broad

smile told her he'd shared, really shared, every minute of that earthshaking experience.

And heaven help her, she wanted to travel there with him again and again, for as long as he'd stay with her.

"You're everything a man could want in a partner or a lover. Tonight you're my woman." He pressed a kiss on her shoulders. Then he laughed. "Bet you're too independent to be anyone's woman."

His kisses, on her lips, on her neck, and on her shoulders said he adored her.

He hadn't said a word about love or tomorrow, but for tonight she'd enjoy every minute in his arms.

Chapter Twenty-Two

It was daylight when Matt woke Valerie. He wore a broad smile. "Hope I didn't tire you out."

She yawned, pulled the sheet higher over her nakedness, and shook her head. "A little exercise is good. And that's the best kind. What time is it?"

"Seven. You hungry?"

"I could pick up some doughnuts, and fix hot tea."

He shook his head. "I don't want you to exert yourself."

"But you have a way of making me do that, one I can't overlook." She grinned.

"How about I take you out to Denny's? You won't have to do anything." He pulled the sheet from her hands, exposing her breasts. She felt heat rise to her face. Shivers of anticipation shimmied down her spine.

"Except, you'd better get dressed, or I'll be in no shape to appear in public." His briefs had a definite bulge.

"Maybe you'd better take a cold shower before we go. Don't think I'm up to spending any more time in bed."

His expression dimmed, making her smile. After a few seconds, she added, "Without food that is."

He pulled at her hand. "You had me going for a moment."

She dressed while he watched. Self-conscious

243

under his continued gaze, she smoothed down her sweat pants. As she reached behind to fasten her bra, his gaze dropped to her chest.

He smiled. "I like it when you stand like that. Makes you look even fuller. Bet you'd look great in a tight-fitting sweater. But then again, I'd have a hard time keeping my mind on what I was eating."

A heated flush rose from her chest to her face. It was nice to be complimented on her figure, but embarrassing too. She turned away and headed for the bathroom. "I need some lipstick."

He grasped her wrist and pulled her to him. "No, you don't. You look fine. Besides, I'll just kiss it off."

"Not in Denny's you won't."

"Then I'll just have to do it here." His lips descended on hers, warm and tender. He nibbled on her lip, and then pressed his lips to her forehead. "Any more and we'll never get to Denny's. Come on. Let's go."

At the restaurant, they talked about making another run to Buck's cabin. Matt said, "I'm convinced he's still holding her there. Maybe they went out to eat. I'll go tomorrow and confront him. See if the real reason he's holding her is because someone wants Gordon to stay in jail, so people won't vote for him."

Valerie frowned, her hands fisting on the Formica tabletop. "Buck won't admit that. He'll claim Christy is staying with him of her own accord."

Matt leaned back. "What if it's true?" His jaw seemed set in stone, perhaps echoing his mind.

She bristled. "It's not either. How can you say that?"

"Knowing your sister, that wouldn't surprise me."

Valerie leaned across the table. "She wouldn't do that to Gordon."

Matt took her hands in his, rubbing his thumbs over the backs of them. "But what if Buck's as persuasive as you say? Remember, she liked him when she was in high school. From what you told me, he was pretty wild then."

"That was a long time ago. She was an impressionable teenager."

"Didn't she see him not long before she married my brother?"

Valerie nodded. "That was before they were engaged. She wouldn't go out with him after agreeing to marry someone else."

"How can you be sure? Are you that close?"

"We don't like all the same things or travel in the same circles, but I know my sister."

Matt rubbed his chin. "I'm still not sure about her."

"But you want to find her, don't you?"

"Of course. I don't want anything bad to happen to her, and I need to exonerate my brother."

"And I think she's in danger, so I'm going with you to that cabin."

"It's dangerous, but you might find out I'm right. Beneath those fancy manners and fine clothes, she's nothing but a high-class alley pussy. One who doesn't mind who pets her. But she's married to my brother, so I treat her like a lady."

Valerie scowled. "Don't talk that way about my sister. She's not Buck's lover, and she's not an alley cat."

Matt clamped his mouth shut. Valerie ate the rest of the meal in stony silence. How could he malign her sister like that and expect her cooperation? He must still believe Christy was staying with Buck willingly.

****

After Matt brought Valerie back to Gordon and Christy's house, Valerie stormed into the bedroom where he'd shared such wonderful lovemaking with her. She marched into the bathroom. Coming out, she waved her toothbrush toward him and frowned. "Just because you gave these to me, I want to throw them away, except I won't because they're the only ones I have with me."

He scowled. "Now, you're acting childish."

She shot him another angry look. "You can have this room. I'll sleep on the couch in the study."

Valerie marched down the stairs, her footsteps echoing on the hardwood stairway.

Minutes later, she faced him, standing at the foot of the steps, holding her toothbrush, comb, and lipstick. "I'll help you find my sister and testify at Gordon's trial, but after that I never want to see you again." She stomped down the hall. However, she wouldn't be able to avoid him all the time since Christy was married to his brother.

Matt heard her determined footsteps all the way to the lavatory next to the living room. He sighed and returned to the guest bedroom. Frowning, he scooped the remaining condoms on the bedside table into a drawer. Obviously he wouldn't need any tonight. And if he couldn't get back in her good graces, even worse than no more mind-blowing sex was the fact the woman he wanted more than any other now hated his guts.

****

Valerie fumed while she waited for Matt to return

from his attorney friend's office. He'd promised to come back for lunch before leaving to search the cabin again. Had she overreacted to his comment about her sister? He'd find out he was wrong, but would he admit it? Like most men, probably not.

Lunch was a silent affair. She stared at him. How could she have practically lost her soul to him before finding out he hated her sister and was a bad judge of character. And if he thought she'd stay behind while he went off half-cocked to confront Buck and Christy, well he had another think coming. Thankful her good sense had finally prevailed over lust, Valerie picked up her empty soup bowl, grabbed the one Matt had left and rinsed them in the sink.

She didn't want to wear the new clothes Matt had bought her, but she had nothing else until she returned home.

Matt strode into the kitchen. "I'll call you after I find them." He opened the back door.

Valerie ran after him and grabbed his arm. "Wait just a damn minute. I'm going with you."

He turned. "No, you're not." He flung her hand away. "It's too dangerous."

Valerie grimaced. Now he was showing his true colors, the rat. "You're going to need help."

"You think I'm a weakling?" His look scorched her. "The only reason I'd need you is if Christy tries to stop me from attacking Buck. And besides, you can't go wearing those gorilla slippers."

Valerie stepped around him, blocking the doorway. "They're all I have, and Christy's shoes don't fit. What if she needs me? If Buck's hurt her, she might."

He glared at her. "Just in case you're right, I'll take

you, but I'm in charge."

She frowned. He hadn't said, in case I'm wrong. That would be too much to admit. "And you think you should be in charge just because you're a man?"

He looked her in the eye. "How many fist fights have you been in?"

"Hey, it's not as if I haven't fought before. I fought an hour a week for three years in order to make it to black belt."

"That's not the same as on the street. Buck won't fight by the rules. Let me take the lead. Then we can get Buck arrested and Christy home safe."

"Aren't you going to call the police first?"

"I did, while you were in the hospital. They went to the cabin and didn't find anyone there. I called them again, but I doubt the police will go there again, so it's up to us."

"Thanks a bunch for finally including me in your plans."

He frowned. "No need to be sarcastic. You can help me locate the road again."

"That's not all I can do, and you know it."

He glared at her, but said nothing.

Half an hour later, Matt turned into the dirt road, which wound through scrubby mesquite trees. Deep ruts made the ride bumpy. She crossed her fingers, hoping this time they'd find Christy. If only Buck hadn't moved her somewhere else by now. After about a mile the road petered out not far from the small clearing around the cabin. A twin trail of flattened weeds led to a parked red Corvette.

Valerie's pulse raced. At least he was here. Now if only Christy were also.

The cabin looked like a mobile home that had just been plopped down amidst the yucca plants, prickly pear cactus, wild grasses, and mesquite trees.

Matt eased his car to a stop and held a finger to his lips. "We need to approach slowly. See what's going on."

Like before, Valerie headed for the right side of the house, and Matt to the left. They had just reached the corners when Valerie heard voices.

"For the last time," Christy shouted. "I won't divorce Gordon, so you might as well take me home."

"Don't raise your voice to me," said a male voice.

Matt beckoned to Valerie. Bending low so no one could see her through the windows, she scurried to him. "That Buck?" he asked.

"Not sure." She rose up to peek in the open window. The guy's back faced her, but it was Buck all right. Valerie nodded. Christy met her gaze, her eyes widening. Valerie ducked and motioned for Matt to back out of sight.

"What's the matter?" Buck growled. "You see something outside?"

"No, I didn't."

Valerie hoped Buck believed her.

Crouching beneath the window, Valerie waited. They could use the advantage of surprise.

"Well then," Buck said, "Fix me something to eat. And not hot dogs again."

"You wouldn't let me buy any microwave dinners at the convenience store."

"Didn't like what they had. Looked cheap, probably tasted like it, too. Didn't your mama teach you how to cook?"

"Just because I'm female doesn't mean I have to learn that. Valerie's the one who likes to cook. Mom always got impatient with me. Said she'd rather do it herself."

Matt moved away from the cabin and beckoned Valerie to join him behind some trees. "Knock on the door. Say you're glad to find her. Offer to take her home. I'll be close by, but just out of sight, in case he threatens you."

Valerie tiptoed up the steps behind Matt. She stopped in front of the door. He took a few steps past the door and stood, his back against the wall.

Valerie knocked.

"Who's there?" Buck growled.

"It's Valerie. I want to talk to my sister." She held her breath. Would he let her in? Would he threaten her?

The door opened a crack. Like Matt, Buck wore a short, well-trimmed beard. But his was blond. He frowned. "What are you doing here?" His gaze raked over her. He laughed. "Those hideous gorilla slippers and the sweats with those too cutesy flowers look ridiculous."

Valerie shoved the door open, bumping him. Heard him grunt. He deserved it for that crack. "Never mind my clothes. I want to see Christy."

He blocked the doorway. "She's not here. You might as well leave."

"She is too. I saw her."

He looked behind him. "Damn you, Christy. You lied when I asked if you saw anyone." He raised his hand to her."

The sound of his slap made Valerie mad. She yanked the door wide open. "Leave my sister alone."

Buck faced her, his blond hair awry. He shoved Christy behind him, leaving only part of her visible. "She deserved it. She lied to me."

"You have no right to hit her."

"That was only a slap. And she's going to divorce Gordon and marry me, so mind your own business."

"I am not divorcing Gordon," Christy shouted.

Valerie swallowed. "Buck, do you really want to marry a woman who doesn't want you?"

Buck pulled Christy to his side and put his arm around her waist. "But she does, don't you, sugar?" He met Christy's frightened gaze. Even to Valerie, he looked threatening.

Christy's cheek was pink where he slapped her. Dark circles lay beneath her listless eyes. "I just want to go home, Buck. Please let me go." She sounded tearful.

Valerie reached for Christy's hand. "She looks tired. Let me take her home to rest."

Christy tried to peel Buck's hand from her waist. He scowled and planted his feet a foot apart. "No." More than six feet tall and broad shouldered, he looked ready for battle.

Could she throw him? Not without knocking Christy down. She gritted her teeth. Time for reinforcements. "Matt!" she called.

Matt stepped inside. "Take your hands off her, Robbins. She wants to return home. You can't keep her against her will."

Buck pulled Christy closer to his side. "She wants to stay with me. Tell them, Christy." He glared at her, then clamped his mouth shut and stared at Matt and Valerie.

"Move away from him, Christy," Matt ordered.

Christy rubbed at her eyes. "Buck took care of me when I-I had a miscarriage, Val. I lost my baby. I wanted it. I really did, but now I want to go home with you."

"Why didn't you tell me you were pregnant?" Valerie asked.

"I didn't know. Not until I started bleeding."

Buck danced away from Matt. "She'd bled a lot…" He stopped to take a breath. "When I found her, it scared the shit outta me."

"When did it happen?"

"The night—" Christy wiped a tear rolling down her cheek. "It happened the night I left. I wouldn't have gone to the Sundown Bar if I'd known."

"What happened?" Valerie asked.

"I only had one drink, well it was a double, before I got in the truck and headed home. I stopped because I had cramps. Then I was bleeding. I must have passed out because the next thing I knew Buck was knocking on the window."

"I told him I thought I might be having a miscarriage. He picked me up and put me in his car."

Buck patted her shoulder. "She didn't look good. I drove like a bat out of hell to the first clinic I could find. Sat in the waiting room for over an hour before they even let me know she was going to be all right."

Christy rubbed at her eyes. "All I remember was they told me I'd lost the baby." She hiccupped. "Th-they said I could go home in a couple of hours." Tears ran down her face.

Buck thrust a handkerchief toward Christy. "Shit, don't go crying again. Tears me up."

Christy wiped her eyes and edged away from Buck.

"He carried me to his car, and I fell asleep, but then he took me to Mexico and wouldn't let me come home."

Valerie grabbed her sister and hugged her. "You poor dear. I'll take care of you now. You need to rest."

Buck grabbed Christy's wrist and yanked her to his side. "She needs to stay with me. That jailbird husband can't do anything for her."

The look in Cristy's eyes galvanized Valerie. She stepped closer, grabbed Christy's hand and pulled. "But he's in jail because she disappeared. Let me show the judge she's not dead, so Gordon can be released."

Buck pried Valerie's fingers from Christy's. "No way. I'm not letting her go back to that jerk. Doesn't treat her right. Must be ashamed of her not to take her to any of those political meetings."

Christy inched away from Buck. "He took me to the very first one where he announced his candidacy."

Matt had his fists ready.

"The San Antonio Express News never showed your name or your picture," Buck said.

Christy yanked her hand from Buck's grasp and stepped away from him. "I wanted to stay in the background. The spotlight should be on him, not me."

"Why didn't you go to other meetings with him?" Valerie asked. "Aren't you proud of Gordon?"

Christy held up her hand. "Of course I am, but he always said the same things in his speeches—how he'd promote the city by making talks all over Texas. I got tired of hearing it. He'd never took me dancing or out to dinner. Most nights after those meetings he'd come home exhausted and fall into bed, too tired for anything else."

Buck reached for her. "See, sugar, that's why you

need to stay with me. I'm never too tired to make love to you."

His gaze spoke of longing, maybe even obsession. Valerie wondered if he and Christy had sex while she was gone. Surely, she had recovered from her miscarriage by now. And he could be persuasive. But Christy was loyal to her husband, wasn't she?

Valerie swallowed. Better not bring it up. She took hold of Christy's hand again and pulled. "Come on, sis. I'll take you home. Matt and I will make sure you get all the treatment and attention you need."

Buck glared at Matt. "She's not leaving with you."

Matt grabbed Buck's forearms, restraining him. Christy struggled, but couldn't get loose. Matt punched Buck's face.

Buck's face reddened, his expression thunderous. He pushed Christy away and socked Matt in the solar plexus.

Matt's "oof" made Valerie cringe. He geared up to hit back. This was her opportunity. She grabbed Christy's hand. "Get in the backseat of Matt's car." She heard a thud from Matt's blow.

Valerie led her sister to the Mustang. She looked for bruises, but only saw small ones on Christy's wrists. Valerie shoved Christy into the backseat. "Lock the doors, and be ready to let us in when this is over."

Valerie waited until she heard the click of the locks and then ran back into the cabin.

Matt lay on the floor. Kneeling, Buck straddled him and punched him in the stomach.

"Stop," Valerie screamed. "Christy wants to go home with us. You might as well give up."

"Never," Buck growled. He reared back to punch

Matt again.

Valerie grabbed Buck's shoulders and tried to pull him off Matt.

Buck turned and scowled at her. "Let go. I might bruise your pretty face."

"You try, and I'll tear your eyes out." She glared at him. Clamping her hands into fists, she flexed her knees, ready to light into him.

Buck rose on one knee and lurched toward her. Matt jumped up and pushed Valerie to one side. "Come on, Robbins. Only cowards take on somebody weaker. Hit her, and you'll answer to me." Adopting a fighting stance, he danced from one foot to the other.

Buck planted both feet on the floor. "I'm no coward." He punched Matt's belly. "Take that."

Matt aimed his next punch at Buck's gut, but Buck jerked to the side, minimizing the effect. He jabbed at Matt's abdomen. Matt tightened his ab muscles and recoiled from the impact. Hopefully, that made it hurt less. Buck was bigger, but Matt was faster. He aimed an upper cut at his opponent, followed by an elbow strike.

His next blow connected with Buck's nose. Blood dripped as Buck howled. "I'll get you for that." He rained punches on Matt's chest.

Valerie cringed. That must hurt a lot. Was Matt tiring? He looked like it. After stepping back, he feinted to Buck's right side, then made a right cross hit to Buck's left mid-section. Buck's "oof" told her the punch had been a hard one.

"Had enough?" Matt asked.

"No, dammit." Again, Buck rained blows on Matt, this time aiming for his face. A few got though Matt's defenses. Blood dripped down Matt's cheek, his lip, and his nose.

Valerie kicked Buck from the side. She wanted to do more, but Matt would hate that. Besides, Buck was tiring, and Matt was winning—wasn't he? She clenched her hands so tightly, her nails bit into her palms.

Matt threw a hard punch, knocking Buck down. Matt grabbed Valerie's hand. "Christy in the car?"

She nodded.

"Run." They raced to the Mustang.

"Unlock the door!" Valerie shouted. Christy did.

Valerie opened the passenger door and slid in. Matt ran around to the driver's side. "Unlock this one, quick."

Both Valerie and Christy reached for the lock. Christy pulled it up. Matt grabbed the door handle.

A shot rang out, and Matt collapsed.

Chapter Twenty-Three

Matt lay on the ground beside the driver's door. "Oh, no." Valerie scooted behind the wheel and took a closer look. He wasn't moving. His eyes were closed, and his face looked pale.

She slid back across the seat. Wrenched the passenger door open. Ran around the car. Matt couldn't be dead. He just couldn't.

She stooped beside his body. "Matt, Matt, speak to me!" He didn't answer. She felt his neck, searching for a pulse. His heart was beating, but just barely. She reaching inside the car and grabbed her cell phone. 9-1-1 had better work out here.

"Hello," answered a voice, much calmer than Valerie felt. "Your location and the nature of the emergency please?"

Valerie took a deep breath. "A man's been shot. He's unconscious. We're next to a cabin on Ridge Road, that's a dirt road off Highway 181."

"Is he breathing?"

"Yes."

"Is he bleeding?"

"I'm not sure. I can't see any blood."

"Did you see where he was shot?" asked the voice.

"I don't know. It happened so fast."

"Look for the wound. I'll keep you on the line. We'll pinpoint your location. Do not move the victim."

Valerie glanced toward Buck. "What if the man with a gun tries to shoot him again?"

Buck just stood there, about thirty yards away. She held her breath.

"That's your decision. A medical team is on the way. We'll send officers also. Keep the line open."

Valerie set the phone on the dirt, rose up about a foot, and scanned the area around the cabin. Was Buck just waiting to shoot her or her sister? "Christy, stay low in case Buck comes closer. Lock the car doors."

Crouching low, Valerie's heart raced. What if Buck came closer and shot Matt again? She wished to hell she had a gun. Matt's was in the glove compartment, but she wasn't going to leave his side. "Matt, can you hear me?" He didn't answer.

He was breathing. She bent down, loosened his shirt. No blood on his chest. She examined his shoulder. Just below his ear. Blood, wet and sticky, now discolored his hair. "Please, God. Let him be all right." She pressed her fingers beside the wound in his shoulder to see if that would slow the bleeding. She couldn't see any noticeable difference. Damn.

She wanted to kneel beside him. To whisper help was coming, to whisper she loved him. But staying stooped would let her react quickly.

"Is he dead?" Buck's voice startled her. He was only ten feet away now.

She stood. "No. Why did you shoot him? The police and an ambulance are on the way." Her heart raced. Would he shoot her too?

"I wasn't trying to kill him. Just wanted to keep him from taking Christy. She's mine. No one can take her from me."

Valerie swallowed. What could she say? Buck wasn't thinking rationally. She resisted the impulse to contradict him. She wouldn't argue. Might send him even more over the edge.

"We aren't going anywhere, Buck. First I have to make sure Matt's all right."

"Does he need CPR? I can do that."

"No. He's breathing."

Buck stepped closer. Deep frown lines creased his forehead. Valerie's breaths came in short gasps, and her pulse raced. Was he only pretending to help? She swallowed. Was he waiting for a chance to shoot again? And would he shoot her this time?

She needed to get him to move. "Buck, he needs plenty of air. Could you step back a bit, please?"

He moved a few paces away. Her tension lessened, but only a little. He was still too close. Still frowning.

Her heart raced. She wanted to control the situation, but wasn't sure what would work. Buck had all the earmarks of an abusive husband—and a gun. But he and Christy weren't married. As a paralegal she tackled those types with protective orders from the court, enforced by local police. Valerie wished she had one against Buck.

He stepped closer and leaned over Matt. Her heart pounded against her ribs. "Stand back, please," she said.

"You won't report me, will you? It was an accident. I wasn't trying to kill him. I was just trying to scare him away from Christy. He should be okay. You don't want to get me in trouble. Sure would make Christy feel bad."

"Uh, no. Of course not." Chills ran down her spine.

She tried to calm herself. Tried to portray an outward semblance of calm with this maniac. It was all she could do to keep her hands from shaking. She hoped Buck couldn't see how terrified she was. She could knock him down, but not with a gun in his hand.

If she could only keep him talking, he might not do anything violent. Might even put the gun in his pocket. She cleared her throat. "Buck, while we're waiting for the ambulance, tell me how your work is going. You travel a lot, don't you?"

He nodded. "Keeps me busy. I go here, there, and everywhere in my business."

"So, are you a salesman?"

He laughed. "Much more than that."

"So exactly what do you do now?"

"I'm an executive sales representative for Blackmore & Blackmore, as well as two other pharmaceutical companies. I do millions of dollars in business a year. I can buy Christy all the Neiman Marcus outfits her little heart desires. Soon as she's free from Larson, I'll move her into a penthouse condo in Lincoln Heights. That's the most exclusive section of San Antonio in case you didn't know." He tilted his head toward the cabin. "This is just my weekend retreat. We've been roughing it here because it's cooler than in town."

Rubbing her fingers against her palm, she shot a furtive glance at Matt to be sure he was breathing. Thank goodness, his chest still rose and fell.

She had to keep Buck talking—had to keep him focused on himself rather than hurting Matt or demanding Christy get out of the Mustang.

"So what cities do you travel to?"

He nodded. "New York, San Francisco, Los Angeles, and all the important cities. I go first class, stay in the best hotels."

He still held the gun, but at least it wasn't pointed at anyone.

Buck continued. "I'm taking Christy with me as soon as she's free. I'll show those stupid drugstore chain executives I can attract the best. She'll wow them, I'm sure."

He stepped closer. Valerie held her breath, then said, "What was your most challenging sale?" She hoped she could keep him talking long enough for the cops and the medics to get here.

He rubbed his chin. "The best one was with a large drugstore chain buyer for the Midwest. Met him in Chicago." He rubbed his fingers on the gun barrel.

She swallowed. "So did you cinch the sale on the spot, or did you have to wine and dine him?"

Buck smiled. Spread his hands in an expansive gesture—but he didn't put the gun away. "Took him to Morton's Steakhouse on State Street downtown. After we stepped down into the restaurant, the waiter pushed a cart displaying plates of steak and lobster next to our table. The distributor drooled over their 24-ounce steak. He loved it. I picked up the hundred-dollar plus bill. After that, the sale was a sure thing."

Wondering if he dealt just in prescription drugs or illegal ones too, Valerie glanced down the dirt road and back at Buck. He'd stuffed the gun into the waistband of his pants, but could pull it out at any moment. If she jumped him, he could shoot her at point-blank range.

Where the hell were the police and the ambulance?

Matt hadn't regained consciousness. That terrified

her, but she couldn't go to pieces now. She had to protect him from Buck. "So did you get the contract?"

He grinned. "Did I? Boy, I'll say. For mega bucks. I'll do even better when I talk with the west coast distributor. I'm sure of it." Stepping closer, he reached toward Valerie.

Standing, she tensed, braced her feet so she could throw him if necessary.

He dropped his hand and started to step over Matt's body.

Valerie planted her hand on his chest. "Stop right there."

"Hey, I won't hurt you. I just want to get Christy out of the car. It's hot. Don't want her to get heat exhaustion. Got a fan inside my cabin that blows cool air. After you and Matt leave, we can get on with what we were doing." He licked his lips and grinned.

"No. And step back so you won't kick any dirt on Matt."

He frowned. "What do you mean no?" He grasped her wrist. "Stand aside so she can get out."

"She can get out whenever she wants to, but she doesn't want to."

"That's not true. She loves me. She wants to be with me always. She's just confused now."

"But she's married to Gordon." Valerie couldn't be sure, but she thought she heard sirens in the distance. They'd better get here soon. She was afraid to do much more for Matt. Buck might interfere. Probably as unpredictable now as he'd been in high school.

Valerie watched him carefully. The sirens sounded louder now. He cocked his head toward the sound, and then grasped her arm. "You've got to tell them it was an accident." He stepped closer, his brows furrowed into deep ridges. "You will, won't you?" He stared at her face as if daring her to disobey his command. He made her insides curl. However, she wouldn't let him see her fear.

She pried his fingers from her arm. "If you say so." At this point she didn't dare refuse. No telling what he might do.

He grabbed her wrist again. "Is that a yes?"

She yanked her arm from his grip. "Let go of me. I said I would. Now step away from Matt. I don't want you kicking any dirt. It might get in his airway." She held her breath, hoping she hadn't given him any ideas. As close as he stood, she'd have a hard time throwing him without spraying dirt onto Matt's face and wound.

Standing between Buck and Matt's unconscious form, she alternated her attention between him and the sounds of help arriving.

Two police cars got there first. They parked behind the Mustang. Getting out, with guns drawn, they shielded themselves behind open car doors. One called to Buck. "Put the gun down, right now."

Buck set it on the ground, but remained standing beside it.

"Now, move away from it," the officer said in a commanding voice. Buck took two steps from the weapon.

"Farther than that," said the officer holding his gun pointed at Buck from behind the open door of the police car. Buck moved farther.

An officer stepped out, picked up the gun, dropped it in a bag, then stepped closer to Valerie. "You all right, miss?"

She nodded, looked down at Matt. "But he's not." She pointed to Buck. "He shot him."

Buck stepped closer. "It was an accident."

A siren heralded the approach of an ambulance. Valerie sighed in relief.

The paramedics parked behind the police cars and rushed to Matt's side. They examined his head, turned him to one side—looking for injuries she guessed—then placed a white collar-type brace around his neck. They shifted Matt onto a stretcher and loaded him into the vehicle. The female paramedic attached an IV to his arm and dragged an oxygen tank next to the cot. She turned on a computer monitor. Valerie was relieved to see a line moving in a steady rhythm before the paramedics shut the back door, but how long would it keep doing that?

"Where are you taking him?" she asked the other paramedic as he opened the front door.

"Southwest General Hospital. Do you want to ride there with us?"

"Ma'am," said one of the officers. "I need to ask you some questions. It will only take a second."

The paramedic beckoned to her. "No time for that if you want to ride with me. Now get in."

She called to the policeman. "Ask the woman in the car what happened. She's my sister, and she saw what happened." She nodded toward Buck. "Keep him away from her so she'll be safe." Valerie headed toward the ambulance.

"I'll take her to the station in my patrol car," said the officer. "If she can't answer all my questions, I'll call you at the hospital."

"Miss," said the ambulance driver, his voice sharp

with impatience. "We're leaving now. Are you coming?"

Valerie hurried toward the ambulance. Buck stepped close to her. "Not so fast. What did you tell him?"

Valerie ran around the front of the ambulance. "I have to go to the hospital with Matt now."

She got in and slammed the door. The driver already had started the engine. The ambulance backed up.

Through the window Valerie watched. The ambulance turned around. It moved forward, slowly at first, and then faster as the road became less rutted.

Valerie craned her neck to look behind. Her sister stood next to one of the policemen. Wishing she could see into the back, she wondered how Matt was doing. She crossed her fingers. He wouldn't die; he mustn't, not before they got to the hospital.

****

Buck called to Christy, who stood beside a cop's car. "Come on over here, sweetheart. You need to stick with me, kid."

She took one hesitant step toward him, and her hands trembled. She moved closer to the policeman beside her. "Maybe later, Buck. I'm sure the officer wants to talk to me."

The officer, dressed in navy pants and a starched blue shirt with a badge that said Miller, faced her. "Did you see him fire the gun?"

"I was in the car. I heard the shot and saw Matt fall to the ground."

"I said, did you see someone fire the shot?"

Christy stepped closer to Officer Miller. "I saw

Buck holding a gun. Then I saw a flash."

Miller put his hand on his holster. His face looked stern. "You two need to come to the station for questioning." He faced Buck and pointed to the other officer. "You'll be riding with him."

Buck stood there, his boots firmly planted at least a foot apart. "What if I refuse?"

The other cop, his shirt buttons straining over his stomach, stepped over to Buck. "Then we'll arrest you, handcuff you, and take you by force to the station."

"I see." Buck pondered that for a moment. "Okay, I'll come with you, but this is strictly voluntary on my part. I should be free to leave whenever I wish. That right?"

The pudgy officer shook his head. "I wouldn't count on it. Now, get in the back of the squad car."

Buck scowled. "Okay, okay." He held out his hand to Christy. "Coming, sweetheart?"

She backed up a step, bit her lip, and waited.

Office Miller shook his head. "She's riding with me."

Buck clamped his mouth shut, and then opened it. "I'll see you there, then." He stood by the squad car, but didn't get in. She edged toward Officer Miller's Crown Victoria.

Officer Miller asked her. "Does your boyfriend have any record that you know of?"

"He's not my boyfriend, just someone I knew when I was in high school. He's been holding me against my will."

"That's not true," Buck insisted. "You said you wanted to go to Monterrey, and I took you there."

"Yes, but you wouldn't take me back home when I

asked." She faced the office. "Something he said once makes me think he might have a warrant out for him in Dallas. He insinuated it was for traffic tickets—not surprising by the way he drives, but I'm wondering if it might be for something else."

Oh, no. Buck held his breath. He was in for it now.

"Like what?" Officer Miller asked.

Christy edged closer to Office Miller. "Like sexual assault. I'm afraid he might have hurt some other women. He slapped me once or twice when I didn't do as he asked. He seems obsessed with me.

Buck shook his head. "That's crazy. I'm not obsessed. I love her."

The officer stared at Buck, then asked her, "Did he beat you?"

"Not really. He just slapped me a few times."

Buck let out his breath. That didn't sound too bad. Maybe if he apologized, things would go better for him at the police station. He stepped closer, and Christy took a step back.

"Look, Christy, I'm sorry if I slapped you. I don't know what I was thinking, but I didn't want you to leave me. I love you. I really do."

Christy shook her head. "You don't love me. You just want to possess me." She faced the policeman. "I usually did what he asked, just to keep him from losing his temper. You wouldn't believe how mad he can get."

"We'll check into it." The office turned toward Buck. "What's your real name?"

"Robbins, but I've always gone by Buck. My first and middle names are Alfred and James, but I hate them."

The officer stared at her. "You look familiar.

What's your name?"

"Christy. Christy Larson. Why?"

"You married to Gordon Larson?"

"Yes. Is he really in jail because I'm missing?"

"That's right."

"Why would anyone think he killed me? We're newlyweds."

"Neighbors said they heard you two arguing the night you disappeared. And we found your blood in his truck."

"That can't be enough to think he killed me. Besides, the blood's from my miscarriage. He might lose his temper sometimes and shout at me, but he's nothing like Buck."

Christy gripped the dashboard and stared at Officer Miller. "You've got to tell them I'm alive. Please take me to the district attorney's office. I've got to get my husband released immediately."

Officer Miller gave her a stern look. "You can do it later. You should have thought about what might happen when you ran away with Robbins."

"I didn't run away with him. He came to my rescue when I had a miscarriage. After he took me to the clinic, I thought he was going to drive me home. I passed out and didn't realize where he was going until we were in Monterrey in Mexico.

"So why didn't you ask him to bring you back to San Antonio?"

"I did. A dozen times, but he wouldn't come back here until a few days ago. "

"Why didn't you leave and return on your own?"

Christy hesitated a moment. "I didn't have any money, and I couldn't get away from him. He threatened to beat me."

"So, why didn't you leave while he was sleeping?"

"I tried to leave once while he was taking a nap, but he woke up and chased me. He slapped my face and dragged me back to the hotel. I was afraid of what he'd do if he caught me leaving again."

"Couldn't you call your folks to come get you?"

She leaned forward and shook her head. "I tried to call my sister, Valerie, in Dallas, but he caught me at it and disconnected the call. He wouldn't let me near a phone after that. Well, once he let me use his cell phone to call Gordon and Valerie, but they weren't home."

The officer frowned. "You don't exactly fit the battered woman profile. You should have tried harder to get away."

"I told you I had no money. I was too sick the few days we spent in Monterrey. When we got to the hotel in El Jardin Bonito, I asked the maid to call the police."

Buck frowned. "I didn't know you did that. I thought you were asking for more blankets."

Christy continued. "The maid didn't understand. When I said policia, I think she thought I was going to call them about her. She ran out the door and never came back to clean the room. I didn't think anyone else in Mexico would help. Buck told everyone I was his woman. Down there, everyone thinks the man is the boss."

"I see. We'd like to question you at the station. And check out your Mr. Robbins, too."

Christy surprised Buck with a dirty look. "He's not my Mr. Robbins. I never want to see him again."

In the car on the way to the station, Buck couldn't get those words out of his head. That hurt more than knowing he'd face charges for attempted murder. He'd need a good lawyer.

The pudgy officer, whose badge said Dalton, grabbed Buck's arm. "Are you coming willingly, or do I need to handcuff you?"

"Yeah, I'm coming," Buck said.

Twenty minutes later, Officer Dalton parked in a lot on Nueva Street, next to the San Antonio police station and stepped out. "Come with me." Buck followed him past a green tiled wall with POLICE in big gold letters, walked up the steps onto a green and white tiled floor. He passed an ATM machine, probably for people to get cash to pay their fines. As big as the place was, this must be the main police station.

Just ahead of them in the lobby, Office Miller stopped and turned to face Christy. "Are you willing to testify that he kidnapped you and held you against your will?"

"Yes."

"I'll notify the U.S. attorney in our area. That's a federal offense. He could be put away for several years."

Buck held his breath. This sounded serious. Office Miller led her down a long hall.

Christy's voice carried across the gray and tan striped terrazzo floor. "I want Buck behind bars or maybe in a mental hospital under guard. If this helps get him there, I'll tell you everything I know."

Buck glared at Office Dalton. "You can't hold me unless you charge me with something."

The pudgy officer beside him nodded. "We need to ask you a few questions about the shooting. If you cooperate, and we determine that it was accidental, this shouldn't take long." The officer pointed to a room with a telephone, a computer monitor on a table, and two chairs. He motioned Buck to a chair facing the desk. Buck sat, mentally rehearsing what to say. It would have to be good.

Dalton slid into a blue high-backed chair behind the desk. "Now, tell me the whole story of the abduction from beginning to end. You don't mind if I tape it, do you?"

He shook his head. "Go ahead. I'm guessing you will anyway." He hoped Christy wouldn't tell Officer Miller about the time he'd handcuffed her to the steering wheel while he went into a store to buy groceries. He'd found her brushing angry tears from her eyes as he unlocked the cuffs. After seeing the marks where she'd tried to get the cuffs off, he'd kissed her wrists and begged her to forgive him. He'd said he hadn't wanted to hurt her, but she said she wished she'd taken karate like Valerie, so she could have knocked him down and gotten away.

Dalton slapped his hand on the table, rousing Buck from his memories. "Pay attention. Matt's the man who got shot, right?"

Buck nodded.

"Did Matt threaten you?"

"Not exactly, but he hit me when I said Christy couldn't leave with him." Buck explained how Matt had fought him earlier—inside the cabin.

Dalton asked a few more questions. Buck tried to answer without incriminating himself.

Officer Miller appeared at the door and knocked. When Dalton nodded, the other officer opened it. "Christy Larson has signed a statement charging you with aggravated kidnapping, assault and battery, and attempted murder.

Dalton rose and gripped Buck's upper arm. "From what the witnesses said, you shot Matt Larson point blank. He may die. Until he's stable and can testify otherwise, you're going to jail for attempted murder, and then there's a charge of assault and battery and a federal charge for kidnapping."

"B-but, it wasn't kidnapping, I swear." I want to call a lawyer."

Dalton snapped handcuffs on Buck's wrists. "I'll schedule your arraignment for nine o'clock in the morning. If you post whatever bond the judge rules on, you can leave, but until then you must remain in custody."

As Dalton and Miller led him down the hall, Buck scowled. "As soon as I get a hold of a good lawyer, I'll sue the lot of you for false arrest."

****

At Southwest General Hospital, Valerie walked into Matt's room, thankful to be finished talking to the police. Matt lay there, his shoulder bandaged. A cart with squeaky wheels rattled down the hall, making it impossible to hear anything. His chest moved ever so slightly, and she let out the breath she'd been holding.

After tiptoeing to the edge of the bed, she stood there, waiting for him to wake up.

He opened his caramel eyes and smiled at her.

Her heart beat faster. "You're awake. How do you feel?"

"My head hurts and my shoulder too—not much—guess they gave me something for pain." He tried to rise up, then dropped back down.

Valerie patted his hand. "Don't try to do too much."

He gave her a stern look and then grinned. "Now who's bossing whom around?"

She squeezed his hand. "I just don't want you to overdo it. Remember you've been shot."

He groaned. "Tell me something I don't know. At least I was only grazed." He pursed his lips. "Valerie, I hate to admit it, but I guess I was wrong about Christy. It's obvious Buck was keeping her against her will."

"I guess it might have looked different to you. I forgive you."

He smiled. "Then we're friends again?"

She nodded and took his hand and squeezed it. "Just get better, okay?"

He smiled. "Come here, and give me a kiss."

Bending, she touched her mouth to his. Her lips tingling, she marveled at the strength of his response as his warm mouth roved all over hers, sending toasty shivers down her spine.

He reached up and stroked her hair with his right hand. "I can't wait until I can get out of here and can kiss you senseless."

She smiled. "You're doing a pretty good job of it already. Hope that means you're getting better."

He held tight to her hand. "Pull up that chair, and talk to me. Do you know what's happening with Christy and Buck? I need to take her to see the D.A."

She patted his hand. "Don't worry about that. I'm sure the police will sort it out. Gordon should be free in a day or two."

"I hope a publicist can do something to repair his image before the election. Damn, I wish I had enough evidence to pin Christy's kidnapping on Frank Carter."

Valerie frowned. "You think he was behind my kidnapping too, don't you?"

"Of course. Don't know why the police haven't found out."

"Hmm," she said. "Maybe I can do some digging."

"Leave it alone. You're not a private eye. If the cops haven't found them, what makes you think you can?"

"It's probably low priority with the police. But it's on top of my list." She let go of his hand.

"Don't do anything rash. I don't want you to get hurt. The last time really scared me."

"Hey, don't worry. I'll be careful." At least he cared about her safety, but being the kind of man he was, he'd care about any friend.

He reached for her hand. "Don't leave now. I like having you beside me. I like seeing you every day."

Valerie watched his face, listened to the tone of his voice. What was he trying to say? Was he leading up to asking her to move in with him? He hadn't actually said he loved her, and he could have his choice of any woman he wanted. From what her co-workers said, she knew he'd dated some gorgeous women. But she wasn't gorgeous. She was just an ordinary woman who loved him, one who wanted more than a charming smile and great sex. Winning his love might be too much to hope for.

She'd better cut him off at the pass. Being a lawyer, he'd use some nice-sounding phrase like she was a wonderful woman, one he'd like for a friend. She didn't want hear that. She pushed his hand away. "I've got to go. I need to check on Christy. I'll see you later."

"Wait." Matt grabbed his wallet from the drawer of his bedside table. "Take this fifty-dollar bill. You'll need cab fare to get to Gordon's house."

Remembering she had no cash, she took it and hurried from his room before he could say anything else.

She walked out of the hospital. What a coward she was for leaving him. How could she go into battle with formidable foes, but walk away from him?

It was the fear of rejection that made her want to put the pain off as long as possible. He seemed to like her. He certainly acted that way in bed. Maybe, if she encouraged him to make love to her again, showed him how much she cared, he might come to feel something stronger.

She bit her lip. It was a gamble, but it was worth it if she could win Matt. And she'd definitely enjoy the effort. Now if only he'd heal quickly.

Chapter Twenty-Four

Leaving the hospital with its smells of antiseptics and cleaning fluids, Valerie rubbed the back of her neck. She took a deep breath of fresh air, tinged with honeysuckle blossoms, and then let it out. Matt was well on the way to recovery, thank goodness. While he slept, she wanted to help the police round up Pierce and Slim. She'd given them a description at the hospital, but so far the police hadn't arrested anyone for kidnapping her.

She reached in her pocket, found the fifty, and hailed a cab. "Take me to the main police station."

Once there, she paid the driver and pocketed the thirty-five bucks left after giving him a tip. She stepped inside the station. After seeing Christy sitting on a wooden bench in the lobby, Valerie hugged her, glad to feel her slim form again. "Christy, I'm so happy to see you're all right. Do they want to question you some more? Is that why you're here?"

Christy shook her head. "I was just waiting for one of the cops to take me home. I don't have any money with me. How is Matt? Will he be okay?"

"I think so. He seemed okay before I left the hospital. You don't need to wait for a ride. I have cab money. Did they arrest Buck?"

Christy nodded. "I heard him cursing and shouting. He threatened to sue the cops for false arrest."

"All the time you were missing I was really worried. How come you didn't try to escape?"

"I was scared. Scared of Buck and what he might do if I tried. I guess I didn't really know him before. From some things he said, I gathered he might have raped some women in Dallas when they resisted him."

"Did he—did he try anything with you?"

Christy sighed. "Every night. I kept telling him I was too sick from the miscarriage." Her eyes looked sad. "It got harder and harder to convince him. I told him I wanted my doctor in San Antonio to examine me before we did anything. Thank goodness you and Matt came when you did. I was running out of excuses. I was afraid he'd force himself on me."

"Why were you staying in a cabin out in the boondocks? Can't he afford a better place?"

"I think he was afraid someone would find me, or I'd try to escape."

"Look, Christy, I'll get a cab to take us to your place, but first I want to look at some mug shots to see if I can help the police find those two guys who kidnapped me."

Christy's eyes opened wide. "You were kidnapped too? When?"

"A few days ago two guys chloroformed me, dragged me off, put me in a wooden crate, loaded it in a truck, and drove off. When I started coming to, I felt every bump in the road. They put that cloth over my nose again before they delivered me in that box to the office where Matt was working on Gordon's defense."

"How awful. Did they hurt you?"

"Duh." She rubbed her shoulder. "I have some aches and bruises, but I'm okay. The worst part was being cooped up and fearing I couldn't get loose. "

Christy looked puzzled. "Strange that we were both kidnapped. Sounds like a conspiracy. Who would do this to us? I mean, we haven't made an enemy of anyone, not that I know of."

"Matt thinks it's a scheme to keep Gordon from winning the election for mayor."

"Man, I didn't realize politics could be so dangerous. I wish Gordon had never gotten involved, but he really wanted to run for mayor."

"Christy, when you were with Buck, did he ever talk to anyone named Slim or Pierce?"

Christy nodded. "Someone named Pierce came to the door while we were at a motel, but I didn't actually see him. I heard them plotting to send me—well, I thought it was me at the time, but it must've been you they were talking about—to Matt in a box, dead or alive." She shivered and her shoulders shook. "I was scared they'd really do it."

"When they did, I feared they were going to kill me." Valerie shuddered, remembering how she'd gasped for air, wondering if she'd run out. She clenched her fists. "If I can identify either of them from a mug shot, I want the police to arrest them. Maybe they can get to the bottom of things. Matt thinks Gordon's opponent, Frank Carter, is behind the kidnappings. I'll bet they even arranged our enforced hospitality at that drug lord's hacienda down near the border."

"You stayed at a drug lord's house? Weren't you scared?"

Valerie nodded and explained about being nabbed, Matt's appearance at the hearing, and stealing Roberto's car to get away.

"Wow," Christy exclaimed. "I didn't know you had it in you."

"Desperation breeds a strange kind of courage. You do things you couldn't imagine doing otherwise." Valerie stepped over to speak to the clerk at the information desk.

A few minutes later an officer wearing a blazer, a tie, and dark pants stepped out. "I'm Detective Brownlee. I understand you want to look at some mug shots."

"Two men chloroformed me and shipped me in a crate to the office of Matt's friend where Matt was working. You probably have a report on that around here."

Valerie pointed to Christy. "This is my sister, Christy. She might have seen them, too."

She told the detective what happened and described the men as best she could. He led Valerie and Christy down a tan and gray striped hallway to his cubicle. "Let me see what I can get." He motioned to a small room nearby. "Wait in there."

A few minutes later, he brought two printouts. Each had six pictures. "We try to narrow them down to the most likely ones." He left them to study the photos.

While Valerie studied them, he stuck his head back in the room. "Do you still need a ride to the hospital, Mrs. Larson?"

Christy rose. "Thanks anyhow, but my sister says my brother-in-law's going to be okay. I'll go later. She's still perusing mug shots."

"Do you recognize anyone?" the detective asked.

Valerie turned to the second page and stared at a pudgy face. "There. This man, the one who looks like he could use a shave. It says here that one of his aliases is Pierce. I think he's one of the men who kidnapped me. The other man called him Pierce."

Christy spoke up. "I heard Buck talking about it with a man called Pierce. Unfortunately, I didn't see him. I bet if you picked him up, you could make him tell who's behind both kidnappings and why they're connected."

Detective Brownlee glared at Christy. "Listen, we're the ones to make those decisions. You weren't able to get away from that guy named Buck. Why do you think you can solve a conspiracy? Are you even sure there is one?"

Christy looked taken aback, but soon adopted a gracious smile as she shifted into her southern gal persona. "Please pardon me, Detective Brownlee. I wasn't trying to suggest how to do your job, just making a humble suggestion."

Christy put her hand on his sleeve. "I thought it might be helpful, that's all." She smiled again.

The detective rubbed his chin. "I see. Well, we might pick him up for questioning and see where that leads. He's already on probation. If we get him for conspiracy, he's in danger of doing time—a lot of it. If we offer a plea bargain on the kidnapping, we might have enough leverage to get him to spill what he knows."

Christy flashed the officer a broad smile. "I'd sure appreciate it if you'd call the D.A.'s office and notify them that I'm alive. And could you please try to find some evidence that Frank Carter's behind all this?"

"Whoa. If you're trying to bust Frank Carter, you'll need plenty of ammunition."

Valerie frowned. "Both Christy and I can testify about Pierce being involved. I bet he works for Carter."

Brownlee picked up the mug shots. "I'll look into it."

While Valerie called a cab, Christy wrote down her phone number for the officer. "Thanks for everything. Sure glad your officers got there when they did. Things were getting scary." She turned to Valerie. "Let's wait outside."

Later, at Christy and Gordon's house, Valerie paid the cab driver and followed Christy inside. "I hope you don't mind Matt and me staying here. Gordon said we could." Christy smiled. "Sure. Make yourself at home. The first thing I have to do is visit the D.A.'s office with some I.D. Now where did I put my passport?" Christy stepped into the room Valerie and Matt had shared and picked up a nightgown. "This yours?"

Standing in the doorway, Valerie nodded. They'd made love half the night, and Matt hadn't complained about his arm. However, when he helped her make the bed in the morning, he'd winced when he tucked in the blanket. She hoped her sister couldn't tell they had slept together. What the hell? Who she slept with was none of her sister's business.

"So is Matt a great lover?"

Valerie's face grew hot. So much for keeping that a secret. "What kind of question is that?"

Christy looked at her inquisitively. "Well, is he? You and Gordon didn't hit it off, but Matt looks so sexy with those bedroom eyes, I just figured he'd be great in bed."

"You're not supposed to think like that about other men. You're married now."

Christy grinned. "I may be married, but there's nothing wrong with my eyes. Matt looks hot. If he is, and he likes you, well, that's great." She rummaged in a drawer of the maple chest. "Here's my passport. Want to come with me to the D.A.'s office?"

"Guess I'd better so I can swear you really are Christy."

****

Valerie waited with Christy for half an hour for an audience with the D.A. Seated in his office in front of his oak desk, they finally convinced him of her identity and that she was okay.

After tucking a signed statement in her purse, Christy drove toward the hospital. "Don't know why there's so much red tape. You'd think they'd release him right away."

"I'm sure it will be just a formality after you appear before the judge."

At the hospital Matt seemed much better. He was sitting up when they walked in his room. He smiled. "How are my best woman and my favorite sister-in-law?"

"We're fine," said Valerie. "How are you?"

"Okay, but I can't wait to leave here. It's certainly not the Hyatt or the Marriott. Come closer, ladies. I'm not up to standing, but I can squeeze your hands."

Valerie walked to one side of the bed, and Christy stepped to the other. Matt reached out to take their hands. "I'm hoping to get released tomorrow. If the x-rays and electro-encephalogram don't show any brain damage, they might let me go."

Christy patted Matt's arm. "Thanks again for rescuing me. I felt like a slave."

"You're welcome. I couldn't have done it without Valerie. She was a great help. Wish those damn bastards hadn't gotten hold of her. I hate what they did to her. Lying in that box must have been awful."

"It was," Valerie said," but after living through that, a night in a Mexican jail and being kidnapped by a drug lord, I feel as if I can tackle anything."

Christy's glanced at Valerie. "You've been through hell to rescue me. I'm grateful for all you did, and I owe you big time. I don't deserve it after taking your fiancé and—"

"Don't bring that up," Valerie interrupted. "That's ancient history. You have always been the best person for Gordon, and I've forgiven him for breaking up with me."

Christy dropped Matt's hand and walked around the bed. She hugged Valerie. "You have such a generous heart. I'm proud to call you my sister."

Valerie smiled. She'd known it was right to forgive Gordon and her sister. Now she realized that she really didn't hate Gordon. Not after Matt had called her sexy and made such glorious love with her. Knowing he thought she was someone special made her feel confident. Made her feel she was worth loving. Seeing the way he grinned at her, she could hardly wait until he was better. She bent and kissed him.

His response warmed her throughout, letting her know he could hardly wait to be with her again. Beaming, he held onto her hand for a long moment, then kissed it before letting go.

"We'd better let you rest," Valerie said. "We'll check tomorrow to see if they'll release you."

Christy blew him a kiss. "Sleep well. We'll be back

tomorrow as soon as we get my husband out of jail."

That night Valerie and Christy shared a few scoops of ice cream in the kitchen. Christy put her hand on top of Valerie's. "I'm really sorry I caused you so much grief. I never dreamed Buck was capable of letting Pierce and what's-his-name tie you up in a box. I overheard him on the phone saying, "No way will I do that to Christy. I bet that's what he was talking about. At least he cared enough about me to refuse to do that, but I hate it that they did it to you."

"Hey, you couldn't help it."

"Yes, but if Gordon hadn't been running for mayor, I bet it wouldn't have happened."

"Politics can be a dirty business."

"At least Gordon hasn't done anything bad." Christy took another spoonful of ice cream, then looked down at the table. "And I guess it was wrong to flirt with Gordon while he was your fiancé. At first I didn't mean anything by it. You know how I enjoy flirting with every handsome man. But Gordon saw something in me, something more than just your little sister. I was impressed."

"When we broke up, I was hurt at first. It was painful to be thrown over, especially because he preferred my sister, but you can be charming to everyone, and that's good for a politician's wife. He picked the right woman. And I like the right brother for me."

Later, Valerie snuggled under the sheets. Catching the faint scent of Matt's aftershave from the pillow, she smiled. Last night had been wonderful. She missed Matt and hoped he'd feel better soon. She could hardly wait to hold him in her arms again. He made her feel so special, so desired. Her heart beat faster just thinking about him.

The next morning Valerie drove Matt's car to court where they met Matt's attorney friend, Joe, who appeared in court with Christy and Valerie. After some discussion, he got the judge to dismiss the case and sign release papers for Gordon.

Several hours later, they approached the jail, a large red brick building in downtown San Antonio and presented the judge's order.

Ten minutes later, Gordon walked into the lobby, wearing a beige knit shirt with a collar and jeans, probably what he'd worn when arrested. At least they'd let him change out of prison clothes. Christy rushed to him and hugged and kissed him. "I'm so glad you're okay. You look thin. Don't they feed prisoners more than bread and water here?"

He shook his head. "I haven't felt like eating much. I've been so worried about you." He grasped her around her waist and pulled her close. "Are you okay?"

Christy nodded. "I am now. I'm just so glad to see you free." She smiled. "I'm really sorry I caused you so much trouble and worry, but I couldn't help it. Buck found me having a miscarriage in your truck."

Gordon let go of her waist and looked her in the eye. "You didn't tell me you were pregnant."

"I wasn't sure until then. Buck found me bleeding in your truck and took me to a clinic, but then he drove me to Mexico and wouldn't let me go until your brother and Valerie found me. Then he shot Matt, and the cops came and arrested him."

Gordon scowled. "I hope they throw the book at him. What he did was unconscionable. Did he hurt you?"

"Not really. He just didn't want to take me back to you. He's obsessed with me."

"Well, I'm not letting him anywhere near you again." He hugged and kissed her once more. Taking the large plastic bag holding the rest of his possessions, he walked with them out to the car.

****

The next day after Matt was released from the hospital, the four of them shared a late lunch, pizza delivered to Gordon and Christy's house. Matt rose. "Hey, brother, now that you're out of the pen, I need you to do a favor for me. Let's go into your study, and I'll explain."

Valerie watched. Matt's step seemed sure and steady. She relaxed, glad they had been able to bring him home so soon.

Christy cleared the table. "Hey, sis, Matt says all your stuff was stolen from the car while you were in that Mexican jail. Let me take you shopping. That's the least I can do."

Soon they were strolling in and out of shops at a mall. Valerie tried on a low cut dress of shimmering gray satin with a lace inset that dipped to reveal the tops of her breasts. The wide neckline spread to the tips of her shoulders.

Christy stood beside her, looking in the mirror. "Now that's stunning. You just have to get it."

Valerie smiled at her reflection. "I love it, but I never go any place where I need a dress this elegant."

Christy smiled. "So. Make Matt take you to some fancy restaurant."

"I'm not asking Matt to take me somewhere

expensive."

"All it takes is a little sweet talk. Most men are pushovers for that."

"Maybe it works for someone as glamorous like you, but I'd feel stupid."

"I'll put a bug in Matt's ear."

"Don't you dare. If he wants to take me someplace like that, he will."

Christy pulled out her credit card. "I'm buying, so take the dress." She glanced down at Valerie's feet, still in gorilla slippers. "You need some shoes to go with it."

Fifteen minutes later, Valerie sat in a shoe store with several boxes of shoes on the floor. She tried on a strappy silver sandal with high heels. They looked really sexy.

Christy nodded. "Those shoes were made for that dress. You have to take them."

Smiling, the salesman tucked her slippers in pale gray tissue in a shoebox. Again Christy whipped out her credit card despite Valerie's protests.

Christy held the packages while Valerie went to the restroom. When Valerie came out, Christy glanced up, said, "Bye, Matt," and turned off her phone.

By five o'clock when they returned, Matt and Gordon were watching a baseball game. Christy touched Matt's shoulder and met his gaze. She whispered something to Matt. Smiling, Matt rose without a backward glance at the game on television. Christy took his hand, led him into the kitchen, and shut the door. Was her sister flirting with Matt? Had she been doing this every time he visited them in San Antonio?

Chapter Twenty-Five

Matt and Christy were still in the kitchen talking with the door closed. Valerie couldn't make out what they were saying.

Matt's deep voice seeped through the wall. "You really think I should?"

What were they talking about? She remembered Christy on the phone at the store. Was Christy bored with Gordon and trying to start an affair with Matt now? Or, despite what Christy said about being sorry she'd flirted with Gordon when he was Valerie's fiancé, had she been seeing Matt on the sly? Valerie's stomach knotted. Had Christy's apology and Matt's criticism of her sister been a smoke screen?

Now she couldn't hear them talking. Were they whispering? Or kissing?

Valerie tried not to think of them together in each other's arms. That image hurt so much, she shut her eyes tightly, trying to block it out.

Her heart quivered like an earthquake was shaking her. She swallowed. When she'd been in the hospital, he'd acted as if he cared for her. He'd shopped for clothes. He waited on her. Later, he made love to her as if she were the only woman he wanted.

Earlier, he said he'd wanted her to be his. But then he laughed. Said she was too independent to be any man's woman. Now she wanted to be his, but did he want her?

This couldn't be happening.

Valerie had endured a lot to get her sister back. They both had reason be grateful to Matt, but Valerie didn't want Christy flirting with her boyfriend.

Not again. She was welcome to Gordon. He thought she was prettier.

Valerie didn't want a man who only held onto a woman to sport a trophy wife on his arm. She wanted to be appreciated for more than her looks. And she'd thought Matt did. Now she wasn't so sure.

She wanted someone who shared the same interests, read the same kinds of books, listened to the same kind of music—like Matt.

Maybe she should have said no when he enticed her into sharing his bed. But the way she felt that night, she couldn't have resisted him, not even knowing it might never happen again. She'd melted when he'd told her she was everything a man could want. Had that been only a line?

Why was she staying out here speculating? She shoved open the swinging door and froze. Christy's hand was on Matt's arm. You've got to tell her," Christy said. "Tell her now so she can be prepared."

Her heart in her throat, Valerie asked, "Tell me what?"

Christy removed her hand from Matt's arm. "He should be the one to say it."

Matt turned his caramel eyes on Valerie and smiled. She met his gaze head on. She wanted to keep on believing—believing he meant it when he'd said she was special and sexy, and everything a man could want.

It would tear her up if he hadn't meant it, but she'd

catch her breath—it might take more than that—but if so, she'd straighten her shoulders and move on. Better find out now. She stuck out her chin and stepped forward, pasting a smile on her face. "Okay, tell me what?"

Her heart quivered. She had to know whether to sing for joy or let her heart beat slowly like the rhythm of a funeral dirge.

Matt took her hand. "Valerie, I was going to surprise you by taking you to dinner at the top of the Tower of the Americas, but Christy says I should let you know now so you can wear your new dress."

Unsure of his intentions, she pulled back her hand.

"Valerie." He touched her arm, warming it. His brown eyes met hers. "Don't you want me to take you out to dinner?"

"Yes, yes, I do." Oh great. Now she'd said, "I do" just like in the wedding ceremony. He hadn't seemed to notice that. She shot a quick glance at her sister.

Christy nodded. "Of course she does. The Chart House Restaurant's an elegant place. It's really neat at 750 feet high with the floor revolving so you can see the whole city. And they've got an apple cinnamon and nut strudel to die for." She patted Valerie's hand. You'll love it. Christy left the kitchen, shutting the door behind her.

Matt looked at Valerie. "I thought Gordon and Christy could use some time alone. They've both been through a lot. You've been through a lot, too. But that's not the real reason. I want to give you some good memories to help you forget the bad ones." He pulled her into his arms and kissed her. It was tender, and hinted at more to come. "I'm so glad you've recovered from what those men did to you."

She smiled. Dare she hope he really cared for her? "I'm fine now."

Walking arm in arm with Matt back to the living room, she hoped this meant he wanted more than friendship.

Later, dressed in her new silver dress with shoes to match, and with silver butterfly clips holding her hair back from her face, she stepped into the living room.

His eyes lit up. "You look absolutely stunning." His words and the look on his face set her senses shimmering. Her whole body tensed with anticipation.

Half an hour later, at the Tower of the Americas, he followed her into the elevator. Alone with Matt, she felt as if she were in a different world as the elevator rose. Through the glass, trees and houses spread out before them. When the doors opened, the crowded restaurant with smells of shrimp and sizzling steaks surrounded her. The hostess seated them at a table in the middle, resplendent with crisp linen, sparkling wineglasses, and gleaming silverware.

"Order anything you like." He was really treating her special. She studied the menu.

Not long after ordering, Valerie felt a chill. Not sure if it were her nerves or the temperature, she lifted the burned-out velvet stole she'd borrowed from Christy. Matt rose and took it from her. "Let me." He spread it around her shoulders, letting portions of her arms and her silver dress show through to emphasize the burned-out design.

His warm fingers caressed her flesh. "Your skin is soft, like velvet. And you have such sexy shoulders." He dipped his head to kiss first one, then her other. The tender touch of his lips on her skin sent a warm glow through her whole body. Feeling deliciously warm, she savored his quick squeeze before he returned to his seat.

When his adoring gaze met hers, she took a deep breath and reached across the table to touch his hand. He grasped hers, then lifted it to his mouth and kissed her fingertips, one by one. "I can hardly wait until I can get you alone."

Speechless for once, she was glad to see the waiter bringing their salads. Minutes later, lifting her fork, she wondered if Matt was only interested in a few nights, or like her, did he want so much more.

"Valerie." His deep voice interrupted her thoughts.

"Yes?" Seeing his serious expression, she waited.

He drummed his fingers on the tablecloth. "I've been thinking."

Valerie watched the waiter, dressed in a gold vest over a white shirt, return and relight the candle on the table. Nervous, she smoothed her skirt.

Matt ran his fingers through his hair and waited until the waiter walked away. Maybe he wasn't seriously involved with his brother's wife, but what about the next attractive woman who caught his eye? After all, there were many more sophisticated and attractive women than she.

"Valerie." Matt spoke her name, interrupting her thoughts.

"Yes?" Meeting his gaze, and noting his serious expression, she waited to hear what he was going to say.

His expression was serious. Uh-oh, was he going to tell her they needed to cool it, that he needed to concentrate on his career or something vague sounding like that? If he did, he wasn't the man for her.

He ran his fingers through his hair. "When I took time off to hunt for Christy, the atmosphere at my firm seemed rather cool. I've been wondering if that were only temporary because I was letting the others take over some of my clients or if my associates no longer have confidence in me."

Leaning back, she let out a breath, one she hadn't realized she'd been holding. Her heart skipped a beat. He wanted her opinion, wanted to know how she felt, what she thought. Maybe he considered her more than just a lover. Maybe dreaming of a future together wasn't foolish.

She looked across the table at him. "I have no way of knowing what's going on at your office. Why do you feel the lawyers have no confidence in you?"

"I don't seem to fit into their culture of anything for a buck."

The waiter set down shrimp and crab fondue with garlic bread. After taking a bite of the garlic toast, Matt continued, "They follow the trail of the almighty dollar. I don't take on cases where the client stands a good chance of losing. I tell them their chances aren't good, and that they'd be wasting their money."

She nibbled on a piece of garlic toast. "What do the other attorneys do?"

"Most of my associates would take their money and go through the motions. There's a lot of pressure to keep my hourly billings high. I'm considering going out on my own."

She studied his face. "You are?"

He nodded. "Might be a financial drain for a while, but I've got savings in my 401K I could rely on."

"Enough for a year?"

"Not quite. I'd have to pay a penalty to take money out, but I could live on it for a while.

She reached out, put her hand on his forearm. "If that's what you want, I say go for it."

"You don't think I'm foolish."

"Going for a dream if you have a good plan is never foolish. Why not do it if that's what you want?"

His face lit up. "I will."

After the waiter had served and cleared their appetizer and salad plates, he brought two plates of herb-seasoned prime rib with roasted ratatouille. Their waiter explained it consisted of several vegetables, which were sautéed separately, layered into a dish and baked.

Matt's smiles seasoned her enjoyment, enhancing each bite.

After they finished, and the waiter cleared the table, he brought a tray of desserts. A strawberry shortcake topped with whipped cream a mile high, a raspberry chipotle chocolate torte, margarita cheesecake, and a light, fluffy Grand Marnier soufflé with raspberry crème anglaise.

Perfect for sharing—the warm apple strudel with ice cream and nuts that Christy had raved about, accompanied by a ball of vanilla ice cream coated with nuts and smothered with caramel sauce also decorated the tray.

"I don't know. I'm pretty full," she said.

"You can't be that full. You didn't eat all your ratatouille." He waved his hand over the tray, grinning impishly. "Bring us one of each and two spoons."

"We can't eat all that."

He grinned. "Maybe not, but we sure can have a good taste of each. And waiter, would you please set it on that table over there by the window, then bring some coffee."

The waiter bowed. "Yes, sir."

Matt looked at her with the same hunger she saw when he eyed the desserts.

He rose and took her hand. "Come on. I want to show you something." He led her to a candlelit table by the windows. After pulling a long white box from his pocket, he set it on the tablecloth. "This is for you."

What could it be? With eager fingers she undid the satin ribbon and opened the box. Large turquoise stones, mounted in silver, lay nestled on black velvet. It was the largest squash blossom necklace she'd ever seen.

He smiled. "I bought it to replace the one you had to give up in Mexico when we bargained for a bucket of gas."

"Oh, thank you." She stared at the blue-green stones. "You didn't have to do this. It must have cost a lot."

"I wanted to, and you're worth every penny. Let me." He reached around her and raised the necklace. Latching the clasp, his hands brushed across her shoulders, sending shivers down her spine. He pressed a tender kiss on each bare shoulder.

Basking in the warmth of his touch, she ran her fingers over the stones and intricate silver leaves. When he skimmed her hair aside and placed a feather-light kiss on her neck, her hand froze on the largest stone nestled in her cleavage. The touch of his lips had her skin tingling all the way to her toes.

"Now sit. There's something else I want to show you." He pulled out the chair for her and gestured to the window.

Below, on the flat roof of a nearby building, Gordon and Christy waved at them. Huge orange cardboard letters lay spread out on the roof. They spelled, "I love you. Marry me?" Fidgeting nervously, Matt looked out the window to his brother and then back at Valerie. "This is what Christy and I were talking about in the kitchen. So, what's your answer? Would you consider marrying an attorney who plans to set out on his own and may be struggling for clients for a while?"

Valerie sat there, speechless. Matt could win any woman he chose, but he wanted her. Her heart danced for joy.

When she didn't respond immediately, he swallowed and said, "If the answer's no, just say so. I don't want to hear any nonsense about let's just be friends."

Feeling deliciously warm, she rose and took both of his hands in hers. "The answer's yes."

He pulled her close and pressed his lips to her bare shoulder. "Now I know you'll always be around so I can kiss those sexy shoulders whenever I want to." He lowered his mouth, stopping a breath away and murmured, "And that contrary mouth of yours, too."

Filled with eager longing, she met his gaze with gladness. Her heart swelled to overflowing with happiness.

He reached in his pocket and handed her a gray velvet box. I almost forgot this. In it lay a huge emerald ring surrounded by diamonds. "To match your eyes."

He kissed her again. Amber highlights gleamed in his brown eyes, warming her soul as he slid the ring on her finger.

When the desserts arrived, they took only a few delicious bites in between kisses. "Wrap it up. We'll finish our dessert later," Matt told the waiter. She knew he had more on his mind than sweets. Never again would she doubt his love. Her heart beat in double time as she floated out the door.

On the way down in the elevator, she stood wrapped in Matt's arms, watching the early stars twinkle in an indigo velvet sky above his shining words of love on the roof. Slowly, the letters faded in the twilight. But she didn't need to read the words. His arms held her tight, and his lips on her shoulder engraved his declaration on her heart for all time.

Epilogue

Gordon Larson laid the newspaper on the breakfast table of the hotel coffee shop. Valerie glanced at The Dallas Morning News. It mentioned everything that was important. On the front page the headlines read San Antonio Drug Salesman Revealed as North Dallas Rapist, Frank Carter under Investigation. Another read San Antonio picks Larson as Mayor. Brimming with happiness, Valerie glanced at Christy who was waving at a baby at the next table. "Sis," Valerie said, "you wowed them two nights ago at the victory party. You'll make a great politician's wife."

Valerie turned to the society section and read her favorite headline once more, San Antonio's New Mayor Best Man for Dallas Attorney, Matthew Larson, Wedding Today.'

Matt pointed to the picture of the four of them. "I guess when you marry the brother of a celebrity, you should expect to share the spotlight."

Valerie smiled. "That's fine with me, but this afternoon at two, you and I will be the ones in the spotlight."

Matt beamed and squeezed her hand. He leaned close to whisper. "The light I want to see you in is the moonlight from the window when we're alone tonight." His brown eyes, shining with love, met hers with a promise of more joy to come.

A word about the author...

As a teenager, Carolyn Rae told stories to kids she babysat. On a long road trip, she entertained her younger sister with stories she made up.

Later she taught home economics and family living in Michigan, Illinois, and Texas, where she earned a master's degree and also taught English. In Illinois, she worked as a researcher for a mincemeat company and met her neighbors by bringing samples of mincemeat pies. She was a teacher and supervisor of ironwork, painting, and carpentry residents at the Fort Worth Federal Correctional Institution in Texas. While there, she also wrote and directed videos on nutrition and fair fighting for married couples.

Carolyn Rae wrote the text and many recipes for *There IS Life After Lettuce*, a cookbook for heart patients and diabetics. Her profile and travel articles have appeared in the Romance Writer's Report, Fort Worth Star Telegram, The Dallas Morning News, Positive Parenting, and AAA World, Hawaii and Alaska. She has worked as a paralegal and follows her passion, writing romantic suspense where bullets are flying, people are dying, and lovers are resisting attraction until they can escape the danger following them.

http://carolynrae.com